FORBIDDEN
Promises

Also by Synithia Williams

The Promise of a Kiss

Look for the next book in Synithia Williams's sexy and
irresistible Jackson Falls series, *Scandalous Secrets*,
coming soon from HQN.

SYNITHIA
WILLIAMS

FORBIDDEN
Promises

HQN

ISBN-13: 978-1-335-01324-8

Forbidden Promises

This edition published by arrangement with Harlequin Books S.A.

For questions and comments about the quality of this book,
please contact us at CustomerService@Harlequin.com.

HQN
22 Adelaide St. West, 40th Floor
Toronto, Ontario M5H 4E3, Canada
www.Harlequin.com

Printed in U.S.A.

Recycling programs
for this product may
not exist in your area.

To my grandmother Lil. I wish you were here, but I know you're smiling down from heaven.

Dear Reader,

When I was younger, I was a big fan of soap operas. I religiously watched the three o'clock soaps because I could catch them as soon as I got home from school. This love of soaps went well into my college years and waned only when I started working nine to five and wasn't able to watch them. The never-ending drama and excitement of the characters' lives captured my attention and kept me enthralled for the entire bumpy ride.

Forbidden Promises introduces you to the Robidoux family, who are a lot like the families in the soap operas I used to devour. They're rich, they have secrets and they may fight, but at the end of the day, they'll always be there for each other. Or, as they'd say in the soaps, always be there for "the family." The Robidoux clan isn't perfect, but as you read their stories, you'll realize they're complicated and worthy of love.

After you've finished *Forbidden Promises*, reach out to me and let me know what you think. I love to hear from readers via email or social media.

Happy reading!

Synithia

CHAPTER ONE

A LARGE CALLA LILY bouquet came entirely too close to slapping India Robidoux in the face the moment she entered her family's home for the first time in four years. Only a quick slide to the right saved her from that indignity.

The woman carrying the flowers rushed by with a barely audible "excuse me."

India jumped back to avoid being hit by another bouquet as a different woman with an equally large arrangement hurried by. The ornate oak-and-glass front door swung open behind her. India stutter-stepped to the right to avoid being hit. Maybe she should have taken up dancing instead of the violin. She clearly had the footwork down.

The front door opened again, and a man carrying a large box rushed through. "Where do you want these?" he asked her. He shifted and the sound of glasses clinking together came from the box.

India's mouth opened, then closed. She glanced around in the hope he was talking to someone who had some clue what was going on.

The man loudly cleared his throat. "Ma'am?"

Blinking rapidly, India pointed down the hall where more noise came from the back of the house. "Um…the kitchen?" That had to be where glasses needed to go.

The man nodded and hurried on his way. Yet another woman carrying a huge bouquet, roses instead of calla lilies, rushed by.

India moved out of the entryway and the line of people going back and forth. She pulled her cell phone out of the back pocket of her jean shorts and checked the date. No one's birthday, no anniversary and no major holiday. Why were there dozens of people zipping around making the already impressive interior of her family home even more extravagant?

People were everywhere, placing flower arrangements, hanging decorations, carrying crates and cleaning every nook and cranny. The effort put into whatever was going on wasn't surprising. Her family didn't do anything half-assed. It was as if four years hadn't passed and she was back home in time for another *Robidoux Family* production.

"I told the caterer there were to be no oysters, at all. If my brother dies from an allergic reaction to oysters at his own party because the caterer is too dumb to remember my instructions, there will be hell to pay." Her sister's cool Southern accent was laced with frustration.

India rolled her eyes and sighed. Apparently, Elaina's tendency for overdramatic threats hadn't diminished recently.

The quick apologetic reply of the unfortunate assistant her sister spoke to accompanied the sound of heels clicking along the marble in India's direction. For a second, she considered hiding, but dismissed the urge. There was no reason to hide from her sister. Their relationship wasn't the closest, but neither were they enemies. Elaina always viewed India as the annoying baby sister in need of her guidance. Adulthood hadn't changed that perception.

Elaina and a woman India didn't recognize came into view. Elaina's deep sepia skin, dark almond-shaped eyes and perfectly flat-ironed hair hadn't changed at all. Even though Elaina was thirty-two, India swore her sister had stopped aging at twenty-five.

Elaina's furious pace didn't slow down even though the other woman struggled to keep up with her. Seeing they would continue right by her—probably assuming India was just another person helping with the party, which apparently was for her brother—India sighed and stepped away from the wall. "Byron isn't going to die from eating an oyster, Elaina, and you know it."

Elaina froze midstride. Surprise registered for a millisecond before her gaze traveled over India's body.

India automatically stood straighter. She was considered the artist of the family, and her brother… Well, he was the son, which made him their father's pride and joy. Everyone agreed Elaina was the beauty, but that didn't stop her big sister from quickly sizing up India every time they were together. That didn't make her sister's scrutiny any less annoying. So, India wasn't dressed to impress. She'd come straight from the airport, leaving her luggage in the car in her rush to get inside and figure out why there were so many vehicles in the long drive. She wore jean shorts with a white tank top that sported the words Plays Well With Others beneath musical notes. Elaina's peach silk blouse and tan pencil skirt easily outshone India's wardrobe, but India had traveled all day and opted for comfort. That had to count for something, right?

Elaina's full lips finally spread into what India assumed was supposed to be a welcoming smile. "Well, you're back. I wondered if you would actually come. I guess Daddy hasn't completely lost his hold on you."

India took a deep breath and smiled just as sincerely as her sister. "I'm not here for—" she looked around at the decorations "—whatever is going on. I have a break in touring and now I'm home."

Elaina's dark eyes widened. "Oh. Well, you're home just in time." She turned to the woman next to her. "Gwendolyn, I've got to get my baby sister up to speed. You go check to make sure the crystal glasses were delivered. Please let Sandra know India's back."

Sandra was the head housekeeper for the estate. India didn't know her—she had started after India had already left. According to Byron, the woman was a saint.

Gwendolyn gave India a curious look before she nodded at Elaina. "I will, and I'll make sure there are no oysters anywhere on the menu."

"Please see that you do," Elaina said in an exaggerated tone.

When Gwendolyn walked away, Elaina strolled over to India. "Gwendolyn is a straight-up pit bull when it comes to party planning. If there is an oyster in the house, she'll make sure it's destroyed."

India's lips twisted. "She sounds delightful."

Elaina smiled ruefully. "Actually, she's a little scary."

"Scarier than you?" India said with disbelief. Elaina was nearly a carbon copy of their late mother. Witty, smart and unwilling to take shit from anyone.

Elaina lifted one slim shoulder and placed the tips of her manicured fingers on the other. "No one's scarier than me."

India smiled and some of the tension eased from her

spine. She'd forgotten that Elaina made her laugh occasionally. "So, this thing is for Byron?"

"You really don't know?" When India shook her head, Elaina motioned for her to follow. "Come on, let's go upstairs. It's a madhouse down here. Byron is running for Senate and he's formally announcing his candidacy tonight."

India froze at the bottom of the curving staircase. Shit. Damn. Motherfucker! She'd hoped to come home, spend a few easy days, maybe a week, catching up with her family and then get the hell out of there. Not arrive in the middle of what was sure to be a full-fledged Robidoux family drama complete with television cameras, adoring friends and political posturing. There was no way her daddy would stand for her popping in and out during her brother's political campaign. If she'd known, she would have gone straight to Los Angeles instead of opting for a family visit.

Elaina either hadn't noticed India wasn't climbing up the stairs or hadn't cared, and continued her assent. India resumed her stride and followed her sister to the second-floor family room. Though the downstairs rooms were ornate and grandiose with their antique furnishings, expensive wall hangings and polished surfaces, the upstairs was relaxed and welcoming. This was where the family got together to talk, watch television and spend time together. Dark carpet covered the family room floor and large leather sofas and recliners filled the space before a large television screen on the left. A pool table and minibar occupied the right side of the room.

Elaina went to the bar and pulled a bottle out of the small fridge and two goblets from the cabinet. "Wine?"

"Please," India answered.

Elaina raised one arched brow. "And here I thought you weren't a day drinker."

"A lot's changed in the years I've been away." Truthfully, nothing had changed. Any other day, she'd say one in the afternoon was too early for wine. But any other day she wouldn't be home facing her demons.

Elaina poured them wine, then walked over and handed a glass to India. She held up her glass. "Welcome home, sister." Elaina's voice didn't carry any warmth or fondness. That was Elaina. Cold beauty and pragmatism. Warm and fuzzy was not her style.

India clinked her glass to Elaina's and took a sip. As the crisp flavor of the wine played across her tongue, she glanced around the room. Pictures of her and her siblings along with the various awards Robidoux Tobacco, the vast empire that supported their lavish lifestyle, had won over the years filled the bookshelf. The faint scent of cigar smoke hung in the room that was the heart of the family.

India took a deep breath. The smell of home. Tobacco had made her family rich and turned Robidoux Tobacco into one of the most profitable tobacco producers in the country. Despite arriving in the middle of a publicity storm, India had missed home.

She walked over to get a closer look at the pictures. "I can't believe Daddy still has these up."

"As if he'd take them down," Elaina said with a trace of humor. "He loves to brag about his children's accomplishments. From fourth grade spelling bees to traveling the world with a renowned orchestra."

India smiled at some of the pictures from the events Elaina mentioned. There was even a framed newspaper clipping of a review of the Transatlantic Orchestra from the *New York Times*. Her dad hadn't wanted her to go, but he'd still been proud enough to brag.

Her gaze slid across Elaina's wedding photo, then jerked back. Her chest tightened as if her heart was in a straitjacket. The photo of Elaina in the arms of her ex-husband, Travis Strickland, during their wedding dance instantly made India wish she'd gone on to LA. They were smiling and staring into each other's eyes. Elaina and Travis had been happy that day, and India had wanted to cry. She hadn't expected to still feel so disappointed.

"I hate that picture," Elaina said. India jumped and whirled around to face her sister. "Daddy loves it," Elaina continued. "He still thinks it's fate the boy he saved fell in love with his daughter." She took a long sip from the glass. "I've considered throwing it out the window, but he'd just print another."

India swirled the wine in her glass. "It is a good story."

Elaina laughed softly and drank the rest of her wine. "The story sounds nice. The ending isn't so happy." She stared at the picture a few more seconds. No emotion on her face, but her hand tight on the wineglass before she turned and sat primly on the edge of the couch. "How long are you here for?" she said in a cool, let's-change-the-subject tone of voice.

Usually, when Elaina intentionally tried to change the subject, India would use the opportunity to keep pushing. That was part of the little sister code of conduct—tease older sister relentlessly. But, when it came to Elaina's marriage, India was more than happy to stray from the habit.

Besides, Elaina and Travis were divorced now. Elaina had called her two years ago to tell her she and Travis were ending things, but because Travis was their brother's best friend and partner in a successful law office, she'd have to keep him in her life. Elaina hadn't said what caused their split, and India hadn't asked, even though she'd wanted to know. In the end, the why didn't matter. She couldn't go after the man she'd always wanted when he was her sister's ex-husband.

"I'm only going to be home a few days." India sat on the other end of the couch. "The orchestra's tour for the year is over. I'm taking some time to recharge. I submitted my request to audition for the Los Angeles Philharmonic."

Elaina tilted her head to the side. "Los Angeles. Impressive."

"Only if I get the job."

"You will. You're persistent and that violin was always attached to your damn hand. You'll be fine." She said the last with a wave of her hand and more than a hint of pride. Elaina may be cold and distant, but India would never call her unsupportive. As if realizing she'd let her pride show, Elaina frowned at India. "How did you get here?"

"My plane landed about an hour ago. I rented a car at the airport."

Elaina looked confused. "Why? Daddy would have had a car waiting for you."

"I didn't want that. I hoped to sneak in. I wasn't ready to see everyone just yet." She looked away from Elaina and turned the glass in her hand. Her dad would be hurt she'd sneaked home, but he'd also be happy to see her. They'd Skyped and video chatted while she'd toured, but she hadn't been home in years. Somehow seeing Travis when he was free of Elaina had seemed harder than seeing them together.

"He'll be happy to know you're here for Byron's announcement," Elaina said. "He's worried your prolonged absence reflects badly on Byron."

India froze with the glass of wine halfway to her mouth. "How?"

"You being away makes it look like our family's torn apart."

"What? Where on earth did that come from?"

Elaina's lips twisted into a small smile and she shook her head. "I wish I could blame it on his overactive imagination, but I do think this is from Byron's campaign manager. You running off and not coming home for years does make it look as if you don't want to be around."

"I didn't run off. I've been touring." That's what she told herself anyway.

"Doesn't matter. You know Daddy only thinks three things are important. God, family and Robidoux Tobacco." Elaina raised a manicured finger with each word. "To him, you've turned your back on two of the three. I'd admire you for doing what you love instead of sticking around here and doing what he wanted, if it hadn't made my life so damn difficult."

"Sure, Elaina, I left just to make your life difficult," India said sarcastically.

The corner of Elaina's mouth lifted for half a second before she sighed. "I'm the one who argues with Daddy. Byron hangs on to his every word and you're the sweet one who can do no wrong. Did you really think you could go traipsing off across the world and Daddy wouldn't shift your share of the pressure to live up to the family's legacy onto me and Byron?" Elaina brought her glass to her lips, frowned when she realized the glass was empty and stood. She quickly crossed the room to the bar.

"I didn't think he'd take things out on you two." Honestly, she hadn't thought about how her leaving would affect Elaina and Byron. She'd only known she couldn't stay and pretend as if her heart wasn't breaking every time she saw Elaina and Travis together.

Elaina poured another glass of wine. "You should have known Daddy wouldn't be easy to deal with after his favorite daughter defied him."

India rolled her eyes and fell back onto the chair. "Don't be dramatic. I didn't *defy* him. Daddy knew about the offer to play with the Transatlantic Orchestra. I told him I wanted to go."

Elaina strolled back to the couch. "Yes, and he said you couldn't go, remember? That meant the case was closed. Even I thought you were staying. You never went against what Daddy wanted. What happened?"

The need to go against her dad's wishes had never been a problem before, because until then their dad hadn't denied her anything she'd wanted. He'd disciplined her when she'd messed up and pushed her to be not just good but great in everything she did. She hadn't fought him on things the way Elaina used to, so he never had a reason to say no to India's requests.

The urge to tell the truth about why she left was on the tip of her tongue. To shed light on things in the open and unravel why events had played out the way they had. India sat forward and swirled the contents of her glass instead. Confessing her sins and fighting with Elaina would make a difficult homecoming worse.

"I wanted to go, that's what happened. I was tired of being Daddy's baby girl. It was time to live my life." That part was true, as well. She'd had no identity before leaving. The youngest Robidoux. The sweet baby sister. Leaving her family behind had allowed her to grow and depend on herself. For that, she'd never regret her decision.

Elaina scoffed and sipped her wine. "You're Grant Robidoux's daughter. You don't get to live the life you want."

India swore there was bitterness in Elaina's voice, but her face held no sarcastic or angry smirk. Instead she stared off into space. Grant Robidoux making demands of his family was no secret. Everyone was expected to do their part to uphold the traditions their paternal grandparents started when they opened Robidoux Tobacco. Their mother had helped market the company before she'd passed away nearly ten years ago when India was twenty. Elaina worked at the company and oversaw some of their other holdings and was primed to take over the helm. Byron had been one of the many legal counsels for them before opening a law firm with Travis. Not to mention all of their aunts, uncles and cousins who also worked somewhere in the company.

India was the only one who hadn't wanted to grow the empire. As his baby girl, her dad had let her indulge in her "little violin hobby" until she got serious about making music her career. He couldn't accept that what he considered a hobby was a passion for her.

"Where is Daddy anyway?" Except for the noise of preparations downstairs, the house was quiet.

Elaina smiled widely. The expression was so unlike Elaina that chills of foreboding skittered down India's spine. "He's off with his new project. You're going to love this." The glee in her voice only increased India's unease.

"Forget the dramatics and let me know where he's gone." Her words were confident, but her stomach quivered.

"He's off with Russell Gilchrist. The newest young executive at Robidoux Tobacco. Marketing division. Daddy's bringing in all this new blood to revitalize the brand. Russell's one of them."

"Okay, so why are you smiling like Cruella de Vil?"

"Because, I heard Daddy say he can't wait for Russell to meet his baby girl."

India started shaking her head before Elaina finished talking. "Don't tell me he's playing matchmaker and he doesn't even know I'm home."

"Daddy's always planning for the future. Apparently since I can't make babies, and Byron won't get married and make any, he needs you to carry on the family line."

India cringed. During her first Skype calls with her dad a few months after she'd left with the Transatlantic Orchestra, he'd told her about Elaina's miscarriage. India hadn't even known her sister was pregnant. When she'd tried to call Elaina afterward, her sister discussed the medical details as if she were going over a business proposal before rushing her off the phone. "Don't talk like that."

Elaina's lips tightened. "Don't patronize me. Look, forget my broken womb and prepare for yours to be claimed faster than the last yeast roll at Sunday dinner. Daddy's ready for you to get married and make little Robidoux children. Our cousins are being fruitful and multiplying. If we don't catch up, the company will end up completely in their hands. So, beware of Russell."

India shook her head. "No, no, no. I'm not going to let him coerce me into anything. I'm only here for a few days."

Elaina sipped from her glass and raised one slim shoulder. "I wouldn't complain. Russell isn't bad. He's young, smart, good-looking. I don't think you'd find it hard to cozy up to him."

India scowled. "Then you cozy up to him."

"I'm not the cozying type." Elaina waved a hand. "Enough about that. I'll wait and see who wins that battle after we get through the party tonight."

"Where's Byron? If this party is for him, I'd expect him to be here."

"As if the favored son would dare take the time to plan his own party," Elaina said without any animosity. Byron had always been spoiled and doted on by their father and late mother. Even India, his baby sister.

"He's off with Travis. They'll be in later," Elaina said.

India's stomach twisted as if she'd had six glasses of wine instead of half of one. "Will Travis be at the party?" she managed to ask in a steady voice.

"Of course, he will. He and Byron are joined at the hip." There was one emotion Elaina wasn't afraid to show and that was irritation, something which was thick in her voice as discussed her ex-husband and brother.

After what happened between her and Travis, every time India saw him with Elaina it felt like jagged claws sinking into her chest. The pain had dulled somewhat over the years, but Travis had never belonged to her. Elaina had been married to him. They'd shared so much. India could only imagine how hard it must be for Elaina to see him so often. "That doesn't bother you?"

Elaina ran a finger over the rim of her wineglass. "Travis and I don't love each other. He worked for the company and is my darling brother's best friend." The words sounded like a carefully crafted public relations statement.

"That doesn't answer the question."

Elaina pointedly looked India in the eye. Her push-me-on-this-and-I'll-eviscerate-you feelings were very clear in her direct gaze. "No. It doesn't bother me," she said carefully. "I don't love Travis and shouldn't have married him. Our divorce was the best thing that could have happened to either of us." She capped off the very mature-sounding words with a serene smile.

The words were little comfort to India. She was happy her sister wasn't heartbroken, but had they really not loved each other? She'd consoled her own bruised feelings and reasoned that Travis had married Elaina because in the end he realized he had loved her. That maybe he'd felt guilty after what happened the night of India's birthday and had tried to make things right. For Elaina to say they never loved each other made the bitter disappointment she'd felt back then come back even more.

That doesn't mean he would have married you. It doesn't mean anything would have been different. She'd been too young, too idealistic and too romantic back then. Maybe the truth was Travis had just been looking for a Robidoux sister to marry so he could further his own goals. Just because he kissed her once on the edge of the tobacco field, whispered words that she'd longed to hear, didn't mean a thing.

She managed a small smile. "I'm glad you two are still friends."

Elaina's shoulders relaxed along with the tightness around her smile. She clearly had not wanted to continue to explore any of her feelings for Travis. "I'd thought Daddy lost his mind, plucking him from that trailer park and training him up, but he's proved himself to be loyal. That's all the family needs."

India opened her mouth to ask what Elaina needed, but footsteps sounded in the hall right before a man walked into the room. India's breath rushed from her lungs.

Time had only enhanced his good looks. Dark brown skin smoother than the finest mahogany. Midnight-black bedroom eyes that used to pierce through her shyness to the bold girl she'd tried to hide from her daddy. He had a swimmer's body. Tall, sleek, well-defined. He wore a maroon polo shirt and dark brown slacks that complemented his dark skin. His full lips were parted in a big smile. He hadn't noticed them, as he looked back and smiled at her brother behind him. Yet flashes went through her mind of his lips brushing her neck and his eyes staring at her beneath lowered lashes in the moonlight.

Byron saw them and his grin brightened the room. "India. You're home."

Travis swung around. His dark gaze collided with hers.

"India?" His deep voice washed over her. She'd forgotten the sound of her name on his lips: low, smooth, intoxicating. As if he savored the syllables as they rolled off his tongue.

Her stomach tightened and she chugged the remaining wine in her glass. Heat prickled across her skin like a thousand needles. She should have gone to LA. She should have realized running from a problem didn't make the problem go away. Her brain screamed *run* and her feet twitched with the urgency to obey as the one answer she'd come home to find out robbed her of the ability speak. She was still in love with her sister's husband.

CHAPTER TWO

TRAVIS MET INDIA'S wide amber-colored eyes and grinned. He knew he'd missed her, but hadn't realized how much until just now. He expected her to smile back. Jump up and greet him and Byron with the enthusiasm years away from home deserved, but she didn't do any of those things. If anything she looked like she wanted to be anywhere but in that room after taking the glass of wine in her hand and completely draining the contents.

Byron rushed past Travis to his sister. "When did you get home?"

India blinked several times before her face brightened and she smiled. She held open her arms and hugged Byron. "A few minutes ago."

Byron picked her up and spun her around. India squealed with delight. Travis brushed off the odd feeling she wasn't happy to see him. Of course, she'd be more excited to see Byron. Not just because he was her brother. Byron was the kind of guy people always cheered for when he entered a room—"Hey, Byron's here!" His best friend was likeable in that way. Good looks, money and confidence didn't hurt either.

Travis strolled over to the siblings. "Welcome home, India."

Her eyes darted to him before her chin jerked up and down in brief acknowledgment. She focused on

Byron again and grinned. "Senate? You're really running for Senate?"

Okay, he hadn't imagined it. She was giving him the cold shoulder. Why? India was a few years younger than him, but next to Byron, he considered her the Robidoux sibling he was closest with. That was the case even before he'd married and divorced Elaina. She was the baby girl of the family, and Mr. Robidoux loved to spoil her and treat her like a precious jewel. Travis was the one who'd seen past the darling daughter act she put on to the impulsive personality she hid. Maybe it was their affinity for the arts. He used to paint; she played the violin. They'd gotten each other.

There was that one night where things had almost gotten out of hand between them, but that was years ago. Surely she wasn't embarrassed about that?

He glanced at Elaina. Her eyes were on him. Cool and calculating as ever. Even after five years of marriage, he still couldn't figure her out. In-depth conversations had never been their thing. She preferred to keep her thoughts and feelings to herself, but her expressions sometimes revealed her emotions. Mainly when she was angry or irritated. Right now she looked at him as if he were an irritation. He nodded in her direction. She turned away and nursed a glass of wine.

He looked from Elaina to India. Had Elaina said something to make India so standoffish toward him?

"I've conquered the State House. Now it's time for me to conquer Washington," Byron was saying to India. "Do some things that will really help the people in our area. How long will you be here? I could really use your help on the campaign."

India's eyes widened and she placed a hand on her chest. "Me? How can I possibly help?"

"We need the entire family here to show everyone I'm a family man."

"You are a family man," India said. "You'd do anything for any one of us."

"I know that, you know that, Travis knows that," Byron said, pointing back at Travis. "But because I don't have a wife and kids to parade in every commercial I put out, the voters don't know that. I need my family to help me build the case. At least until I pick someone worth marrying."

Elaina sniffed disdainfully. "You've got to stop sleeping with every woman who flirts with you to find someone worth marrying, Byron."

Byron's shoulders straightened. He tugged on the front of his pink-and-blue-striped button-down shirt. "I don't sleep with all of them. Just a quarter." He grinned and winked.

India slapped Byron's shoulder. "Stop it. You're too old to be trolling the streets."

"I don't troll. The women come to me." He looked at Travis. "Don't they?"

Travis shrugged and raised a hand. "You're not pulling me into your fight with your sisters. Though I can attest to at least three different women calling your phone while we were out today."

Elaina grunted. "Thank you for proving my point."

India shook her head. "How on earth are you going to be a senator?"

Byron placed an arm around India's shoulders. "By putting my two beautiful sisters on camera telling everyone about what a loving and supportive brother I've always been."

"He's gonna need you two on camera a lot," Travis teased. Byron was a loving and supportive brother. One of the few people Travis knew who really believed in truth, justice, the American way and all that *we are the world* stuff. If he hadn't been raised by a smartly calculating family, Byron might have been beaten up by the injustices of the world. Instead, he used his privileges to try to make things better.

Travis grinned at India again so she could pick up where he left off. Whenever he teased Byron, she usually joined in. Instead, she glanced away quickly. What was going on with her?

"You know we'll talk about all this later," India said. "I've got to get my bags out of the car and apparently prepare for a party. Is Daddy with you?"

Byron shook his head. "He went down to the offices this morning. Said he'll be back in time for the party. You know he's going to be happy as hell to see you."

India's full lips lifted in a sweet smile. "I can't wait to see him, too." She hugged Byron again. "It's good to be home. Even if you're fighting an uphill battle to the Senate."

"Not quite uphill," Travis said. "The primaries aren't that far, and he's already considered a favorite."

She didn't even glance his way. "Good. I'll come home and vote for you."

"Are you serious? You have to stay for the entire race." Byron's handsome face was covered in a wounded look.

India shook her head. "Don't even try that with me.

It doesn't work anymore." She kissed his cheek. "I'm going to get my bags, and I'll talk about your race later."

She headed toward the door. Travis followed. "I'll help out."

Her steps faltered. If he hadn't been paying attention, he wouldn't have noticed. She finally met his gaze. Man, she had the prettiest eyes. A soft brown that became tawny when the sunlight caught them, in a cute heart-shaped face. Her Cupid's bow of a mouth pursed in a slight frown. A mouth that made a man think about how soft those lips would feel on various parts of his body.

Time to rein in those thoughts.

He'd promised to stay away from India years ago, and he damn sure couldn't break that promise now. Shit. She had been his sister-in-law. He respected her family, including Elaina despite their tumultuous relationship, too much to daydream about India's sexy little mouth touching him in any way. Daydreaming usually led to actions. Actions he'd surely enjoy but later regret.

India shook her head, sending her ponytail swinging. "I'm good. I don't need any help."

"It's no problem. I was going home to shower and change for the party anyway. Might as well help you before I go." He looked back at Byron. "Don't drink all the whiskey before I get back."

Byron laughed. "I'm not drinking anything tonight. I've got to keep a clear head." He tapped his temple.

"You with no whiskey before shaking down donors should be fun." Byron wanted to run for Senate, but hated the fund-raising side of politics. He looked at Elaina, nodded again. She turned her head away.

Suppressing an annoyed sigh, he turned back to India. "Come on."

Instead of giving her another chance to say she didn't need his help, he left the room. Her softer footsteps followed him. They moved in silence down the hall to the stairs. She looked straight ahead.

"Are you happy to be home?" he asked.

"Yes." The word came out quick and hard.

Travis rubbed the back of his neck. Her icy reception made his muscles tighten. They walked down the stairs into the whirlwind of preparations for the party. "I tell you what, your family knows how to throw a party."

"Mmm-hmm." She went to the front door and opened it.

Okay, so she obviously didn't want to tell him why she was upset with him. Years of dealing with Elaina refusing to say what she felt and picking a fight instead of dealing with a problem should have prepared him for this. Except he and India had never had that type of relationship. They used to talk, a lot, about everything. Whatever he'd done, he needed to know so he could fix it. He'd missed India. More than he'd realized, and he didn't want them to not be at least cordial with each other.

"How was Rome?"

"I was in Paris last," was her clipped reply.

He followed her to a red Kia Optima with a rental company tag on the back. "Last I heard it was Rome."

"Well, you heard wrong." She pulled the keys out of the pocket of her shorts. The lights flashed and the car beeped before the trunk popped.

Travis sighed. He was not about to do the silent treatment with her. "All right, India, what gives?"

She reached into the trunk and pulled out a carry-on. "What do you mean?"

"This cold shoulder you're giving me? Did Elaina say something to you?"

She glared at him over her shoulder. "What would Elaina have to say to me about you?"

"The hell if I know. That's the only thing I can think of to explain why you're acting like talking to me is a chore."

She jerked on one of the large suitcases in the trunk. "What do you want me to do, Travis? I'm not the little girl that used to follow you around."

Travis hurried over, brushed her hand aside and pulled out the suitcase. After setting it next to her, he took a good look at her. Her shorts stopped right below the curve of her ass. She had nice thighs and toned calves. The tank top she wore clung to breasts that were just the right size. No, she definitely wasn't a little girl anymore.

"I'm not asking you to follow me around, but damn, can you at least smile and act like you're happy to see me?" He slammed the trunk shut.

India crossed her arms beneath her breasts. "You're my sister's ex-husband. I didn't realize we were supposed to be friends."

"I didn't realize that meant we had to be enemies." He tried to say it lightly. Like her words hadn't felt like a slap in the face, but his confusion couldn't be hidden. He'd been so damn happy to see her, and being friends with him wasn't even a possibility for her?

"I just… I can't…" She took a deep breath. "Look, I'm only in town for a few days, all right? I've changed. I'm not your little buddy anymore, okay?"

Her words hurt. More than they should have. He broke eye contact, grabbed her bags and carried them to the front door. He knew things had been awkward after the night he'd kissed her. More than kissed her, if he allowed himself to be truthful. The night he'd helped her ring in her twenty-first birthday with whiskey shots under the moonlight. India's mother used to love celebrating her children's birthdays. After her mother died, India had a hard time on her birthday. She'd been so sad and in need of a distraction from her pain, and she'd planned to go to a party with people from his old neighborhood. A party that had been busted up late thanks to a drug deal and gunfire.

Even though he didn't regret convincing her to stay and skip the party, he did regret the kiss that steamrollered out of hand and resulted in India going from friend to a temptation he had to fight to ignore. After that night, he'd promised to keep his hands off of India. And he had. They'd never talked about that night. When Elaina came to him later with news that changed everything, he'd decided a night of whiskey shots and impulsive kisses did not need to be revisited.

"I can take them inside," India said when he reached the front door.

Travis turned to face her. She still avoided meeting his gaze. His friend was gone and had been for a while. "You're right. Things have changed. That doesn't mean we can't start over."

She lifted the handle on one of the suitcases and opened the door. "Consider this us starting over. I'll see you around, Travis." She lifted the carry-on with the other and went inside. She shut the door firmly in his face.

Travis stared at the front door. The urge to follow her inside and try to clear the air wrestled with good sense. India was right. Time had passed. Decisions had been made. Their old friendship was over and done with. He'd accepted that when he'd taken up Mr. Robidoux's offer, accepted responsibility for his actions and proposed to Elaina.

He shook his head and walked to his Cadillac Escalade. He got in and tried to push aside the musings of what might have happened if he'd done things differently.

CHAPTER THREE

INDIA STARED AT the black dress on her bed and frowned. The dress was her staple. The one she wore whenever she performed. A simple shift dress that was functional and slightly cute. She really liked the dress for sitting on a stage playing her violin. Not so much for going to a party at her family home. A party where Travis would be in attendance.

Someone knocked on the door. Giving the bland dress one last glare, she went to the door. Party attendance hadn't been on her mind when she'd come home. She didn't have anything nicer to wear. Asking Elaina was out of the question. Her sister wasn't big on sharing her designer clothes with anyone.

India opened the door. "Daddy!" She rushed forward into his arms.

Grant Robidoux wrapped his strong arms around her. The faint smell of cigars, the same scent that reminded her of home, clung to his suit.

"Someone told me my baby girl was home." He squeezed her again before stepping back. "Why didn't you tell me you were coming?"

Her father was a handsome man. Skin the color of dark honey, light brown eyes, curly hair that was a distinguished salt-and-pepper color, and a smile that brightened every time she walked into the room. He was ruthless when it came to his business, but when it came to her he had always been her big teddy bear.

"I wanted to surprise everyone. I didn't want this to be a big deal."

"Big deal?" he asked in his larger-than-life voice. "Of course, it's a big deal when my baby comes home." He looked her over. Not quite as critical as Elaina, but an inspection nonetheless. "You've lost weight. Your mama, God rest her soul, would lose her mind if she saw you so skinny."

India laughed and shook her head. She went back into her room and her dad followed her. "I'm far from skinny, Daddy."

"You were a lot thicker before you left. They aren't feeding you in that Transatlantic Orchestra?" he asked, as if he were about to file a formal complaint for negligence. He would if she gave any indication of wrongdoing.

"They're feeding us just fine. We travel a lot. I eat a lot. I'm also not eating a bunch of junk."

"Well, I'll make sure Patricia makes all your favorite foods while you're home."

India's happiness dimmed. "Patricia still works here?"

Grant's gaze sharpened. "Of course, she does. Why wouldn't she?" he asked in a slow drawl that dared her to voice any objection.

India went to her suitcase and pulled out more clothes instead of facing that stare. "It's been years. Just wondering."

India loved her daddy more than anything, but she still hadn't forgiven him for going to their family cook's bed while their mother fought a breast cancer battle.

She'd already had that fight with him. A fight that made Patricia leave for nearly a year, but she was right back in their kitchen one month after her mother's funeral.

"Well, she'll be happy to see you," Grant said as if India should be thrilled about Patricia's efforts to play nice. "You know how much Patricia loves to spoil you kids."

Patricia liked to spoil her daddy. Not them. "So, Byron's going for Senate, huh?"

Grant shook his head but let her change the subject. He smiled and sat on the edge of her bed. "He sure is. I couldn't be prouder of that boy."

"I thought you wanted him to work at Robidoux Tobacco?"

"I did, but he can do a lot more for us in Washington. Keep the legislation going in favor of us large tobacco producers. Help calm down some of the complaints that cigars and cigarettes are bad for you."

She cut a glance at him. "Daddy, they aren't exactly good for you."

Grant grunted and waved his hand dismissively. "Neither is liquor, but you don't see anyone doing mass media campaigns against the alcohol industry. Besides, we've got an entire division dedicated to making smoking less harmful. Hired a new scientist and everything."

She lifted a brow. "That's good."

"Yeah…that's what they say. How long you staying in town?"

"Just for a few days."

He stood and shook his head. "No, your brother needs you here longer."

India's spine stiffened. She heard the demand in her father's voice. "Daddy, I've got my own plans."

"And you've also got a family. You haven't been home in four years. Now it's time to do your part for the family."

"Seriously? I've been home a few hours and I'm already getting the family-first speech."

"Yes, and you're going to keep getting the speech." He pointed one long, perfectly manicured finger her way. "You're a Robidoux. You benefit from all the hard work everyone in this family puts in. You can stay for longer than a few days and help get your brother to Washington so he can continue to help the family."

"Daddy—"

"We'll discuss this more tomorrow. After the official announcement in the morning, we're all meeting to talk about the best way to help Byron win. Come prepared to help." He looked at his watch. "I've got to change for the party. Your sister put this entire thing together and has everything running like clockwork. She might not be able to hold together a marriage, but she sure can throw a party."

"Don't say that." Her dad threw out his opinions with little thought of how they may hurt.

He shrugged. "It's the truth." He met her eyes. "I'm encouraging Travis to find a good woman to marry. Someone not connected to our family. No need to stir up any trouble with Elaina."

Heat spread over her cheeks. "Why are you telling me this?"

"Just thought you should know. He needs to move on. I've got a good idea of who he should move on with, and when he does, Elaina will move on, too."

"Is she having a hard time?" Was her sister still in love with Travis?

"I just know she hasn't dated anyone since her divorce and who knows how long it'll be before she does date someone if Travis doesn't start?" He went to the door and stopped. "I'm glad you're home, baby." He winked, then exited.

India released a heavy sigh and fell back on the bed. Her dad was like a hurricane. He came in, tossed things around the way he wanted and destroyed his opponent's good intentions. She didn't want to stay, but she'd bet her Fiddlerman violin he'd maneuver things for her to stick around. Just like he was maneuvering Travis to find another wife.

Was Elaina really not dating after the divorce? She must not be. Her dad didn't say things unless he was sure. Did that mean she was waiting on Travis? Did she hold on to the hope they'd get back together? If that was the case, why had they split in the first place? The idea of Elaina still in love with Travis made India feel like the worst sister on the planet for still wanting him.

She slapped her forehead. None of that mattered. She couldn't even entertain any lingering feelings she still had for Travis. He treated her as if she were still the young kid who had followed him around all those years. The only reason he'd kissed her that night was because they'd chased the flavor of the newest Robidoux cigar with whiskey shots on her birthday. He'd overheard her planning to go partying with her cousin Ashiya. He'd told her she didn't need to get drunk with people he used to hang out with.

Then why don't I get drunk with you? She'd thrown out the taunt with a flirty smile.

God, she'd wanted so badly for him to see her as a woman instead of a kid. She'd known he and Elaina had been sneaking off together for years. Then she'd overheard them fighting. Heard Travis say he wasn't going back and forth with Elaina anymore and Elaina say she was done with him. When she'd asked Elaina about it later, her sister had told her to mind her own business right before she'd left the house with *to hell with Travis* the last words on her lips. India had assumed they were done.

He'd taken her to the edge of one of the fields, where they'd lit cigars, talked art and music and downed too many shots. Then made out like cats in heat.

For years she'd analyzed that night. The words they'd spoken. The look in his eye. The way he'd touched her. The way he'd brought her pleasure. Each touch and kiss she'd taken as proof that he really did care about her. But the next day he'd told her they'd been drunk and made a mistake. He'd avoided her for two weeks, then proposed to Elaina.

Her dad was right. Travis needed to find a new woman and he needed to find her quickly. Then she and her sister would be able to move on. Maybe.

THE BAND PLAYED upbeat jazz, champagne flowed like a stream, and everyone who was anyone in the county filled the grounds behind the Robidoux estate. After Robidoux Tobacco became one of the top tobacco producers in the state, their grandfather, whose own grandfather had once been a sharecropper on the land, vowed to build a home fit for a king. The huge brick mansion sported towers, spiraling staircases and grand entrances. He'd named the place Robidoux Castle, and sometimes India was sure her father believed they really were black royalty.

Now, as India looked over the backyard with the strung lights, full bars and mixture of people over the lawn, she wished her grandfather was still alive to see all the people playing court at his castle. He'd died when she was seven, but she remembered him taking her, Elaina and Byron out to the fields and telling them about the process of growing tobacco. How he'd bought the land, grown the business and become a leader in their community. She didn't smoke and hated the pomp and circumstance that came with being a Robidoux sometimes, but she was proud of her family's achievements.

She scanned the crowd. Her gaze landed on a woman in an elegant emerald green one-shoulder dress, tall like her father with the same dark honey complexion and thick, beautiful, salt-and-pepper hair in a tapered style that accented her smiling face. India hurried down the brick patio stairs to the bar on the lawn.

"Aunt Liz," she said.

Her father's sister stopped speaking to some people India didn't recognize and turned toward her. A huge grin broke out on her face. "India, baby girl, why didn't anyone tell me you were here?" She excused herself and strolled over to India.

India reached out for a hug. Liz had always been her favorite aunt. After India's mother died, Liz had stepped in as a second mother to India and her siblings. India loved her almost as if she were her mother.

"I'm surprised Daddy didn't say anything."

Elizabeth Robidoux Waters pulled back but kept India's hands in hers. "You know your daddy likes to make a grand entrance. He hasn't made it down yet."

"True. What about Byron? He's just as much of a showboat as Daddy."

Liz laughed and pointed across the lawn. "The man of the hour is over there, charming a few men from the local chamber of commerce. I haven't gone over to speak to him yet. I'll let him work the crowd for now and get my hug in later. Your sister is also doing her duty as the diligent hostess. She reminds me so much of your mama in that way. Virginia knew how to throw a party."

India remembered the lavish parties her mom would coordinate. She never seemed stressed or frustrated when things went wrong. A trait India wished she possessed. Virginia always laughed and said things would work out. They always did, and no one left a Robidoux party disappointed. Every day India missed her mom. Elaina had done a great job with the party, but their mom would have made everything sparkle just from the pride she would have felt with the idea of her son running for Senate.

India looked at Elaina, charming the crowd in a dazzling black-and-silver cocktail dress, her long hair pulled up in a sleek twist. She looked so much like their mom. Tears welled in India's eyes. "Daddy says she's just like mama."

"Which is why they butt heads so much," Liz said with a raised brow. The unexpected comment made India chuckle and washed away the melancholy feelings. "Elaina is as stubborn and strong-willed as your mom was. I think your dad married Virginia in a macho attempt to try to tame her. Impossible, but Grant never could back down from a challenge." Warmth didn't fill her voice. Aunt Liz and her mama hadn't been best of friends, but they'd both loved her dad and therefore they'd gotten along.

"Everyone's here then?" India said, choosing to pull Aunt Liz out of the past, as well. India once again scanned the crowd, her brain automatically searching for a certain person even though common sense said she shouldn't.

Liz gasped. "What in the world? I can't believe it."

India looked back at her aunt. "What?"

Liz pointed toward the patio, a scowl on her face. "Travis brought a date. Sweet Jesus, I know your dad wants him to move on, but he didn't have to move on tonight."

India turned toward the patio. Her breath locked in her lungs. Sure, it was hard for a man to look bad in a tuxedo. But it damn sure wasn't fair for Travis to look delectable in one. A beautiful woman with dark brown skin wearing a sexy black cocktail dress clung to his arm. Her dark hair was swept up into a complicated style that showed off her slender neck. Travis leaned to the side while the woman whispered something in his ear that made him smile.

Okay, so maybe believing things would be easier if Travis moved on to someone else had been wishful thinking. "Who's that?"

Aunt Liz moved closer to India. "A daughter of one of your dad's friends, I think. Her family makes craft beer and they're the newest toast of the town. I can't remember her name."

The woman ran her hand over Travis's chest. He wrapped his hand around her wrist. Before India could be relieved he'd stopped her from groping him, he brought her hand to his mouth and kissed the back of it.

India's stomach twisted. "Are they dating?"

"I don't know. Sure looks like they're doing something. I hope this doesn't cause any problems tonight."

"Why would it cause problems?"

"Because your sister doesn't have a date, and her ex-husband is here with a beautiful woman. Elaina doesn't like being humiliated."

No, she didn't. Reluctantly, India dragged her gaze away from Travis and the beauty to Elaina. Her sister watched them with cool eyes, but then her chin lifted and she turned her back to Travis.

"Go over there and talk to him. Try to lure him away from her." Liz pushed India forward.

"What? Why?" The tempo of her heartbeat skyrocketed. She couldn't talk to Travis after making a big deal about them keeping their distance. Seeing him up close and personal with another woman on his arm was the last thing she wanted.

"Because, if you go over there, it'll look like you're helping Elaina welcome new people." Aunt Liz placed a hand on India's shoulder and turned her in Travis's direction. "You can also remind him he doesn't need to poke the hornet's nest that is Elaina Robidoux at your brother's campaign party," she said under her breath as she gave the people passing them a pleasant smile.

India held stiff against her aunt's attempts to push her forward. "He knows that."

"He also knows how to press your sister's buttons. Remind him. This is for the family." Liz gave India a quick shove.

India stumbled a few steps, then glared at her aunt.

Liz's eyes sparkled with humor. "Welcome home, baby girl."

"Yeah, some welcome," she mumbled. She took a fortifying breath and turned toward Travis.

Her legs shook as she made her way over to him. A few people recognized her and stopped her. India took the time to say hello. She caught Liz's eye. Liz raised a brow and waved her hand in a *go ahead* motion. India swallowed the nervousness in her throat and stopped talking to walk on shaky legs toward Travis.

Travis leaned in and said something to the woman that made her swat at his chest. Raw jealousy had India's hand clenched into a fist. She shook out her hand and rolled her shoulders. God, this wasn't her. This jealous, shaky, uncertain person. She was smart and accomplished. She'd traveled the world, dated men she'd met on her travels who were sophisticated, assertive and handsome. She should not be thrown off her game by a guy from eastern North Carolina whom she'd had a silly crush on when she was younger.

The time to get over Travis was now, and dammit, she was going to force herself to stop loving him if it killed her. Her stride lengthened and her shoulders straightened.

"India!" a female's voice called.

India jerked in the direction of the voice and grinned. "Ashiya!"

Aunt Liz's only daughter hurried over. Of all the people she'd seen today, she was most excited to see Ashiya, who was closer in age to India than her sister. She and Ashiya had been inseparable growing up.

"Oh, my God, Elaina said you were back." Ashiya

wrapped India in a huge hug, then stepped back. "You don't know how happy I am that you're home."

Ashiya's hazel eyes, more green than brown, were bright with happiness and excitement. Her cousin was shorter than her by a few inches, her chestnut hair cut in a stylish chin-length bob, and a dark blue sheath dress accented her hourglass figure perfectly. Diamond studs sparkled in her ears almost as brightly as her smile.

"Why are you so happy?"

Ashiya linked her arm through India's. "Because now I have someone to make rude remarks under my breath to during your brother's campaign. You know it's going to be nothing but the family on parade, sporting our best behavior while this is going on."

Being snarky with Ashiya did sound like a lot of fun. Even though India was delighted to see her cousin and wanted to fall back into their old habits, the parade Ashiya mentioned was exactly why she didn't want to stick around for it. "I know. Daddy is already telling me I have to do my part."

"Most of the time I'd disagree with what Uncle Grant tells you, but this time I'm with him. Please tell me you're sticking around." Ashiya's voice went from light-hearted to serious.

"I only plan to stay in town for a few days." Her voice held the apology she didn't speak. The part of her that was happy to be back around family urged her to stay, but the idea of being swept into a political drama pushed her toward the nearest airport.

Ashiya shook her head. "No, ma'am. You've been gone way too long to say you're only sticking around for a few days. Video chats and text messages do not make up for having you here in person. You owe me weeks if not months of stories about all the fine men you seduced while traveling."

India laughed and placed her hand over Ashiya's. "I didn't seduce a lot of fine men."

"Oh well, make it up. How the hell will I know the difference anyway?" Ashiya said with an eye roll. "Just promise me you'll think about staying longer?"

The weight of her father's guilt trip was nothing compared to the wave that Ashiya's pleading eyes inspired. India sighed and smiled. "I'll think about it."

Ashiya beamed and squeezed India tighter to her side. "Good, now where were you going looking like you're ready for battle?"

India glanced over her shoulder. Aunt Liz's nudging look from earlier was now outright annoyed. "Your mama wants me to separate Travis from the woman on his arm."

"Who? Camille Ferguson?" Ashiya said with a laugh. "You'd have better luck prying your teeth out with a spoon. That woman is crazy about Travis."

"So, they are dating?" Disappointment entered her voice. Ashiya raised a brow. "Aunt Liz wasn't sure," India said in a rush.

"Not officially, but Uncle Grant's encouraging Camille's crush. Though I would agree with Mama that tonight isn't the night to get your sister riled up."

More speculation Elaina was holding out because of Travis. Why? That was a mystery she'd have to solve another day. Right now, Aunt Liz was giving her the evil eye and Elaina was glaring at Travis again.

"Then grab your proverbial spoon and help me." She pulled on her arm linked with Ashiya's and headed toward Travis.

"Why do I have to help?" Ashiya said in an exaggerated whine.

"Because I want you to," India said, realizing she sounded a lot like her mother used to when giving them rules they didn't want to follow.

"You're as demanding as your daddy," Ashiya said, but her voice held no malice. She grinned at India. "Watch this. I bet you Camille will find a way to mention her family's brewery or their beer in the first five seconds of our conversation."

Travis turned in their direction as they walked up the steps onto the large circular patio. Despite her brush-off earlier, his lips tilted up in a small smile and his dark gaze latched on to hers. Sweat slicked India's palms and her pulse matched tempo with the jazz beat from the band. The man had too much of an effect on her. She wanted to turn and run, and she hated that.

"Camille, I love that dress," Ashiya said with false cheer.

Camille must not have heard the insincerity in Ashiya's voice because she beamed and ran a hand over the front of the dress. "Thank you. I got it last week in New York. I was up there introducing some of our craft beers to several interested restaurants."

Ashiya gave India a told-you-so look. "Oh really? How nice."

India suppressed a laugh and unlinked her arm from Ashiya. "I'm India Robidoux." She held out her hand.

Camille let go of Travis and shook India's hand. "The long-lost daughter. Travis has told me so much about you."

India's gaze jumped to Travis. "Really?"

Travis shrugged. "You're talented on the violin. The entire family is proud of you."

Camille moved closer to Travis. "He brags as if he's still a part of the family." Camille said the words as if Travis claimed he could jump to the moon.

India met Camille's eyes. "He *is* still a part of the family." India softened her hard tone with a reproachful smile.

Camille's lips pressed together in a thin line. "Of course."

India felt the pressure of Travis's stare on her. She didn't meet his gaze. Camille's sly effort to shove Travis away from their family hit a nerve she hadn't known was exposed.

Ashiya stepped forward. "You know, Camille, my mom is going to New York in a couple of weeks. I bet she'd love to hear about the restaurants considering your family's beer. She likes to try new places and why not someplace that will support someone we know?"

"Oh, I'd love to tell her exactly where to go," Camille said eagerly. She took a step forward, then glanced back at Travis. "Can you excuse me for just a second?"

Travis nodded. "Go ahead. I'm here all night."

Camille laughed as if Travis was the funniest guy in the world before turning to Ashiya. Camille rambled on about the restaurants she recommended. Ashiya threw India a *you owe me* glare over her shoulder as she walked away with Camille.

"Let me guess," Travis said close to her side. "You were told to separate me and Camille."

A sizzle of awareness made her breath stutter. India quickly faced him. "Why would you say that?"

"Because I saw your aunt practically shove you in my direction," he said with a quirk of his lip.

"Then you know why," she said irritably.

Travis shifted his stance and slid a hand in his pocket, mirroring her annoyance. "Elaina and I are divorced. Have been for two years. I can't keep hiding my dating life from her."

"You've been hiding it from her?" He had been dating? Smiling and flirting with other women? Kissing other women? *Sleeping* with other women?

He shook his head. "I haven't had much of a dating life, but the little bit I have I don't exactly want to talk to her about."

"Is she still in love with you?" she blurted out. Subtlety was not one of her virtues.

Travis looked genuinely surprised. "In love with me? Doubtful. I don't know if your sister was ever in love with me."

Then why did he marry her? The question was on the tip of her tongue. Was it just to get closer to the family? But the regret in his voice brought another thought. Had he loved Elaina and she'd broken his heart?

She swallowed the words. In the end, the whys and hows didn't matter. He'd married Elaina, and that choice had killed any chance of them ever being together. "Just don't do anything to intentionally provoke her."

"I never intentionally provoke her, but you know as well as I do if Elaina wants to be insulted, she will be."

She couldn't argue that. "Then my work here is done." She turned to walk away.

Travis's hand gently clasped her forearm. The heat of his touch shot through her like a bullet. She pulled away from his touch and took a quick step back, her heart racing in her chest.

"What?" she asked in a breathless rush.

"You look nice. I like the dress."

Her boring, functional, black dress that wasn't nearly as fancy or showy as his date's. She hated it, but the compliment made her chest tighten. "It's old and practical but it works."

His dark gaze caressed her face, a look of appreciation in his eye. "I don't care about any of that. It looks good on you."

Warmth spread down her cheeks, neck and chest. Now was the time to go before those feelings she didn't want to acknowledge made her say or do something stupid. "I should go check on…something." She turned to leave again.

He touched her again. A soft brush of fingertips that had the warmth in her chest drifting farther down to parts that didn't need heat right now. "No, that's not all. Have a drink with me."

She spun and faced him. "Why?"

"Because we need to talk about earlier." He took a step forward. The scent of his cologne caressed her senses. His dark eyes lured her into their depths. "There's a few things we need to get straight. Tonight."

CHAPTER FOUR

TRAVIS HAD NO idea what he wanted to say to India. He just knew he couldn't go through the next few days, weeks, months or however long she was going to be in town with whatever wall she was trying to erect between them.

India looked left, then right. Reminding him of a kid trying to come up with an excuse to get out of school. She sucked in a corner of her lower lip, a habit she had when thinking or concentrating hard. It gave her mouth a pouty, kissable look. One he wished he'd never noticed.

"Are you afraid to talk to me?" He threw out the taunt intentionally.

The words hit their mark. Her shoulders stiffened, and she met his gaze directly. Her lower lip slipped from between her teeth and her head tilted to the side. "Fine. Let's talk."

India had never backed down from a challenge before. She was just as stubborn as the rest of her family, but India had a softer touch when directing things to her advantage. The art of a compromise was her strong suit and one of the things he admired about her. Her ability to always find common ground had helped him whenever he'd argued with his parents about spending too much time with the Robidoux family.

"This way." In true Robidoux fashion, there were multiple bars set up for the party. Travis held out a hand toward one of the four behind the house.

He placed a hand near the small of India's back. Not touching her, but that was worse than if he had put his hand on her. India was warmth, happiness and innocence. Things he hadn't known growing up. Just being near her made him feel as if her aura touched him. No wonder he'd been drawn to her.

"Bourbon neat," he told the bartender before looking at India. "What about you?"

"Vodka tonic."

He ordered her drink, then raised a brow. "I thought you preferred brown liquor."

"I lost my taste for it over the years." Soft brown eyes met his, then looked away. Tightness framed her full lips.

"Why are you angry with me?" he asked.

The bartender put their drinks on the bar. Over India's shoulder he saw someone who recognized her, an old classmate if he wasn't mistaken. Travis picked up their drinks and motioned for India to follow him before they could be interrupted. He picked a table far away from the bar where they were less likely to be interrupted.

He held out her drink and she calmly took it from him. "I'm not mad at you," India said.

"We're friends, India," he said surely, not letting any of his doubts bleed into his voice.

"Were friends," she corrected in a tight voice. "We *were* friends. Now we're just former in-laws."

The incredulous way she said *in-laws* told him everything he needed to know. The situation he'd avoided talking about, thinking about and pretending never happened. They'd been friends. Then they'd almost made love that night. But instead of clearing the air with India, he'd been thrown by Elaina saying she was pregnant and keeping it. He'd proposed to Elaina and, under Grant's order, kept the pregnancy a secret until after the quick wedding. How could he explain now?

Did India know the reason they got married? Elaina had originally told him no when he'd asked her to marry him. Two weeks later, she'd come back and agreed. Had she told India?

"We never talked about that night," he stated simply. He didn't beat around the bush. His mom had punished him enough as a kid when he hinted around instead of getting to the point. If he wanted to know how much India knew, he might as well bring up the subject.

Her eyes snapped to his. In that second when the flash of hurt and denial lit her gaze, he knew he was right. "I'm not mad about that."

"Then what's going on?"

India took a small sip of her drink. Licked her lips. Travis's stomach tightened. He looked away. Attraction or not, anything other than a strictly platonic relationship with India was nothing but trouble.

"I was wrong for seducing you that night," she said in a rush. "I knew you and Elaina were…" She rotated her hand in a circle.

"Sleeping together," he finished for her.

She took another sip of her drink. "I shouldn't have done that."

The corner of his mouth tilted up. "You seduced me?" He took a sip of his drink. Relished the smooth flavor and hints of caramel in the bourbon.

"I asked you out there because I knew what might happen."

Travis leaned back in his chair. "Did you, really?" He met her eyes. His voice lowered. "Did you really think there was a chance we'd have sex?" He'd come so close. Only the good Lord and every shred of decency in him had kept him from doing more.

India sucked in a fast breath. Her breasts rose and fell with the movement. She took another swallow of her drink. Even in the dim lights of the party, he could see the faint flush of her sienna skin. Innocence and warmth. After all these years, she still blushed.

"I'd hoped we would. I didn't expect you to be such a gentleman about things." Her voice shook slightly, but she didn't shy away.

Her softly spoken words touched something long forgotten inside of him. The feeling of being a prop for the Robidoux family. Grant's good deed. Elaina's rebellious affair. Had he also been India's walk on the wild side? He didn't want to believe that. He didn't want to think he'd romanticized something that didn't mean as much to her.

"I shouldn't have let it go as far as it did. I'm sorry for what happened that night. It was a mistake." He said the words and meant them. Even though he wouldn't take back a second of the time he'd held her in his arms, tasted her lips and felt the silk of her skin, he never should have crossed that line. Not with India. The one person who'd always been on his side in the Robidoux family.

"A mistake?" She shook her head and let out a small chuckle. "You know what, Travis, you're right. That night was a mistake. It was my birthday. We'd had way too many shots. That's all. I'm more than happy to pretend it didn't happen."

The hurt that flickered across her features almost made him take back the words. Almost. Nothing came of reliving one night years ago. Not if they were going to go back to being cool with each other. Not if they were going to be near each other.

"If we do that, does that mean you're no longer mad at me?"

"I'm not mad at you." The words stumbled from her lips. "Really, I'm mad at myself."

"Why?"

She glanced around the backyard. "I'm mad at being coerced into staying. Once again, I'm drawn into the Robidoux drama. It never ends."

"You mean Byron's run for Senate?"

She nodded. "Yes. I'm happy for my brother. I wish him lots of luck, but that doesn't mean I want to stay here and be a part of the parade."

Travis slowly turned his half-touched glass of bourbon on the table. "Try not to be upset. Your brother really cares and wants to help the constituents. He wants to win, and while your sister can help him strategize, he needs your compassion."

"My compassion?" Interest sparked in her eyes as she looked at him over the rim of her glass. An almost flirty look that made him shift in his seat.

Travis dropped his gaze and picked up his drink. "You'll help him win the voters' hearts."

"Why, because I'm the baby girl of the family?" she asked in a droll tone.

Travis chuckled. Some things never changed. She'd never liked being only viewed as the baby of the family. He knew that was part of the reason she'd struck out on her own with the Transatlantic Orchestra. She'd wanted to make a name for herself that wasn't tied to her family's empire. He'd always admired that about her.

"No, because you have a heart. Out of all of them—" he pointed toward the yard where the rest of her family payed homage to their court of fans and followers "—you're the one most likely to really give a damn." He knocked back half of his drink. "Byron needs that. Someone to remind him not to sell his soul to politics." Something Travis feared Byron would succumb to in order to win.

"You really think I can do that?" She didn't sound convinced.

"I know you can. He listens to you and your sister. He'll take whatever advice you give to heart."

Byron always considered any guidance his sisters gave. He may not always do what they recommended, but he never blithely dismissed what they had to say. With India back in town, there was a good chance Byron wouldn't become a political cliché.

"I get that, but my plan was to go to California in a few weeks." India pulled the corner of her bottom lip between her teeth.

Travis straightened and downed the rest of his drink, refusing to be distracted by her mouth. Those soft lips. "What's in California?"

"I requested an audition with the LA Philharmonic." Excitement crept into her voice. "I loved traveling with the Transatlantic, but I kind of want to settle down. Put in some roots and make a home for myself."

Roots? Was she looking to settle down? If so, with whom? "Can you settle down here?" Unless she had some guy waiting for her out in California.

"I don't want to live here," she said quickly and firmly.

"Why not? It's your home." Was there a guy? He

wanted to ask, but that wasn't his business. He shouldn't... didn't care.

She glanced at him, then finished her drink. "I have my reasons. Mostly, I want to build my life without the pressure of my family reputation hovering over me."

He was only slightly put at ease by her answer. India had never wanted to be governed by family pressure. She'd traveled across the world just to prove that. Still, her family missed her. They'd enjoy having her home longer.

Her family, or you?

"Having a family reputation behind you can be beneficial," Travis said. "Especially when your family has a reputation worth being proud of." Bitterness crept into his voice and she stiffened before concern etched across her face.

"How is your family?" she asked hesitantly.

Travis smiled and twirled his empty glass on the table. "You don't have to ask like that."

Her eye widened. "Like what?"

"As if you're afraid to bring up the subject."

She placed a hand on her chest. "I'm not afraid to bring up the subject."

Travis smiled, sat forward and leaned his arm on the table. "My family is the same. Still living in Sunnyside Acres, despite my efforts to move them out. My mom says she's not bothering to mingle with bougie people that don't want her around. My dad is still calling me a sellout."

"Why is he still being so stubborn? You've only wanted to do something great with your life and help people."

Her eyes sparked with anger and indignation. She

looked like a mother bear ready to defend her young. That's what he'd loved about India. The way she instantly jumped to the defense of people she cared about. Would she still react that way once she understood the latest reason his family had chosen to hate him?

"I can understand his anger this time," he said slowly. "I took on a case defending the guy who shot my cousin."

She sucked in a breath. "What?"

He longed for another drink. The drama with the case and his family was more than he wanted to deal with tonight. "My cousin Antwan was going back and forth with Zachariah King. You remember him?"

"The shady loan shark?"

"Alleged shady loan shark." The response was automatic. He was a defense attorney. His personal feelings toward Zachariah had nothing to do with how he defended the man. Zachariah owned several title loan and payday lending businesses. He took people's cars, property and last paychecks without qualms. Many people in town hated him, but still went to Zachariah when the banks said no.

"Antwan went to Mr. King's business with the intent of robbing him. Possibly more. Mr. King acted in self-defense."

Everyone knew that, but Zachariah's history of shady behavior meant there were those who thought Antwan was doing the county a favor taking him out. Things had gone south quick. His cousin was dead, and his family wanted vengeance.

He and Antwan had been close. Almost like brothers. But like the rest of his family, the closer Travis got to Grant and Byron, the more Antwan believed Travis thought he was too good to hang with them. He and Antwan hadn't talked in years before his death, but when he'd learned his cousin was dead, Travis had been angry. Angry at the path his cousin had taken, the loss of the relationship they'd once had and the unfairness of a life cut short.

India's hand rested on his. "Are you okay?"

Her touch was light, but he felt the connection in every cell of his body. Not many people asked him that. Everyone took him at face value when he said his job was to defend his client no matter the situation. His relationship with his family was already strained. Had been strained from the moment Travis went to work for Robidoux Tobacco as a young adult, though he never understood the reason for his father's animosity over that decision. He had no idea why his father considered him a sellout, and though he'd once hoped to fix his strained relationship with his parents, he doubted that was a possibility after this case.

He glanced down at India's hand on his own. The simple, caring gesture made him want to spill everything in his soul. All the confusion, pain and disgust he felt with himself, this case and the choices he'd made with his life. His other hand lifted to rest on top of hers. Movement in his periphery caught his eye attention.

"There you are." Camille's voice. "I was looking for you."

India pulled her hand from his quickly. Their eyes met. An infinity passed in that second he held her gaze. So many words. So many feelings bubbled inside. He wanted to both walk away from her without another glance and pull her into his arms and hold her tight. The scary thing was, he thought he saw the same longing in her eyes.

"You found me," he said, not looking at Camille.

"I've got to go find Byron," India said. She rose from her seat. Travis immediately stood, as well. Old-school chivalry was still ingrained in him.

India met his eyes and raised a brow. "Remember what I said. Let's make the night go smoothly."

They were back to the original reason she'd sought him out. Not because she'd wanted to talk to him. Not because they were back to the way things were before he'd screwed everything up and kissed her. Elaina was her priority. The one she cared about. The one that would always keep them apart.

"There's nothing smooth about this family," he said dryly. "But it's time to move on. I think we all have to accept that." Himself included. He turned from the frown forming on India's face to Camille. "Let's dance."

Camille nodded and slipped her arm through his. She threw a quick, uncertain glace in India's direction. He led her toward the dance floor before she could verbalize whatever thought was forming in her head.

He put his empty glass on a passing waiter's tray. No more alcohol for him tonight. He already felt unstable just from how quickly India had seen the stress in him from this case. How easily he'd been ready to confess all of his uncertainties and regrets just from a simple touch that still tickled across his senses.

She was back. She still saw things in him no one else picked up on. He'd have to be more guarded around her if he had any hopes of ignoring the longing for her that still swirled inside him.

CHAPTER FIVE

"Did Aunt Liz tell you to keep Travis away from me?"

India turned toward her sister. The party was in full swing. People laughing, mingling and opening their wallets in support of Byron's campaign. India had finally gotten a second to breathe and walk away from the constant small talk and smiling. Just beyond the manicured lawn where the party took place was an area her mom had left more or less natural. Tall pine trees with azalea bushes in between flanked unpaved walkways that led to the pool house to the east, lake to the west and south toward the first tobacco fields. Of course, Elaina would find her sitting quietly on a bench near one of the pine trees.

Elaina watched her with cool eyes. She held a half-full champagne glass in one hand, her arm bent so the glass hovered near her face. Her other arm crossed her slim midsection, her hand resting beneath her bent elbow in a pose that would look good on any runway model.

"Actually, she asked me to tell Travis to play nice with you tonight," India said. There was no reason to lie. Between her, Ashiya and Aunt Liz, they'd all managed to ensure Elaina and Travis were never in the same area of the party. Elaina wasn't foolish. She would have noticed their efforts to keep them separated.

Elaina rolled her eyes, took a long sip of her champagne. "I'm not going to make a scene. Not at Byron's party. This is to launch his candidacy. He's got a long road to win the primaries. I won't be the reason he loses."

That was a relief. India had been surprised by the passion in Byron's voice as he promised to do everything in his power to serve the people of this area if elected. She'd never seen her brother passionate about anything except women or his own self-interests. A lot had changed in the time since she'd been on tour.

"If it weren't a party for Byron, would you make a scene?" She watched Elaina closely. Was everyone right? Was her sister still holding a torch for her ex-husband?

"Travis would love for me to make a scene." Elaina walked over and sat next to India on the stone bench. The smell of the night-blooming jasmine that grew on the arch over the bench filled the air and mingled with Elaina's expensive perfume.

"Why do you think he'd want that?"

"Because then he could accuse me of actually having a heart." Elaina finished the champagne in her glass. "He thinks I'm cold," she said with an eye roll.

"You're not cold." India tried to sound sincere. Elaina cut her a dubious glance. She'd work harder on being believable next time. "You're not overly affectionate, but you aren't coldhearted or mean, Elaina. Even though you try to pretend to be."

The corner of Elaina's mouth tilted up. "I'm sensible and realistic. That's more important when it comes to our family."

That was the truth. Their family was always under

a spotlight in their town. The people of Jackson Falls, North Carolina, looked to the Robidoux family as one of their most influential. Being under that constant spotlight meant they never knew a person's true motives for coming into their lives. It's why they stuck together no matter what. They might not always be able to trust each other, but they were certain they couldn't always trust people outside of their family circle.

"You still haven't answered my question," India asked. "Would you... Do you want to make a scene?"

Elaina lifted the glass to her mouth. Frowned at the empty crystal flute and placed it on the bench next to her. "No. I don't want to make a scene. Scenes don't change things or make things better. I knew eventually he'd move on. I didn't think it would be with that Ferguson twit. I thought he was smarter than that."

"Guys aren't always smart when it comes to the women they sleep with. Byron is proof of that."

Again, Elaina's mouth twitched. "True."

"Why did you two..."

Elaina turned and eyed her.

The warning was clear, but India didn't back down from her sister's sharp glare. "I mean, if you still love him."

Elaina lifted a hand, effectively shushing India. "I didn't come out here for a heart-to-heart."

"Then why did you come out here, Elaina?" India snapped back. Her shoulders tightened at Elaina's quick dismissal. No matter how conflicted she was about her feelings for Travis, she didn't want her sister to hurt.

"To tell you the efforts to keep me and Travis apart aren't needed. I'm not fragile. I'm not going to break."

Elaina pushed a lock of thick hair that had escaped the sleek twist behind her ear.

India swore her sister's hand trembled, but she'd dropped her hand before India could be sure. Though no one else was around, Elaina held herself rigid. Back ramrod straight, shoulders stiff, tightness around her full lips. Her sister was wound even tighter than usual. Concern wormed its way through India's irritation. The feeling was unusual. Elaina never appeared to be on the verge of breaking down. She was always so calm and in control. What was really going on?

India placed a hand over her Elaina's. Her sister's fingers were cold despite the warm evening. "Elaina, you can talk to me. You don't have to hold everything in."

Elaina stood abruptly, the movement swift and graceful despite the speed of her efforts to get out of India's reach. "I came for another reason. Daddy sent me to find you." One of her perfectly manicured brows arched and the semblance of a true smile graced Elaina's lips. "He'd like you to meet Russell Gilchrist."

India winced. She'd forgotten all about Daddy's "project," as Elaina had called him earlier. "I'm not interested in dating anyone."

In Paris she'd casually dated an art professor she'd met in a café. He'd talked to her about his students and passion for art while showing her the city. The entire situation had been sweet and sexy, but she'd known it wasn't forever. She wasn't ready to get back out there again.

"Either meet him now or have him invited to dinner unexpectedly later." Elaina's reply was pragmatic as usual.

"I'm not going to let Daddy run my life," India said.

Elaina placed a hand on her hip and made India feel like a pouting five-year-old with one look. "Will you stop whining? Russell is really a decent guy. He's not stupid and doesn't follow Daddy around like a mindless minion. Plus, Daddy isn't asking you to marry the guy, just to meet him. So, play along. Be nice, maybe go to coffee and then quietly send Russell off on his merry way and Daddy will be none the wiser."

"That won't work."

"Oh really? Do you think Daddy hasn't tried to hook me up in the two years since my divorce?" She held up her left hand. "Still not married or engaged. Trust me. Once you've gone on a date, he loses interest and doesn't pay attention again until you've already sent the schmuck on his way."

Laughter burst from India. She doubted her dad lost interest in anything he set in motion, but she was fairly certain he'd tried to get Elaina remarried or in a new relationship. If Elaina had avoided one of his setups, then she had a point.

"Fine." India stood and brushed off the front and back of her dress.

You look nice. I like the dress.

Hardly the world's most debonair or sophisticated compliment. But those simple words, combined with Travis's dark gaze and smooth drawl, had made her body flare.

Stop it right now! She was not going there. No fantasizing about Travis. His eyes, voice, body or anything else. The air between them was clear. They'd made a mistake that night. He'd gone with her too-many-shots excuse and looked exceedingly relieved to have the entire situation resolved. Obviously, she'd read too much into that night.

Uh, ya think? He married your sister. No more acting the fool over Travis.

She and Elaina found their dad surrounded by friends and colleagues all laughing while he told a story. His eyes lit up and became calculating as he introduced her to Russell. Russell actually took her breath away for a second. The man was movie-star handsome. His tall, lean but muscular form was accentuated by a well-tailored suit, sandy brown skin and green eyes.

After she got over how good-looking he was, she expected him to be arrogant and conceited. But as they talked, she realized he was not only intelligent and well-spoken, but humble. Elaina threw her a told-you-so glance before grabbing a glass of champagne from a passing waiter and excusing herself.

Russell deftly broke her away from the group so they could talk alone. "Mr. Robidoux told me about your travels with the Transatlantic Orchestra," he said after they settled at one of the round tables around the dance floor. "I saw the orchestra two years ago in New York. Were you playing with them then?"

India nodded. "I was. Did you enjoy the show?"

"Yes. I've always been a fan of classical music. I guess it's the old band nerd in me," he said, looking slightly bashful. "You know the art museum has an Arts and Drafts night every month? Would you like to go with me sometime?"

And there it was. The invitation for a date. Over Russell's shoulder, there was movement on the edge of the dance floor. Travis held Camille in his arms. Closely in his arms. Camille smiled up at him and he returned the smile. Her heart clenched.

Travis looked away from Camille. Their gazes locked. His dark stare erased her ability to breathe. He whispered something to Camille but didn't break eye contact with her. India's body shivered as if he'd spoken to her. As if he'd whispered something soft and seductive in her ear. As if his lips were mere inches away and the warm caress of his breath was a prelude to them tracing the edges of her ear. Desire washed over her body like a summer rain, her nipples hardening and tingles flaring out from the apex of her thighs.

He twirled Camille, and the moment was broken.

India felt like she'd just fallen off a roller coaster. Completely thrown for a loop while he danced without a care in the world. What the hell was wrong with her?

A warm hand rested on her shoulder. She jerked her head up. Met Russell's concerned gaze. "Are you okay?"

She nodded, tried to smile. "Sorry, I…I felt a little off for a second. I just got back today—jet lag must be setting in."

Russell nodded. "You're probably exhausted. Do you need me to get you anything?"

She shook her head. "No, I'm good now. Let's go sit closer to the house, if you don't mind. The smoke isn't helping." She indicated the couple sitting across from them at the round table. The man held a Robidoux cigar in his hand.

The smoke wasn't a problem. She loved the smell of her family's cigars, but she needed to get away. Needed to avoid seeing Travis with Camille in his arms. Needed to focus on the gorgeous, considerate man in front of her.

"Of course." Russell stood and held out a hand.

He helped her rise, the strength of his grip surprising and unexpected. She bumped into his front. He quickly stepped back with a mumbled "Excuse me," slipped her arm through his and led her toward the house.

She knew she shouldn't, but she glanced over her shoulder. Travis watched them walk away. The crowd on the dance floor swallowed him and Camille before she could make out the expression in his eyes.

India turned away, placed her other hand over the warmth of Russell's strong biceps and tried to ignore the way Travis made her forget everything with just a damn look.

CHAPTER SIX

TRAVIS TOOK A DEEP, steadying breath as he maneuvered his Cadillac down the gravel drive into the Sunnyside Acres mobile home park. Dozens of single-wide homes were arranged in neat lines down each side of the drive. Pink flamingos, garden gnomes and University of North Carolina flags adorned various trailers, the ornaments the only distinguishing features from one home to the next.

He didn't come home often. If at all. Not because he was ashamed of where he came from, as his parents frequently accused him. He wasn't ashamed. He had too many good memories. Running through the park playing with his friends as kids. Listening to Mr. Jenkins play old-school music and preach to him and his friends about the right way to woo a woman. Losing his virginity between lots nineteen and twenty on the Fourth of July at the age of sixteen while fireworks went off overhead.

He'd known his family didn't have much. His mom didn't work, and his dad barely held down a job, but he'd been happy. He and his friends had hustled and snatched stuff from the houses of the rich folks on the other side of town to help make ends meet.

Until he'd tried stealing from Grant Robidoux. Gotten his ass kicked by the old man. Then told to come work off his debt in the Robidoux tobacco fields instead of going to jail. He'd worked three weekends before Grant gave him a job. After that, he'd become a pet project of Grant's. That's when his parents began to change.

Sellout. Bougie. Wannabe. All things his parents called him when he spent more and more time at the Robidoux estate. Pretty soon his friends caught on. The neighbors. Until going back home became uncomfortable and he went back less and less.

Now, as he drove through the place that had once felt as comfortable as his favorite pajamas, he felt like an outsider.

You need to stop trying.

Yeah, maybe he needed to. But when he saw balloons swaying in the breeze tied to the door of the trailer he grew up in, he knew today wasn't the day. Of course his mom probably wouldn't care that he'd driven here for her birthday.

There were at least twenty people outside of their place. Some hanging around a cooler, others sitting at the picnic table, a few at another table watching a game of cards while the rest walked around laughing and talking with red Solo cups in their hands. The sound of hip-hop echoed in the air. The bass vibrating the windows of his car.

As his car slowed to a stop in front of the party, the laughter died down. Smiles turned into looks of disbelief, astonishment and hostility. The hostility from his dad's side of the family. He wasn't ashamed for taking Zachariah's case, but he didn't know how to get his family to understand without sounding like the betrayer they accused him of being.

He cut the engine, picked up the dozen long-stemmed

roses and card on the seat next to him. He'd considered buying his mom something, but since they didn't talk regularly, he figured the two thousand dollars in the card would be enough. Cash. No check. No way was he giving his family access to his bank routing and account number.

Stepping out of the car, Travis didn't try for waves or fake smiles. He was here to wish his mother a happy birthday in person. Give her a present. Then get the hell out of there.

She doesn't want you here. You could have mailed the money.

True, but he wanted her to see him. Wanted her to accept that despite them turning their backs on him, he wasn't doing the same. He was still their son. They couldn't wish him away.

He felt the bass of the music deep in his bones. Along with the unwavering stares of family and former friends as he crossed the Astroturf his dad put over the dirt in front of the trailer for parties. He stopped at the wooden picnic table in the center of the group.

"Happy birthday, Mom." He held out the roses and card.

Juanita lifted her chin and eyed him. Her dark skin was marked with lines around her mouth and eyes. Mostly from frowning and smoking cigarettes. Her long black hair hung in limp, thin strands around her narrow face. Her dark gaze wasn't outright hostile, but it wasn't welcoming either. She'd dressed up in a lavender sundress that appeared loose and baggy on her slim body.

After several seconds, she reached out and took the flowers and card out of his hand. "Why did you come?"

He could always count on his mom to go straight

to knocking him in the head. He glanced around and pointed to the balloons attached to her chair floating over her head. "I came for the party."

Her lip twisted. "I would have thought you'd know to stay away."

He straightened his shoulders. That's what they wanted him to do. "I don't have a reason to stay away."

He heard grumblings from the direction of his cousins. His mom's two sisters shifted in their seats next to her, eye rolls and grunts accompanying the movements. He fought not to let his hands clench into fists.

The door to the trailer slammed open. "Why is the music down?" His dad's loud voice echoed through the tense silence.

Mac Strickland's eyes landed on his son and the grin on his face transformed into a glower. More grumblings rippled through the gathered guests. A ripple of excitement for an upcoming altercation vibrated in the air. His dad could be considered handsome, if he didn't let his anger for the world and everyone in it show on his face. He and Travis were similar, tall, dark skinned, broad shouldered, but Mac's once solid build was softened with years of beer and neglect. His stomach protruded over the waistband of his jeans and stretched the buttons of what was supposed to be a loose-fitting jean button-down shirt.

He stomped down the stairs. "Well, well, well. Look who came slumming."

Travis held his ground. "I'm not slumming. I came to wish Mom a happy birthday."

"She don't want your happy birthday," Mac sneered. "Not when you're selling out your family." He positioned himself behind Juanita, his beefy hands clutching the back of her chair. His eyes narrowed in on his son.

"I'm not selling out my family. I'm doing my job." Something his dad might have understood if he'd been able to hold on to a job long enough to take pride in his work. Mac had fallen and hurt his back at work seven years ago and rode the wave of worker's comp, unemployment and disability as far as he could.

"Your job," Mac boomed, pointing a thick finger at Travis, "is to look out for family, but you would know that if you didn't have your nose so far up the asses of those Robidoux. You don't know what loyalty means."

Travis had heard the jab before. The accusation no longer stung. That didn't mean hearing his father's bitterness didn't feel like a kick in the nuts.

"I guess I learned from the best." He shouldn't have reacted. Shouldn't let his dad know how much his attitude bothered him. Yet he spent his days defending people. Not defending himself wasn't an option.

Mac pounded his chest. "I know what loyalty means."

"I also know the difference between right and wrong," Travis countered. "What I'm doing is right."

Juanita jumped from her chair. Mac stumbled back. Travis's mom didn't pay any attention to her husband. "What's right is looking out for your family," she said. "Not helping the person who killed your cousin."

"It's not that simple and you know that," Travis said.

Mac pushed Juanita aside and rushed forward. "It is that simple. My brother lost his oldest boy because of your *client*. Instead of helping us, you're over there helping him get off."

"Helping you?" Travis looked between his parents. "Help you do what? I called and asked if y'all needed anything. I paid for the funeral." Because his cousin hadn't had life insurance. Hadn't thought he'd need it at the young age of thirty-three, despite having two kids.

"Don't nobody want your handouts," his dad spat. "Trying to show us how rich you are."

Travis clenched his teeth. No matter what the topic, everything always went back to the same old argument. He'd done well for himself and instead of being happy or proud, his parents resented him. No matter what he did. How much he tried to show them he was still their son and would never forget them or where he came from, they didn't believe him. They took every gesture he made as something for him to show off.

"What do you want me to do, then?" The years of frustration with this constant back-and-forth entered his voice.

"Help us get revenge," his dad said.

The words scrambled like a bad puzzle in his head. Had they completely lost their minds? "What? You can't mean that."

Mac stalked around the picnic table. "I mean it. You better figure out what side you're on real quick. Don't get caught in the cross fire."

A sliver of unease went through Travis. His family didn't mind dipping into petty crimes, but this was beyond that. "You do realize you're threatening my client? I can go to the police with this."

"But you won't," Mac said with a sinister smile. "Not unless you really want to prove you've turned your back on your family."

"I've never turned my back on my family."

His dad grunted and rolled his eyes. The standard reply whenever Travis said he wasn't turning his back on his family. Mac's chin lifted. He looked over Travis's shoulder and crossed his arms over his chest. "Time for you to go. Before you ruin the party."

The back of Travis's neck prickled. Slowly, he turned his head and looked over his shoulder. His uncle Mitch and his youngest son, Devon, flanked him. He fought to not curse and keep all expression off his face. Unlike Mac, Mitch hadn't neglected his body. He was built as if he spent as much time lifting weights as he did breathing. Devon was a younger version of Mitch. Thick necks, beady eyes and square jaws.

Mitch ran drugs through the county. Travis knew because his uncle had tried to get him to sell. Travis hadn't wanted anything to do with that scene and never took his uncle up on the offer. Mitch wasn't a big-time dealer by any means, but he was smart enough to make the link between him and the guys selling on the streets fuzzy enough to prevent the local sheriff's department from taking him in.

Travis eased around and faced Mitch and Devon. He hadn't seen them since before the funeral. When the family had gathered after Antwan's death. He hadn't gone to the funeral. By then he'd agreed to take Zachariah's case and his father told Travis if he showed up at the funeral he'd personally help Mitch beat him out of the church.

"I didn't come here to start trouble." Travis kept his voice calm and cool, even as adrenaline dumped into his system.

Devon lifted the edge of his T-shirt. The butt of a gun protruded from the waistband of his jeans. Mitch smiled, but it was full of malice.

"Then it's time for you to leave," Mitch said.

Travis glanced over his shoulder at his parents. Juanita stepped forward. Mac took her by the arm and shoved her behind him. His dad always forced Juanita into taking his side. But this, he never expected his dad to silently condone such a threat on him. Anger rushed over him like a train out of hell. Hot and fast. Why did he keep trying? Why did he still let their rejection taunt him like a bully on the playground? They hadn't cared. Had left him to his own wits as he grew up. Hadn't cared when he'd started petty theft to make extra money. They'd only cared when he'd gotten close to the Robidoux family. Cared enough to call him a family traitor. To be honest, when had his family *ever* had his back?

The pain of that thought made his throat tighten. He swallowed hard. Getting sentimental wouldn't change this situation.

"Happy birthday, Mama," Travis said grimly over his shoulder. He turned back to his uncle and cousin and stepped forward. They blocked his path to his car. He met their gazes with his own angry glare. Sweat trickled down his back. His heart beat wildly in his chest, but he didn't back down.

Devon chuckled and stepped aside. Without looking back, Travis went to his car and was thankful they at least had the decency not to shoot him in the back. For now.

CHAPTER SEVEN

INDIA CHECKED HER WATCH. For the past hour she'd been held captive in the upstairs family room while Byron's campaign manager, Roy Bouknight, outlined the strategy for her brother's campaign. The primary elections were a few months away. There was another person in Byron's party also running for the seat departed by a senator who'd retired after serving for twenty-five years. The field was wide-open and people in the area were itching for a change. All good news for Byron. India wanted her brother to win, and had succumbed to family pressure by deciding to help out until she heard more about the LA audition, but she was going to kick someone if she had to spend another minute in here plotting politics.

"Now that we've covered the basics..." Roy said in his brisk, no-nonsense tone of voice.

India sat forward on the leather sofa. She was making a beeline for the door as soon as this was over.

"We can discuss the two most pressing challenges of Byron's campaign."

India cocked her head to the side. "Now?" Annoyance crept into her voice. She didn't give a damn. They'd been in here too long to just be getting to the important stuff.

Elaina shot India a don't-be-difficult look. Aunt

Liz glared. Byron and her dad both tried to hide their smiles. Ashiya, who was next to India on the couch, elbowed her lightly in the side.

"I'm just saying. We've been here an hour," India said without remorse.

Byron's grin didn't fade. There was a red tint to Roy's cheeks and the muscle in his jaw jerked. Roy wasn't bad, and he had good ideas for a successful campaign. She'd probably like him if he wasn't the reason she hadn't been able to enjoy her first Saturday morning back home in years.

"This won't take long, India," Byron said. "Besides, we have food. I know you get…irritable when you're hungry."

She glared at her brother, but without any real anger. The irritable retort on the tip of her tongue disappeared with the soft growl of her stomach. She did become bitchy when she hadn't eaten. She should have realized this "quick family meeting" was going to take up all her morning when her dad had the staff bring in fresh fruit, bagels, cheese, coffee and juice.

Late breakfast together my ass.

She stood and crossed the room. She'd had a plate of fruit when they'd first come in. A more substantial meal was what she really wanted. Until she escaped, this would have to do.

Roy straightened his square frame glasses and cleared his throat. "As I was saying." The look he threw her way said before-I-was-rudely-interrupted. India fought the petty urge to stick out her tongue and stacked grapes on a clean china saucer instead. "There are two important things we need to address as part of Byron's campaign. First is his best friend."

India's hand slipped. The fork she was using to pick up pineapple slices clattered to the buffet. All eyes turned to her. Her dad's narrowed.

"Sorry," she mumbled and looked back at the food.

"What about Travis?" Grant asked in a warning tone.

"We need a role for him," Roy answered quickly.

India turned away from the food and gave Roy her full attention. A role for Travis? What did that mean? He was Byron's best friend, that was his role.

Elaina zeroed in on Roy like a predator ready to eviscerate its prey. "Why does he need a role? He's not family."

Byron shifted forward in his seat opposite of Elaina. "Come on, you've got to stop that."

"No. I don't," Elaina replied evenly. "I did not say anything that wasn't a fact."

Roy, good campaign manager that he was, jumped in before the disagreement could boil over into a full argument. "Maybe not, but he's a prominent figure in Byron's life. He and Byron are often seen together. We can't ignore him."

Byron spoke up. "I won't ignore him. He's the person whose advice I value the most."

Roy held up a hand. He looked like he'd already been through this argument and wasn't ready for the replay. "Fine, but it's no secret he isn't on speaking terms with all family members."

Everyone looked at Elaina. She rose to her feet and paced to the window. "What does that have to do with anything?" Elaina asked.

Aunt Liz cocked her head to the side. "Come on, Elaina. You aren't that naive."

Grant faced his oldest daughter. "It's a weak point

people can use to attack. Byron is best friends with his sister's ex-husband, whom she doesn't talk to. I told you it's time for you to move on and at least pretend to be happy."

Elaina's shoulders tightened. "I'm sure we're not the only family in that particular situation."

"Those families aren't getting into national politics," Grant replied. "Our reputation is important. We have to do whatever is necessary to show them not only that Byron is a good candidate, but that our family is strong and sticks together. No hint of dysfunction."

"He's my ex. What did you expect? Us to be best friends forever? I don't have to be nice to him."

"Since you both agreed to the divorce," Grant countered, "you both can be amicable."

"Sorry to disappoint," Elaina replied caustically.

India had noticed the tension between Travis and Elaina. If they weren't on speaking terms, then India wanted to know why. From what India had heard, Elaina moved back to the estate after her divorce, even though Travis offered to move, and sold their home after they split.

"You can't ignore him," Byron's voice interrupted India's speculation.

Irritation blanketed Elaina's face. Roy jumped in before Elaina went in on Byron. "And we need him to help the campaign by showing a different, more urban side of Byron."

Byron's eyebrows shot up. "Excuse me?"

That comment got a range of reactions from the family. Amusement from Ashiya. An indignant frown on her aunt's face. Grant raised a brow. Annoyance welled in India. Urban? What the hell was that supposed to mean?

"Hear me out," Roy said, not breaking a sweat after throwing out that firebomb. "Byron, the perception of you is a spoiled rich boy. That'll make you unrelatable to some people. You're charming and personable, which means you're able to draw people in, but will they trust you in the Senate? Travis grew up hard. Literally in the trailer park across town that's known for drugs and destitution."

Byron rolled his eyes. "I think destitution is a bit dramatic."

"Either way," Roy continued. "Travis made a name for himself. Despite your differences growing up, you two are friends. That friendship makes you approachable. Likeable."

"Glad to know my growing up in destitution makes Byron likeable." Travis's lazy drawl came from the door.

India's heart nearly jumped out her chest. She spun toward the door. Travis didn't look the least bit offended. He looked like he'd stepped off the pages of a catalog with a lazy smile on his face. Handsome, confident and completely in control in a navy button-down and khakis. His dark gaze did a quick sweep of the room. Stopped for an extra second when he met India's gaze, then he looked back at Roy. He strolled into the room over to Byron.

Byron grinned and stood. He clasped Travis's hand and they gave each other a quick hug. "I'm only likeable because I have a friend who grew up on the wrong side of town."

"Make fun all you want," Roy said again, not bothered by being caught talking about Travis. "But everything we can do to prove you're a relatable guy is going to help this campaign."

Byron clasped a hand on Travis's shoulder. "We don't have to bring you into this if you don't want us digging into your family history."

Travis shrugged. "Man, my past is my past. I'm not ashamed of it or my family."

Byron nodded, slapped his friend's shoulder, then dropped his hand. "Even so, we won't be bringing it up or parading you around like you're some urchin we took off the streets." Byron's voice hardened, and he looked directly at Roy. Roy held up his hands in acquiescence.

Elaina looked over her shoulder and grunted. "He *is* some urchin Daddy took off the street."

India's hands clenched into fists. Her eyes jumped to Travis. Again, he was unfazed. His shoulders shook with a silent laugh.

"Sweet and loving as always, Elaina," he said in a mocking voice.

Grant's brows drew together in a scowl. "Elaina, angry and bitter doesn't look good on you."

Elaina crossed her arms tightly over her chest and turned back to the window.

Roy pointed first at Elaina and then Travis. "See, this is what I mean. Travis is obviously going to be part of Byron's campaign, but this animosity between you two won't play out well. You aren't the person to pair with Travis."

Grant turned his attention away from Elaina back to Roy. "Pair. What do you mean pair?"

"For public appearances or fund-raisers. We can't have Travis with Elaina at any events. They'll be too busy tearing each other apart instead of campaigning for you. We need everyone else in the family to demonstrate the family and friendships are still strong despite the divorce. I'm pairing Travis up with Byron and India."

India's jaw dropped. Everyone turned to her. Everyone except Elaina. Who stood even more rigid next to the window.

"Me? Why me?" The words came out in a weird croak and she cleared her throat.

"Because you make sense," Roy explained. "That and Byron has no other siblings." He glanced at Grant. "Right?"

Grant's eyes narrowed. "I don't have any bastards, if that's what you're asking."

"Daddy, crude and offensive don't look good on you," Elaina said in a sweet voice. Grant glared. She responded with a smug smile. Elaina never quivered under one of their father's angry looks.

Getting no response from Elaina, Grant swung his dangerous stare toward Roy. The look had the typical effect on Roy. Color rose in his cheeks. At least he was smart enough not to repeat the statement. Offend Grant Robidoux and he could make your life a living hell.

Roy nodded and rubbed his hands together. "Then India it is."

Travis crossed the room to the food. India quickly stepped out of his way. Her hip bumped the table, rattling the platters set on the surface. Travis raised an eyebrow. She forced herself to relax and nod congenially. She wasn't supposed to *react* when he was near. They were cool now. They'd cleared the air. Deemed what happened years ago a mistake. She couldn't run and hide when he came near.

She focused on Roy. "What do I have to do?"

"There will be a few times when we'll need family members to campaign for Byron if he can't be there personally. We've got a lot of ground to cover and if we can show a united front, I'd recommend having at least two family members together in those cases. I'll partner you with Travis for those appearances. The two of you can play up how great he is as a brother and friend."

Roy made it all sound so easy. Sure, everything seemed simple to everyone else. They didn't realize the easy friendship she'd once shared with Travis was gone. No one knew she could barely look at him without thinking about how she'd loved him. How she'd dreamed about his kiss even after he'd married Elaina. Fought to forget the feel of his hands on her body as she'd stood next to her sister at their wedding.

"Now that that's settled," Roy said, obviously taking India's silence as agreement, "we can get to the next point."

"Are you okay with spending time with me?" Travis asked in a low voice.

India's heart did a triplet beat. He'd slid close to her as Roy moved on. His proximity was like an electric current vibrating against her skin.

"Of course," she said quickly. "Why wouldn't I be?"

"You wouldn't be the only person not wanting my company lately."

The disappointment in his voice made her look up. He wasn't looking at her. He frowned at the floor. His lips pressed into a tight line. She wanted to reach out and touch him. To attempt to erase the sadness from his features. "I'll always want your company."

His head snapped up and he studied her face. She really shouldn't have said that. The words were too close to how she really felt. Too close to breaking the stupid it-was-a-mistake agreement they'd made the night before.

"We'll need to pick out a suitable fiancée for him."

Roy's voice and the randomness of his words broke India from the captivating hold of Travis's eyes. She tuned back into the conversation. "Fiancée? Who needs a fiancée?"

Byron chuckled and placed a hand on his chest. "I do."

She dropped the plate of fruit back on the table. "What? When? To who?" she sputtered.

Grant stood and clamped a hand on Byron's shoulder. "To the perfect woman who will help him become the next senator in this area. She has impeccable lineage, her family is already in politics, and she's smart as a whip. A former law professor with UNC School of Law and on her way to making partner in a prestigious firm."

India looked from her father to Byron. Were they serious? "You didn't mention you were getting married."

Byron shrugged as if not mentioning a possible fiancée wasn't a huge deal. "I didn't decide to ask her until recently. We've been dating for a few months."

Dating for a few months? Wasn't he the same guy Travis teased about three women calling him just yesterday? Her brother was a ladies' man, but he wasn't a dog. He wouldn't be considering marriage to someone if he still had multiple women calling his phone. Would he? Had he changed that much while she'd been gone?

"Do you love her?"

Byron blinked rapidly as if shocked by her question before he smiled his carefree, don't-be-silly smile. "Of course I wouldn't ask her to marry me if I didn't."

"What's her name?" India crossed her arms. Bullshit

her brother was in love. If he was in love, he would've said something. He hadn't mentioned this woman since she'd been home. She wasn't buying what he was trying to sell.

"Yolanda Simms," he said with a smug smile. "You'll meet her at dinner later this week. But don't mention the engagement. I want to surprise her."

"We're doing it later in the campaign," Roy said eagerly. "Not long before the primaries." He looked at his watch. "Okay, that's it. Thanks for your time this morning, everyone."

With that bombshell, the family session ended. Elaina rushed out without a backward glance. Aunt Liz joined Byron, her dad and Roy as they talked more strategy. India stood frozen and watched as her brother smiled, laughed and strategized his way into a Senate seat. They were announcing their engagement closer to the primaries? Was he really getting married just to win?

She spun toward Travis. "You aren't letting him do this, are you?" She pointed over her shoulder at her brother.

Travis stilled with a chocolate croissant halfway to his mouth. "Do what?"

She stepped closer and lowered her voice. "Marry this Yolanda person. Who is she? Are they really dating?"

Travis sighed. "They've gone back and forth for a while."

Which really meant her brother had been sleeping with her for a few months, but there was no commitment. Her hands balled into fists. She couldn't believe this!

"Don't spout off the campaign bullshit with me,"

she said in a low voice that wouldn't carry to her plotting relatives still in the room. "Not with me. This is a campaign maneuver."

"Roy has a point." Travis said the words slowly, as if he couldn't believe he was agreeing with Roy. "Your brother can't be a senator if he's out there picking up women in bars. He's got to settle down. Yolanda is who he chose."

"Did he choose her?" She wouldn't doubt that Roy, or their dad, had picked the perfect woman for him.

"He said he chose her."

"Do you believe him?"

Travis glanced at the group huddled together. "I want to believe him. Giving up what you want for an unhappy marriage isn't worth the price of a Senate seat." He turned a heavy gaze on her. "Not when it ruins a true chance at happiness."

India leaned back. Stunned into silence. Her throat was dry and her stomach fell to her feet. The regret in his eyes created a deep ache in her chest. Had he given up something for an unhappy marriage? Before the words could spill from her lips, he took a bite of the croissant and strolled over to join the strategizing team, leaving India with another unanswered question to taunt her at night.

CHAPTER EIGHT

TRAVIS RARELY LEFT his office at the edge of Jackson Falls to brave the downtown lunch rush, but today he did so to visit Byron's campaign office in the heart of the city. The campaign headquarters was located on the bottom floor of a two-story home renovated into commercial space. The building sat comfortably between an Italian restaurant to the left and a bookstore on the right. A dance studio that overflowed with young kids learning ballet, tap and hip-hop after school occupied the top floor. Travis grabbed the last available space in the parking lot on the side of the building.

Byron's campaign office buzzed with activity. Even before Byron officially announced his intention to run for office, he'd already gathered a group of loyal supporters. Volunteers answered the phones, scheduled appearances and created signs that would soon plaster all of Jackson Falls and beyond. Travis was a regular in the office, so several people waved or spoke as he walked toward the office door in the back.

He knocked twice before a muffled voice said, "Come in," and Travis opened the door. Byron sat behind the desk. He didn't look up from the notecards in his hand. The top button of his blue dress shirt was undone, and the two ends of the blue-and-gray-striped tie hung loosely around his neck.

"Still can't get used to wearing a tie daily," Travis teased.

Byron tossed the cards on the table. Relief washed over his features and he jumped up from the leather chair behind his desk. "Thank God you're here."

"I know I'm great, but what's all this excitement for?" Travis shut the door and came into the room.

Byron came around the desk and leaned on the edge. "I'm going to lose my mind if I have to go over the campaign speech Roy wrote for me one more time." He rubbed his eyes and looked way too tired for it to only be noon. "He's running me ragged."

"You wanted the best campaign manager there was, and he's the best." Before he took on Travis's campaign, Roy had been behind the successful run of an underdog candidate in the Southwestern part of the state. The upset had overthrown a representative who'd held the seat firmly for over a decade. He'd pulled off a miracle. Byron's campaign should be a cakewalk after that.

"True." Byron dropped his hands from his eyes. "I want to win." His voice hardened like concrete.

Travis had seen determination on Byron's face before, but rarely like this. Byron had taken the only-son, golden-child, rich-boy role and ridden that persona to achieve every success in his life. He was a good lawyer and cared about his clients, but becoming a lawyer wasn't a way to improve his life, as it had been for Travis. To see his friend so focused on the campaign gave Travis a mixed sense of pride and discomfort. Byron didn't like losing. How far would he go to win?

"Is that why you're proposing to Yolanda?" Travis asked. He walked over and sat in one of the chairs in front of Byron's desk.

Byron looked everywhere but at Travis. "I want to marry her."

"You can't play politician with me. You and Yolanda had a few regular hookups, but the relationship wasn't exclusive. At least, you weren't. Now you're ready to marry her?"

Byron finally met his gaze. "I need to appear stable."

"Did Roy put you up to this?"

"It wasn't Roy's idea."

Travis bit back a curse. "Was it your dad?" Grant Robidoux liked to manipulate things to work out in his favor. If he thought something needed to change to get the outcome he wanted, then he'd do everything in his power to make that change. Travis bet the man thought he could change the Earth's rotation if he concentrated hard enough.

"Believe it or not, it was my idea," Byron said.

Travis searched his friend's face. There was no trace of deceit. Travis leaned forward, stunned. "Why would you choose her?"

"For all the reasons my dad mentioned. Don't worry, she knows the deal. She doesn't love me any more than I love her, but she's got her own political aspirations. She knew what my intentions were when I first mentioned the possibility of us getting married. She's smart, and she knows how to run a campaign. With her by my side, I'll win."

Travis shook his head. Byron made a marriage of convenience sound so simple and easy. If only that were true. "Did you not witness me in a bad marriage for years? Elaina and I weren't right together."

Byron shrugged off his warning. "That was after the miscarriage. Before…before, you two were okay."

Travis's throat tightened. The reminder like a punch in the chest. He looked away from Byron, not wanting his friend to see the pain that still crept up whenever he thought of the miscarriage. They'd tried to make their marriage work, even though they both knew they'd been forced into the situation. The idea of a baby had brought hope to them both. Hope that was snuffed out at fourteen weeks.

"Even before…" He let his voice trail off. He'd never told Byron that Grant had insisted he marry Elaina. Byron looked up to his father. Travis didn't have that with his dad. As Byron's friend, Travis hadn't wanted to take away his respect for the man he admired most in his life.

"Things weren't always perfect before either," Travis said. "After we realized we'd rushed into things. The loss didn't help."

"Your situation is different from mine. Yolanda and I know what we're getting into."

"Still—"

Byron stood and walked around his desk, his shoulders tense and his face set in a stubborn frown. "I'm not budging on this. Love, romance, all that is a bunch of mumbo jumbo anyway. Foolishness that gets people hurt. I don't need love. Just a perfect wife. We'll both look the other way if we want a little fun on the side."

There was a knock on the door before Travis could tell Byron that was the stupidest thing he'd ever heard. Byron could try his love-is-mumbo-jumbo excuse on someone else. He knew his friend had loved once before. Loved hard and sacrificed a bit of himself. After that experience, he hadn't bothered to get close to another woman.

Byron relaxed and smiled. "Good, she's here."

"Who's here?" Travis turned to the door.

"India. I asked both of you to come by today." He crossed the room and opened the door.

Travis immediately stood and straightened his clothes. Not that he had to. His black pants and butter-yellow shirt were freshly pressed from the dry cleaner's. He reached up to smooth the back of his faded hair-cut, then dropped his hands. There was not going to be anything between him and India. If he thought Grant had nearly skinned him years ago for kissing India, he could imagine the torture he'd plan if he hooked up with her now. He'd kill him faster than his cousin and uncle would.

India walked in, a bright smile on her face as she hugged Byron. She was breathtaking in a soft, mint-green top that hung off one of her shoulders. A long, flowy black skirt draped her curves and brushed the tops of her sandaled feet. Her curly dark hair was pulled away from her face in a high bun. When her eyes spot-ted him, her smile stiffened before she relaxed.

"Travis, I didn't expect you to be here."

There was nothing in her voice to indicate she wasn't happy to see him, but he got the feeling she'd rather him be somewhere else. "Apparently Byron has sum-moned us both," he said, trying to sound carefree. Not like he wanted to cross the room, pull her into his arms and taste the smooth skin bared by the loose neckline of her top.

"Oh really." She raised a brow at Byron. "What for?"

"I want to hold another campaign fund-raiser din-ner, but not at the Robidoux estate," Byron said. He was back to business and led India over to the chair next to

Travis in front of his desk. "I want something a little more informal. To try to draw in voters who aren't able to pay $500 per plate."

India settled into the chair. The faint scent of her perfume, soft and feminine, drifted over. Toyed with his sensibilities. "Okay, what does that have to do with us?" Travis asked.

"I'd like you two to put it together." Byron said it as if Travis and India planned fund-raisers every day in their sleep.

India shifted forward in her seat. "Why in the world would you choose us?"

"Because neither of you think like the rest of the family. Roy may have been a jerk when he said it, but he was right. I can be a little…spoiled."

"Ya think?" Travis replied. India chuckled.

Byron gave him a warning look, then kept talking. "I wouldn't know how to plan something simple if I tried. You two, on the other hand, are more…"

"Destitute?" Travis grinned and made air quotes with his fingers. He wasn't offended by Roy's position. That was his job, to think of how to play every angle. Besides, it wasn't as if Travis had grown up in the lap of luxury.

"If you're destitute," India said, placing a hand on the arm of his chair. "What does that make me?" Her eyes sparkled with amusement.

He rubbed his chin and pretended to mull over her words. "I think you're the relatable one. The heart of the family, remember?"

India nodded. "Ahh, yes, that's right. We make him more human."

They laughed and their eyes met. In that second,

they connected like they had before he'd screwed up and almost had sex with her. Back when he and India would poke fun at the pompousness and absurdity that was the Robidoux family sometimes.

"Call it what you want," Byron cut in, unfazed by their teasing. "You'll come up with a great idea. And I need it to happen at the end of next month."

The deadline cut short their laughter. India narrowed her eyes at her brother. "Wait, you want us to plan a fantastic, budget-friendly campaign dinner, and you want it to happen next month? Are you insane?"

Byron sank into the chair behind his desk, his don't-argue-with-me stare a perfect replica of Grant's. "No, I'm determined. There's a difference. Can you do it?"

"Byron, in case you don't remember," Travis said, "I'm in the middle of a big case that's probably going to make my family kill me." He kept his voice light but the memory of his cousin flashing a gun popped into his mind. They didn't need to know he was serious.

"You come up with the idea, then delegate the actual planning of the event." Byron pointed to the door. "I've got tons of volunteers. Just tell them what they need to do to make it happen."

"You really think planning a campaign event is that easy, don't you?" India asked dryly.

Byron clasped his hands together on top of his desk. His eyes pleading, they passed between India and Travis. "Please, guys, I really need something that isn't going to cost people an arm and a leg to attend. I know I need to make money and big sponsors are great, but I'm also running to help people who don't have thousands of dollars to give. I get it, I'm asking a lot, but this would really ease my mind with everything else going on." He finished by looking at Travis.

Everything else, like an upcoming engagement. Travis didn't agree with all of Byron's tactics for getting into office, but his heart was in the right place with this idea. Travis's caseload was full, but he had other attorneys in the practice who could help with the work. The King case was his biggest, and helping India do a low-cost event shouldn't be too much of a distraction.

"Fine, I'll see what I can move around," Travis said. He turned and faced India. "If you've got the time to help." Was she still planning to leave for California soon? She'd agreed to help with Byron's campaign, but that didn't guarantee she would be in town for a long time. She could decide go to California and fly back to Jackson Falls for important events.

India chewed on the corner of her lip. She eyed Byron, who returned her look with his own please-help-me face. Rolling her eyes, she met Travis's gaze. "I can help."

"Are you sure? What about California?"

"You're not still going? I thought you were helping the campaign," Byron chimed in.

India held up a hand and stopped Byron before he could ask more questions. "I won't know about the audition for two months or so. I can help plan this event and still fly out there for the audition."

Byron sagged in relief. Travis was relieved as well, but held back the joy her answer caused. She wasn't leaving soon. He'd get to see her more. He wanted more time to repair their relationship. Rebuild the friendship they'd lost. That was all.

"Good, I knew I could count on you two." The phone

on Byron's desk rang. "Excuse me a second." He answered the phone.

Travis focused on India. "Thank you for agreeing to help with this. I'm not sure I would know where to start."

"I don't know if I'm the best person to tell you," she replied. "But we'll think of something."

"Let's get together later this week and go over ideas."

India stilled for a second. He hadn't meant to make the suggestion sound like a date. It wasn't a date. There was no way they would ever date.

"You can come by the office," he said quickly. "Call my receptionist and she'll let you know when I'm free. I have some appointments on my phone calendar, but she keeps up with everything else."

India nodded and smiled. He tried not to be offended that she looked relieved. "Sure, of course. I'll give her a call." She checked her watch. "You know, I've got to go."

She stood and Travis got up, as well. Byron covered the mouth of his phone. "You're leaving already?"

"Yeah, I promised Ashiya I'd stop by her store, and I've got a few other errands I need to run."

"Thanks for coming by, India," Byron said. He dropped his hand on the phone. "Sorry, I was speaking to my sister. Can you repeat that?"

Travis turned to India. "I'll walk you out."

She looked as if she wanted to argue, but he had no reason to stick around with Byron's phone call still going. She must have realized the same because her lips tilted up in a stiff smile. Travis waved at Byron, who threw up two fingers in a peace sign. He opened the door for

India and they were silent as they walked through the busy office.

Outside, the sun caught the highlights of India's hair. She squinted and slipped a pair of large black shades out of her purse and onto her face. They made her look like a sexy Hollywood diva.

"Well, I guess I'll see you later this week," she said.

"I'm usually free in the mornings. I also come in early, so feel free to set up a time before eight if that works for you." He was stalling, and he knew it. Trying to find a reason to keep her around a little longer.

"Cool, I'll keep that in mind."

A few seconds passed. There wasn't much else he could say to prolong their conversation. That didn't stop him from trying to think of a reason. He couldn't see her eyes through the dark shades, but he felt her gaze on him. She tugged the corner of her lip in between her teeth. His stomach tightened, and desire stirred farther south.

He looked away first. Staring at her for too long only made his thoughts want to go places they had no business going. "Have a good one."

India stepped back from him. "Yeah, you, too." She turned and nearly sprinted to her car parked several spaces over from his.

Travis walked to his own vehicle. India waved as she pulled out of the lot. He stood at his car door and watched her drive away. Watched and wondered if he'd ever drop this longing he had for India.

CHAPTER NINE

INDIA DECIDED TO get started sooner rather than later with planning Byron's campaign fund-raiser. She called the receptionist and confirmed that Travis came in earlier than the rest of the staff. His receptionist also confirmed he had no morning meetings on Thursday and she could catch him first thing. Which was why India had gotten up early and headed straight for Travis's office. She'd made the appointment for eight fifteen with his receptionist, but knowing he'd be here long before then pushed her to arrive early. If she put off working on this with him, she was more likely to avoid planning all together.

She wanted to strangle Byron for asking her to work with Travis. Then again, it wasn't like he knew about their history. Byron wanted to win, and she'd agreed to be officially partnered with Travis during his campaign. Besides, they were "cool" with each other now. Avoiding him wasn't an option. Not the best option anyway. And it wasn't as if Travis was burning with desire for her. He still treated her like his good friend. She was the only one still hung up on a night of almost having sex from years ago.

She pulled into his parking lot at seven forty-five and sure enough his Cadillac was already in the parking lot. She expected the door of his office to be locked but it swung open easily even though no one sat behind the desk in the reception area.

The office was decorated tastefully. Leather and wood made the space comfortable and professional. Painted landscapes on the wall created a welcoming feeling. She recognized his work instantly. Travis painted with bold, sweeping strokes that intricately blended light and shadow.

She liked seeing his paintings prominently on display. He was still painting. She'd worried the time with her family might have killed his creativity. Grant Robidoux was a superficial lover of the arts. Great to entertain a person for a few hours, but not something worth cultivating seriously.

"Hello," she called out into the empty space. No answer.

She waited for a minute before walking down the hall. His car was outside, so he had to be in here somewhere. The thick gray carpet muffled her footsteps as she passed a conference room and several empty offices. In the back corner was a closed door with Travis's name emblazoned on a gold plate beside the door.

She knocked and waited. The muffled sound of Travis's voice came from the other side of the door. Taking that as acknowledgment of her knock, she opened the door and walked in.

Her feet froze on the threshold. Travis stopped in the middle of singing and slipping on a shirt. One arm was in the sleeve of his white button-down, the other poised to slip into the other sleeve. Wireless earbuds were in his ear.

She shouldn't look. She really should keep her eyes up, but since when did eyes follow rules when there was a handsome, half-naked man in a room? She barely breathed as she took in the chiseled chest, defined abs and decadent brown skin. His pants were unzipped, providing a glimpse of red boxer briefs. She swallowed hard. Fire spread through her body, fast and dangerous like an out-of-control forest fire. It consumed her nerves faster than dried leaves on the forest floor.

Travis pulled the earbuds out and music drifted from the devices. He dropped his arms, the shirt still half on his body. "India?"

Her lungs finally decided to function again. She sucked in air. "Travis…sorry. I called out." She took in his really nice muscles and licked her lips. "You're not dressed."

"I came here straight from the gym." He tapped the screen of his phone and the music stopped before pointing to a door in the corner of his office. "I showered in my bathroom there. What are you doing here?"

"Your receptionist mentioned you didn't have meetings this morning. I know our appointment was at eight fifteen, but I came early to catch you before your day started." Her eyes dipped to his chest again. Then slid lower to the red fabric peeking below his navel. She pulled her lower lip between her teeth. Her pulse jumped to a fast, erratic tempo as she tried not to imagine what lay behind the red.

"You definitely caught me before my day started."

Her gaze jumped up at the sound of his voice. If he noticed her blatant staring at his body, he didn't let on. "Give me a second and I'll get dressed so this won't be weird."

"It's not weird," she said quickly. His abs rippled as he stretched and slipped his other arm in the shirt. Her gaze dropped again. She bit her lip to stop the goofy, embarrassing, you're-naked-and-sexy grin trying to take over her mouth.

Travis raised a brow. He put his hands on his hips instead of buttoning the shirt. "Having this conversation without me wearing a shirt wouldn't be weird?"

The fire in her system roared to life. She fought not to squirm as prickles of desire played hopscotch over her skin while her face burned with embarrassment. Weird was not the word that came to mind. Tempting, distracting, mouthwatering maybe.

I am so pathetic.

Here she was tripping over her words and ogling him like a dog waiting for their owner to drop a morsel from the dinner table when he only wanted to get dressed. Of course this was weird.

"I didn't mean it that way. Just I'm not weirded out by a man with no shirt. I've seen shirtless men before. Tons actually. In fact we visited this nude beach in—"

"I get the picture." He grinned and buttoned his shirt. "My naked chest is not that big of a deal."

His tone was casual, but she swore he was disappointed. She bit her lip instead of immediately rushing to reassure him. Telling him how much of a big deal seeing him shirtless actually was would only further her embarrassment. Unless he wanted her to admit she liked his bare chest.

Not following that dangerous path, India turned and examined his office. "You've got a nice place here."

"Thank you. When Byron and I decided to open our own practice, we had no idea how successful we'd be. He could take on cases when he was in State House, but now that he's running for Senate, it's pretty much all on me."

She turned back to him. His shirt was completely buttoned, tucked in, and his pants zipped. He was perfectly presentable, which shouldn't make her want to pout. "Are you cool with that? Having more of the workload now that Byron is moving on?"

"I am. I have no desire to run for public office. I'd rather help defend people who need help. If Byron wins, he's going to sign over his part in the practice to me."

"Wow. Is that what you want?"

"It's a little scary, the idea of me being in charge of everything, but that's normal. If I wasn't a little nervous about it, then I'd be too confident and maybe make mistakes. But, yeah, I want this. I want to stand on my own. Without having to rely on my connections to your family."

She could understand that. She looked around his office again. The perfect decor, cool, professional ambience, and no hint of Travis's personality except for the landscapes on the wall.

"Good for you," she said, turning back to the painting.

She recognized the location. A creek near the back of the Robidoux estate. The area was pristine, beautiful and quiet. Nothing but the sounds of water trickling and the wind rustling through the leaves of the trees along the banks. He captured the peace of the place so perfectly. Would all of the creativity inside of him be lost once he was sole owner of the firm?

Travis chuckled. She turned away from admiring the landscape on the wall to him and raised a brow. "That sounded really sincere."

Heat rose in her cheeks. Yeah, she could've tried to sound more enthusiastic about a big change in his life. "Sorry. I am happy for you, really."

"But?"

She pointed to the painting on the wall. "But I remember when all you wanted to do was paint. Your dream was to open your own studio and teach others how to paint. I'd always pictured you would do that one day."

Understanding filled his eyes. He crossed the room with slow measured steps. When he moved like that, she couldn't help but notice the grace of his slim and toned body. He stopped close enough for her to be aware of the tall strength of him and smell the subtle scent of his cologne, but not so close that she would accidentally bump into him if she moved. She ran a hand over her arm, but the movement didn't soothe the tingling awareness buzzing over her skin.

"I pictured that, too," he said, sliding his hands into his pants pockets. "Then life happened. Your dad helped me through college. I needed to be able to support a wife. The job at Robidoux Tobacco in their legal department was hard to turn down. When I was tired of corporate law and Byron suggested starting our own firm, I was ready to make the move. I like being a defense attorney. Most days anyway." He said the last part with a half smile that made her heart kick.

She understood that. Travis's father hadn't been reliable for him and his mom. That's why Travis had become a petty hustler to make more money before her dad decided to get him off the streets. He would have wanted to be reliable once he had a family depending on him.

"Okay, I get why you decided to work for the company, but after the divorce… Once you left Robidoux Tobacco, why didn't you decide to pursue your dream?"

He stared at the painting. "I don't really know." He looked at her. "The idea of opening a studio didn't cross my mind. I just knew I wanted to be on my own, and I needed to find a way to do that." His voice and the line between his brows hinted at his regret for letting that dream go.

She looked at the painting and remembered going to that same spot after graduation when her dad tried to force her into choosing a college with a great business program over one with a great music program. "Did Daddy make you work for Robidoux Tobacco?" Was that the reason he'd chosen law over art?

Travis's eyes shuttered as if someone had snapped closed the curtains to what he really felt. "He didn't make me. Not really. I always had a choice."

"Then why do you sound like you regret the choice?"

He faced her, his dark eyes intent as he studied her features. "When you're younger, things seem a lot harder to overcome. A lot more difficult to survive."

"Do the things that seemed so hard then still seem hard now?" After all these years, she still found it difficult to ask what had changed between them. Mostly because she didn't want him to confirm that their night together had been a whiskey-fueled mistake.

He considered her words, then shook his head. "No. I would have done everything differently. I would have chosen what I wanted. Who I…" He trailed off.

Her heart jumped erratically again. Conflicting emotions followed, bouncing here and there as her mind raced with uncertainties. Who what?

"Chosen what?" she whispered.

Travis turned his back to the painting. They faced each other. Separated by a few feet physically and a thousand miles emotionally. His face was an unreadable mask as he watched her.

Unreadable except for his eyes. They were dark, intent and swirled with something hot and primal that made her body respond. Her mouth got dry and she sucked in a short, shallow breath. The silence in the room vibrated with the force of the attraction snapping between them. His gaze dropped to her mouth. She was chewing the corner of her lip. She stopped immediately and licked her lips. Travis's eyes narrowed slightly. His own breathing seemed shallow. The pulse in his throat just as erratic as hers.

They were friends. That night had been a mistake. *We can't go there!*

Sure, all of those things were reason enough for her to step away. Break the sensual spell she was falling under. She *couldn't* look away. Couldn't shake the anticipation of hearing what he would have done differently.

Travis lifted a hand. His fingertips barely brushed her chin. The featherlight touch radiated through her veins. "Chosen not to make so many rash decisions. I messed up more than once."

His hand dropped. He broke eye contact, took a step back and walked to his desk.

India let out a breath. Her heart went from overdrive to bitter disappointment. He'd messed up with her. She'd been one of those rash decisions. He didn't see what could have been when he looked at her, he just saw another mistake.

India kept her back to him. Pretended to look at the

painting while she tried to wrestle the embarrassment and frustration churning in her midsection back into a confined space of her heart. She had to stop looking for signs Travis would have done things differently. He wouldn't have. If she left town with a broken heart again, it would be her fault.

"I still don't think you should give up your dream of painting," she said, trying to appear as if his words hadn't been a blade in her heart.

"I still paint when I can," he said.

She plastered what she hoped was a nonchalant look on her face before turning around. Travis leaned back against the edge of his desk. "Do you?"

"Not as much as I'd like, but I haven't given it up completely. Me not painting would be like you never playing again."

Her eyes widened, and she shuddered. "I couldn't stop playing if I tried." Music was her life. Part of her soul. There was no way she'd be able to give up her violin.

"Exactly, but I just haven't been as fortunate as you to make it my career."

"I could have a permanent position." She crossed the room and rested her hands on the back of one of the chairs before his desk.

"Here in Jackson Falls?" He sounded almost enthusiastic about the idea.

She shook her head. "The LA Philharmonic, remember?"

He rubbed his jaw. "Oh yeah, that's right."

She chuckled and crossed her arms. "You don't have to sound so enthusiastic."

He held up his hands in a you-got-me gesture. "My

bad. You're right. I just don't get why you have to settle across the country."

She needed to move to California. She needed to be away from him. "I want the opportunity and California is just as good a place as any."

He took a few seconds to respond. "Then I wish you luck." He spoke slowly, like he'd had to search for the right words.

Her heart wanted to believe his hesitation came because he wanted her close. The rash-decisions comment from earlier killed that hope. Her damn heart was going to get her into trouble. "Thank you."

He rubbed his hands together. "So, about Byron's fund-raiser. That is the reason you dropped in so early. Did you have an idea?"

Yes, the real reason she was here. To talk about the campaign. Not talk about his art, her audition or wonder what could have been. "I'd thought about a family fun day at the park. Maybe partnering with the local community center to hold it."

His brows drew together. "How would that raise money?"

"The proceeds from the food and game sales could go toward Byron's campaign."

"We'd have to work out deals with the vendors," he said thoughtfully. She could see him thinking over the possibilities.

"Have you had any thoughts?"

He shook his head, and fatigue that went beyond a bad night's sleep covered his face. He looked depleted. "Honestly, no. I've been preoccupied with the upcoming trial. The state is bringing in new evidence to smear

Mr. King's reputation. I spent most of last night going over solutions to that."

The case that pitted him against his family. She was in front of him with a comforting hand on his arm before she'd registered moving. "Are you sure you're okay?"

A light of appreciation filled his eyes. His hand, strong and warm, covered hers. "I'm fine but thank you for asking. Comes with the territory."

"But your family."

He squeezed her hand. His fingers were firm but gentle on hers. The muscles of his arms steady and strong beneath her touch. "Will understand that I'm only doing my job. My job is to defend my client. Even imperfect people deserve a fair trial."

She didn't know the particulars of the case, but she didn't like the look in his eye when he discussed the upcoming trial. "If you need to talk or anything…"

"Are you offering your shoulder for me to lean on?" he asked with an upturn of his lips.

Her heart sighed. Her body melted. "I'm here for you."

Something, longing maybe, flashed in his eyes. He lifted his hand away and dropped his eyes. "I appreciate that. I'll be fine but thank you."

India pulled her hand off his arm. Once again, she felt foolish. She had to get a hold of her reactions to him. "You know, you're really busy, and I'm just here waiting until it's time to go to LA. Why don't I handle things so you don't have to worry about it?"

Travis shook his head before she even finished. "I'm not putting all of this on you. I may not be able to do much, but I'm willing to help however I can. A family day at the park sounds great. We can partner with a local restaurant to sell food. Make it like a cookout or something."

"A family reunion vibe," she said.

"Yeah, I like that. Invite people over. Get to know the candidate. Byron can give a speech and work the crowd. No cost to attend."

"You think he'll go for it?"

"Byron? Yes. He wants something easy, and we'll make this easy. Great job with the idea. Let's make it happen."

She relaxed. That was easy. "I can work on finding a restaurant and reserving the park near the town square. We can communicate through email to make it easier with your schedule."

"Sure, but if you need me, feel free to drop in again."

And catch him half naked. She didn't think so. "I'll call first and not arrive thirty minutes early."

"I didn't mind you coming early," he said. Their eyes met. Electric heat rushed through her.

"Still, I think it's better if I don't pop in on you again." She let out a stiff laugh.

"Yeah," he said with a smile. "Next time you might catch me without pants."

The image of Travis in nothing but those red boxer briefs filled her mind. Her nipples hardened. Heat exploded in her midsection. She crossed her arms and rubbed the back of her neck. "Nah." She cleared her throat. "We wouldn't want that."

CHAPTER TEN

INDIA MET ASHIYA for breakfast while she was in town after her meeting with Travis. Ashiya owned a high-end consignment shop downtown. She'd opened the place after working as a nurse for five years before realizing fashion was her passion. Breakfast had been fun, but the real reason India needed to see her cousin burst from her lips.

"You've got to help me find a man."

Ashiya's eyes nearly popped out of her head. She'd just taken a sip of iced tea as she and India walked down Main Street from the bistro where they'd had breakfast toward Ashiya's shop. India's hastily blurted request must have caught Ashiya off guard because she coughed and held up one finger. She stopped walking and faced India.

"Hold up," Ashiya said in a wheezy voice. She wiped a tear from her eye. "Where is this coming from?"

Oh, just a regular old lusting-for-my-sister's-ex-husband situation.

She couldn't say that. After meeting with Travis and nearly losing her mind at the sight of all that rich, dark skin exposed, there was only one thing for India to do: find a distraction. Ignoring her feelings for Travis had been a lot easier when there was an ocean between them. Now nothing separated them—she was even going to be working with him as they planned Byron's campaign event. At home, she had her violin and her family, but that wasn't enough to keep her thoughts from straying to Travis. She needed to get her life right and finally move on.

"It's been a while," India said. She stepped out of the way for a woman walking a dog. "I'm ready to get back out there."

The sun was high, and the air unseasonably warm for early March. The sidewalks were filled with people in business suits, college students who congregated at some of the coffee shops along Main Street, and a group of students going to the art museum.

Ashiya tilted her head to the side. She wore round blue-tinted shades that matched her nonconforming personality. "How long is a while?"

"Does it really matter?"

Ashiya gave her a don't-be-silly look. "Yes, it matters. If we're talking weeks, then I can take a little time and find the right guy. If we're talking months or years, then I can point you in the direction of a guy who'd be good in a pinch just to take the edge off."

India covered her mouth and laughed. "You've got serious problems."

"Apparently you're the one with the problem. So spill. Weeks, months or years?" She sipped her tea and batted long lashes while waiting on India's reply.

India sighed and thought back to the art professor she'd last dated in Paris. They'd both known it was temporary, and he had been good with his hands, but outside of the bedroom, they'd had little in common. "Months."

Ashiya lowered her shades and peered at India over the edge. "How many months?"

India counted and couldn't bring herself to answer. Five months was a while, but not long enough for her to be desperate for a quick hookup. "Will you stop worrying about the details and fill me in on the available single men in the area?"

"Damn, that long." Ashiya shook her head and pushed up her shades.

India bumped Ashiya with her elbow. "Just stop and give me some ideas. Nothing long-term though. I'm still waiting to hear back about going to LA."

Ashiya rolled her eyes. "You're still on that?"

"Yes, I'm still on that. I've done a lot with Transatlantic, but now I want to build my own career. Going to LA would be huge. Staying here and being another Robidoux on the campaign trail won't." She held up a finger when Ashiya opened her mouth to argue. "So before you tell me I've been away too long, how about you give me some suggestions so I can have a little fun while I'm home?"

Ashiya glowered for another second before letting out a breath in a huff and moving on. "Well, lucky for you your dad has already introduced you to the most eligible bachelor in town." She started walking down the sidewalk again.

India matched her pace. "Russell?"

Ashiya chuckled. "I can't believe you're saying his name as if it's a surprise. The guy is gorgeous."

"He is. I just didn't realize he was the most eligible man in town." Though she shouldn't be surprised. The man had taken her breath away. Despite his looks, he hadn't made her body yearn to get closer.

"He's rich, good-looking, and he's not an asshole," Ashiya said. "That pushes him to the top of most people's lists. Have you talked to him since the party?"

India shook her head. "No, he's still calling and texting. He's not being pushy, but he's letting me know he's interested. I haven't really made myself open to him." She still wasn't warm on the idea of going for the guy her dad was pushing her toward. Not until she knew the ulterior motive.

"Why not? You can't tell me you don't think he's good-looking." Ashiya bumped India's shoulder with hers and winked.

"He is good-looking," she conceded. "He's the best looking man I've ever met."

"Then what's the problem?"

He wasn't the man she wanted. "My dad wants us together. I don't want to be forced into a relationship."

Ashiya nodded and sipped her tea as she processed India's reason. "On the real, I get that. But this time your dad actually picked someone who's pretty decent."

"If you think he's so great, why haven't you gone out with him?"

Ashiya stumbled. India reached out to keep her from falling. She checked the sidewalk to see what her cousin tripped on, but there'd been nothing in their path.

Ashiya waved India off. "Sorry, still getting used to these heels. What were we talking about?"

"I asked why you haven't gone out with Russell."

Color tinged Ashiya's cheeks. She shrugged and adjusted her shades. "Don't be silly. I'm with Stephen."

"Still? I thought you two broke up a year ago."

Ashiya and Stephen had been on-again, off-again since the summer after high school. When they'd first gotten together, their relationship had been filled with drama, arguments over nothing and dragging others into their foolishness. He'd been Ashiya's first love, which made moving on for good hard for her cousin.

"We had a fight a year ago." Ashiya's tone was defensive. "Mama loves him. Daddy thinks he's great. He's finally starting to talk about marriage."

"Marriage? Do you want to marry him?" God, India hoped not. She didn't like Stephen. He took advantage of Ashiya's love for him and wasn't shy about proving he still had control over her emotionally.

Ashiya waved a hand. "Why not? We've made it this far."

"Making it this far is almost as bad as that song that says you're not getting younger, so you might as well get hitched," India said with a shudder.

"India, you're so optimistic. Which is what I love about you, but life isn't a fairy tale. Stephen and I have history. We're well suited…most of the time, and our families are connected. Not marrying him because I'm waiting for some perfect love is foolish."

Was this what her family had succumbed to? People willing to settle for relationships that weren't exactly what they wanted. Byron was ready to marry a woman for the sake of his campaign. Ashiya entertaining the idea of marrying a man whom she'd sworn to never speak to again just a year before.

Are you very different? Ready to date someone else when you know who you want.

But her situation was completely different. The person she wanted was so off-limits he was damn near taboo. Crossing the sibling's-ex line was a hard no. Do not pass go. Do not collect two hundred dollars. Not only would she lose the fragile relationship she had with her sister, but the scandal in the town would hover over the family for years. Finding someone else to date wasn't settling, it was necessary.

"I'm going to call Russell," she said. She wanted to enjoy the rest of her time with Ashiya. The conversation about her and Stephen could wait until another day. "I'll see if he wants to go out this weekend."

"There's a new art exhibit at the museum. You should go to that."

"What if he doesn't like art?" Russell asking her to Arts and Drafts didn't mean he was into that. She'd had guys ask her to museums because they were trying to impress her. India loved the arts, but she'd discovered few men were as addicted as she was. Travis was the exception. He could discuss painting or a piece of music with her for as long as she wanted without ever looking bored. Talk about a hard act to follow.

"I've seen him there before when I've gone to the museum for a quick lunch break," Ashiya said. "A guy that hangs out at an art museum must like art."

India nodded. Hanging out in an art museum was promising. Ashiya said he wasn't an asshole. Despite the misgivings she had of her dad introducing him, Russell didn't have much going against him. "Cool. I'll see if he wants to check out the exhibit."

BY THE TIME Travis left the office to meet with his last client of the day, he still hadn't gotten the interaction with India out of his mind. He hadn't mistaken the look in her eye when she'd caught him shirtless in his office. Clearly, India still found him attractive. Which made pretending like he didn't want to have her body against his whenever they were in a room together extremely difficult.

He needed to get his mind on something else. Quickly. The meeting with his client should succeed where the other meetings today had failed.

Zachariah King was out on bond. Despite the general animosity thrown his way by those who wanted revenge for Antwan's death or thought he deserved to be thrown in jail, he'd strut around town like a tourist on vacation.

"When are you going to get these damn ankle bracelets off me?" Zachariah said as soon as Travis joined him in his study that afternoon.

Travis suppressed a sigh and pulled his brown leather messenger bag over his head. "Zach, I've told you staying on house arrest is best for you right now. There are people in the town who aren't happy about what you've done."

Zachariah snorted. He strode across the study to sit heavily on one of the oversize leather couches. "I did this town a favor, getting rid of that punk."

Travis clenched his teeth. He counted to ten before responding. Antwan hadn't been close to Travis in years, but that didn't mean Travis wanted to hear him talked about with disgust. "You killed someone."

Zachariah tugged on his sweatpants and settled more comfortably on the couch. "I killed a gang member. A gang member who was trying to rob me."

"Rob you of money you took from hardworking people around town," Travis countered.

"What? You're trying me now? I thought you were supposed to be defending me."

Travis shoved up his shirtsleeves. They stopped midforearm because he hadn't loosened the button and that only frustrated him more. "I am, and as your attorney, I have to warn you that going around bragging about the killing won't help your chances with the jury."

"If you play your cards right, the jury will think I did a public service."

Travis's hands clenched into fists. "Are you forgetting he was my cousin?"

Zachariah leaned forward and rested his arms on his knees. His eyes sharpened. "Are you forgetting I'm paying you a lot of money to make sure I don't go to prison for this?"

Travis did remember. He didn't agree with his cousin's lifestyle. Didn't agree with what his uncle constantly got away with, but he hadn't wanted to see his cousin dead. Just as he didn't agree with Zachariah's allegedly shady undercover dealings. He'd agreed to defend him before learning exactly whom Zachariah had shot. Honor wouldn't let him go back on his word. There'd be a shortage of defense attorneys if they only agreed to defend perfect citizens.

Antwan had been wrong. He'd forcefully entered Zachariah's business. Held him at gunpoint and stolen cash and jewelry. He'd made the fatal mistake of turning his back on his target. Zachariah had a right to defend himself against someone breaking into his business. Travis had a duty as Zachariah's lawyer to make sure he didn't go to jail just for being a shitty person.

"I haven't forgotten," Travis muttered. "That doesn't mean I have to like what you have to say. Show some damn remorse. Don't let everyone see just how much of an asshole you really are. Because if you don't calm down, your own arrogance is going to send you to jail regardless of how much you pay me."

Zachariah glared for several seconds. His square jaw worked as if he wanted to spit out angry words. After a few seconds, he sat up. "Fine. I'll try to pretend like I feel guilty for killing the little punk."

Travis inhaled and exhaled slowly. He didn't have time for this. "Is that all you called me over here for?"

"When is jury selection?"

"Next week. I'm reviewing the candidate pool now."

"And?"

Finding a local juror who wasn't familiar with the rumors surrounding Zachariah was going to be harder than finding a contact lens in a mountain of sand. "It's going to be tough, but we've got enough to work with to put together a group who will hopefully understand where you're coming from."

"Good." Zachariah nodded. "What about this house arrest?"

"Stay in the house and work on looking repentant." Travis picked up his bag. "Don't call me unless it's really an emergency."

Travis left Zachariah's home more frustrated than when he'd arrived. He'd known Zachariah was a cold-hearted, vindictive man before he'd agreed to take the case. Growing up in Sunnyside Acres and having Grant Robidoux as a mentor for twenty years had taught Travis not to be too scrupulous in whom he associated with. People both good and bad had a purpose in this world and sometimes you needed both.

Just because Zachariah was a dick didn't mean he needed to go to jail for the rest of his life. Not for this anyway. Still, the looks on the faces of Travis's parents... The threats from his uncle Mitch and cousin Devon made his neck tighten. Regardless of the outcome of this case, people weren't going to be happy. Calls for retribution would be made, and Travis would be right in the middle of the fire.

Shit! You should have stuck with corporate law.

Yeah, and stayed under Grant's thumb? He'd rather take his chances with the backlash from this case.

Travis mentally went through the details of the jury selection pool for the case as he drove back to his office. He could've gone directly home, but there were a few things he needed to finish at the office.

Finding jurors who would look past Zachariah's less than stellar personality and not use this case as a reason to punish him was going to be difficult. There were a few on the list he wanted to have in the final selection. He also had to pull more information on Antwan's illegal activities to show he had a history of violent break-ins. The challenge would be doing so without putting too much undue scrutiny on his uncle.

When are you going to stop trying to protect a family that doesn't want to protect you?

He doubted that would ever happen. He'd learned loyalty from Grant. His family was imperfect, but they were his. He wouldn't plot to make their lives miserable.

He pulled into the parking area of his law firm and frowned. Grant's car was parked beside his building. His driver stood outside and leaned against the driver's side door while smoking a cigarette. Travis got out of his car and strolled over.

"Hello, Barry," Travis said.

"Travis, what's up?"

"You tell me?" He glanced at the back of the car, then back at Barry.

Barry shrugged and took another drag of his cigarette. "I just drove him here. He's waiting on you inside."

Travis suppressed a curse. He nodded to Barry and made his way inside. Grant didn't make trips down to Travis's office. He'd come to the grand opening and that was the last time he'd been here.

Travis walked in and found Grant flirting with his receptionist, Frances. He leaned on the tall circular desk and smiled down at the young woman. Frances leaned forward, her arms crossed on the desk and her head cocked jauntily to the side. She batted thick lashes at Grant.

Travis shook his head. Grant loved Patricia, but he had a personality that made women swoon. "Grant, what brings you down here?"

Grant looked away from Frances. The smile still on his face, but the laughter in his eyes died away. "Just came down to see how things were going."

Travis's neck tightened. Grant didn't just check on things. "Things are going fine. Come on into my office."

Grant winked at Frances. "You have a good time at the book festival this weekend."

"Thank you, Mr. Robidoux. Maybe I'll see you there."

Grant's smile widened. "Maybe you will."

Travis led Grant to his office. He pointed to one of the leather chairs for Grant to sit in and closed the door. "I'd prefer it if you didn't flirt with my receptionist."

"I wasn't flirting. Just talking to her," Grant said innocently.

Travis lip quirked as he tried to suppress a smirk. He hung his bag on the hook next to the door, then walked to his desk. "The look you gave her was a little more than just talking."

"Oh really." Grant sat and crossed his legs. "Kind of like the looks you were giving India the other day."

Travis froze. All traces of a smile were gone from Grant's face. "Say what you came here to say, Grant." He fought the urge to fidget with the buttons of his suit jacket under Grant's hard stare. After all these years, Travis still swore Grant could see past his bullshit to the truth.

Grant leaned back in his chair. "What I told you before about India hasn't changed."

Travis sat stiffly in his chair. "Why do you think I need a reminder?"

"You're free. She's here. I don't need you getting any ideas."

"I'm not getting ideas." The fact that he could look Grant in the eye and say that without flinching proved how good of a lawyer he was. Guilt swelled in his chest as he remembered the way India had looked at him this morning. The hot, hungry look in those bright amber eyes of hers.

Grant studied him before nodding slowly. "Good. Byron is running for Senate. We don't need to screw things up because you decide to play around with my baby girl again."

For the second time today, Travis's hand clenched. His nails dug into his palms. "I never played around with her." He shouldn't have let things get so far that night, but he hadn't been playing with her. He'd felt something with India he hadn't been able to forget. Something he would do his best to ignore out of respect for her family and what they'd done for him.

"That's not how it looked to me," Grant said in a cold

voice. "I let that time pass because you fixed things. You walked away from India and did right by Elaina."

"You didn't leave me much choice." None of the regret he felt came through in his voice. Again, being a good lawyer had its perks.

"I like you, Travis, but I wasn't going to let you disgrace both of my girls. India deserved better than to be the rebound of her sister's ex-boyfriend."

"She wasn't going to be a rebound."

"But you weren't planning to make her your wife. Were you?"

Travis clenched his teeth. He hadn't thought past that night with India in his arms. He didn't know what he would have done with his split with Elaina so new. That's why he'd initially pushed her away. He'd needed time to think.

None of that mattered though. Elaina's pregnancy sealed their fate. He may not have initially considered marrying Elaina, but neither had he planned to leave her to deal with things on her own. Grant put the idea in his head, and Travis made the decision to ask because he'd been afraid of ruining his relationship with Grant. Now it was too late to entertain thoughts of what would have been or what could be now.

"I'm not doing anything to or with India." He let the conviction he felt come through in his tone.

"Keep it that way. I don't agree with you two paired together, but I understand why. As long as we're clear you aren't to start up any trouble by trying to rekindle what you started in that tobacco field."

"I'm not rekindling anything. India and I are working on a project for Byron, but we've both moved on from one night years ago and too many whiskey shots in a tobacco field. Give both of us some credit."

Grant watched him for several long seconds. Clearly evaluating whether he believed Travis or not. But Travis meant what he'd said. He shouldn't think about India as more than a friend. He wasn't so sure about their base instincts though… The heated look in India's eye. The tension that hummed between them in his office earlier. They both put on a good show pretending there was nothing there. How long could they keep it up?

"I'll give you the benefit of the doubt, but if I get one hint you're trying to fool around with my baby girl, I will make your life miserable."

"India is an adult."

"And she still deserves better."

Travis stood, tired of this conversation. Tired of this day. Tired of the reminder that he wasn't good enough. He was emotionally and physically spent. "It was good seeing you again, Grant."

Grant grinned and eased to his feet. "Come over for dinner on Friday. We miss you around the house, son."

The words *I'm not your son* were on the tip of Travis's tongue, but he bit them back. Grant had done more for him than almost anyone else. He didn't like what Grant said, but Travis understood where he was coming from. Pursuing anything with India would cause a scandal and turmoil in the family that wouldn't help anyone involved.

"I'm going out with Camille on Friday. Maybe another night."

Grant nodded with approval. "Another night, then."

CHAPTER ELEVEN

INDIA SMILED AND accepted the beer Russell handed to her. The crowd at the art museum was thick. People milled around inside, viewing the exhibits or talking to people at the various tables set up with simple arts and crafts, while local indie bands played everything from rock to R & B. Vendors selling craft beers were inside and out, and a fortune-teller predicted attendees' futures in one of the auditoriums. Outside, along with the beer and food vendors, a DJ played old-school and contemporary hits. This was India's first time at the event, and she was enjoying herself.

In the weeks since telling Ashiya she needed a man, she'd stopped avoiding Russell's calls and texts. Her first impression of him hadn't changed. He was a nice guy. Attentive, considerate and funny. She'd expected dating him would be difficult, but that wasn't the case.

Russell placed his hand on her lower back and leaned in close. "What do you think of the band?" His lips brushed her ear when he spoke. The music was loud and unless he got close he had to nearly yell to be heard, so he'd been speaking into her ear all night. This was the first time his lips had touched her, and surprisingly the sensation wasn't unpleasant.

"They're good." She sipped her beer and leaned slightly away.

Russell's thumb slowly rubbed back and forth over her back. She'd worn a thin sheath dress, with leggings and knee-high boots. The material of her dress did little to block the heat of his hands or the softness of his caress. Was he trying to seduce her? After realizing she needed a distraction they'd casually hung out, and they'd only kissed. Kissed enough for her to be very aware it had been way too long since she'd been with a man and for her to stop analyzing how he kissed and just enjoy being kissed. Enough for her to almost forget her dad had orchestrated this entire setup for a reason. Almost.

"I'd like to hear you play one day," Russell said close to her ear again.

Her palms were slick on the cup in her hands. Nerves. From anticipation or anxiety was yet to be determined.

"I'm just playing for myself while I'm here. I need to practice in case I'm called in for the audition in California."

That wasn't a lie. She spent most afternoons locked in the music room of her family's estate practicing. She knew the pieces backward and forward by now, but she still practiced. She wanted them to be automatic. To be so lost in the music that she didn't think about the difficult parts and just became the music. That was the only way she would get the coveted spot.

His hand stopped caressing her back. He pulled his head back. India let out a sigh. Relief, disappointment? She really should figure out which. Maybe a bit of both.

"I'd almost forgotten about your plans to go to California."

She nodded and took another sip of her beer. "I'm really excited about the opportunity."

He shifted until he stood in front of her. Blocking the view of the band playing. His hand slid with him from her back to rest on her waist.

"Maybe you'll find a reason to stick around a little longer."

He really was good-looking. She hadn't missed the interested looks thrown his way by other women. Here she was, on the arm of arguably the finest guy in the room, who was showing particular interest in taking their dating to the next level, and she still got panicky and nervous at the thought. What the hell was wrong with her?

"I do have a reason. Byron's campaign."

Russell eased her body closer to his. "There are other reasons."

The look in his eye definitely said he hoped she'd consider him a reason. For a second she felt bad that he hadn't been a part of her stay-or-go considerations, then his hips shifted. Something hard brushed against her belly. She sucked in a breath. Had he really just given her a dick nudge? She let out a shocked laugh, and he must have taken it for encouragement. His lips curved and he nudged her again. Oh yeah, that was definitely a rising mass between them.

"Russell, I..." She struggled for the right words. They'd kissed but he'd never been so sexually blatant. He hadn't come across as the pressuring type, but it wouldn't be the first time she'd read a man's signals wrong.

Russell's lids lowered. His lips puckered and he came in for a kiss.

India pressed her free hand firmly on his chest and pushed. "It's kind of hot in here. Let's go outside and get some air." Her voice was firm and steady, but inside her pulse skyrocketed as she worried if he'd make a scene or not.

He blinked a few times. His gaze cleared, and he immediately stepped back. Color rose in his cheeks and he nodded. "Yeah, let's get some air."

She let out a breath but didn't relax when he took her hand in his and led her through the crowd outside. The cool early-spring night was welcome after the heat and press of bodies inside the museum. He led her away from the DJ to the far side of the plaza. They stopped next to one of the pillars. The music was up, but not as loud since they were outside.

Russell let go of her hand and rubbed his face. He wouldn't meet her eye. The silence between them was long and awkward.

She broke it first. "What was that?"

He finally met her eye, his face embarrassed and regretful. "I'm sorry. I've got a lot on my mind. I'm stressed, but I don't want you to think I'm trying to pressure you into anything." He looked at the ground. Lines bracketed his mouth and his brow was furrowed.

His move had been juvenile and stupid, but it didn't warrant the devastation in his eyes. India put a hand on his arm and kept it there until he looked at her again. "Hey, apology accepted, but never do that again. If something is going on, you can talk to me about it."

He let out a heavy breath and met her eyes. "It's nothing you want to hear about."

"Try me. If anything, we're friends."

"That's the thing, I'd like us to be more than that, but I've got this other...thing going on in my life."

India dropped her hand and stepped back. If her dad

hooked her up with a guy who was married, she would kill him.

He shook his head and reached for her. "Nothing crazy. I promise. Just drama from an ex." He closed his eyes and let out a rueful bitter laugh. "Exactly what I shouldn't bring up when I'm trying to start something new."

India's panic subsided. Drama with an ex she could talk about. "I can relate," she said. Russell bringing up his ex didn't bother her, probably because even though she liked him and enjoyed the time they'd spent together, in her heart she knew she didn't want things to get too serious between them.

His head popped up. A curious but wary look in his eyes. "You can?"

She leaned back against the pillar. The coolness of the marble seeped through her thin dress. "There was this guy I had a really hard time getting out of my system. Even though I knew nothing would come of it. Some people just get beneath your skin like that."

His shoulders relaxed. "My ex. She's…manipulative. I know that. I broke things off with her over a year ago. We're done, but she still pops up asking for help."

Help that, she could tell by the disgust in his voice, he continued to give. "Because you're a good guy."

"And good guys finish last."

She bit her lip. "Russell, you don't have to keep helping her. You're very attractive, you could have—"

"A ton of women," he finished for her. This time when he laughed it wasn't bitter, but neither was it happy. "I get it. I know the effect I can have on women." He said it without an ounce of arrogance. He sounded almost as if his good looks were an annoyance. "I took advantage of that in high school and college. Then I got caught by the ultimate player's trap. I fell for the wrong woman. She turned the tables on me. Hit me with the same games and tricks I used to play. Before I knew it, I was the one heartbroken."

He shook his head. "Getting over that wasn't fun, but it taught me a lesson. I don't want to play around anymore. I want what my parents have. I know marriage isn't easy, but if I'm going to deal with drama, I'd rather it be with a woman I love and who loves me instead of a bunch of meaningless women."

"Do you miss it? The freedom of nights of meaningless sex with no emotional ties."

Russell laughed and leaned a hand next to her head on the pillar. "Not as much as I thought I would. Once I realized what I wanted, it's kind of hard to give up the dream."

Russell's sincerely spoken confession made her like him even more. He deserved a maturity medal or something. Bronze, not gold for that stunt back there. She didn't know how many players reformed their ways because someone broke their heart. If anything, she would have expected that to make them want to play the field more.

"Why did you agree to date me? We'd never met, and I know my dad put you up to it."

His eyes flickered with an emotion she couldn't name. His body stiffened, and he dropped his hand. "Your dad wanted to introduce us. He had nothing to do with me calling you after the party."

His tone didn't waver, nor did his gaze. Still, she didn't believe that was the entire story. Her dad had something on Russell. What could it be? Obviously, something big enough to make Russell agree to date her. That was enough for her to know she couldn't keep trying.

"You know, I don't think it's a good idea for us to take this further romantically," she said.

"Because your dad introduced us, the thing with my ex, or that really bad move back in the museum?"

"A bit of the first two, and since you apologized, I'm not going to hold the thing in the museum against you. As a friend, I hope you realize you can do better and cut her out of your life. The thing with my dad... I don't want to be a part of his game."

She moved to go around him.

Russell placed a hand on her waist and stopped her. "India, your dad doesn't have anything on me. He always brags about you. I'd seen pictures and heard him mention you were his favorite. When he told me you were in town and that he thought I'd like you, yes, I was intrigued. Then I met you and I didn't care about anything else. Even if we never go out again, I want you to know that."

She nodded and his grip on her loosened. She believed him and appreciated his words. She was so paranoid when it came to things related to her dad. Grant didn't do anything without some type of motive, especially when it came to introducing people to his family. Byron may not be a part of whatever her dad planned, but India didn't doubt Grant hoped something specific would come of them getting together.

"I'm sorry for accusing you of playing games."

He shrugged. "After what my ex put me through, believe me I don't want to toy with anyone's emotions." He nodded toward the museum. "Want to go back and try to salvage the night? I promise no more high school prom moves."

India chuckled and took his hand when he held it out to her. "Sure."

He took her hand and stepped back. India looked into the crowd and her gaze collided with Travis's. He stood in front of the DJ booth, a beer in one hand, the other slipped into the pocket of his dark slacks. His focus solely on her. Her legs and lungs stiffened while her heart did a Travis-is-near dance.

Travis looked away from her to the woman by his side. Camille. He said something that made Camille smile and laugh. Her hand rested on his chest. He took it in his, slipped her arm through his and led her inside the museum.

The entire episode couldn't have taken more than a second, but she felt as if she'd just run a race. Her heart pumped wildly, and she struggled to breathe. He'd seen her, looked almost upset to have spotted her, then in a blink flirted with Camille and moved on as if they hadn't made eye contact. So that was his game now? Grab her attention, rob her of breath, then pretend as if she didn't exist?

Uh, yeah, because his heart isn't skipping beats when he looks at you.

"You okay?" Russell asked warily.

India had stopped in her tracks when she'd seen Travis. Embarrassment blazed through her. She wanted to hate him, because she hated the way her world came to a standstill every time while he felt absolutely nothing whenever he saw her.

She turned, lifted up on her toes and kissed Russell. He froze for a second, then his arms were around her waist and he kissed her back. She didn't care they were in a crowded square, surrounded by people. That two minutes ago she'd told him they should count their losses and move on. She didn't even care part of her passion was fueled by a need to channel the stirrings of desire from the intense look in Travis's eyes.

Well, maybe she cared a little, but that wasn't the point. The point was she wasn't going to continue to be the stupid girl who'd fallen in love with a man she couldn't have. She was going to be the girl she'd been on tour. Young, carefree and not succumbing to anyone else's expectations.

When she pulled back, Russell's eyes were wide with surprise. "What was that for?"

"Because you are a nice guy. Forget your ex, my father, everything. Let's just enjoy tonight and have a good time."

He smiled and nodded. "Good with me."

He STAYED AWAY from her as long as he could. Travis had tried to pretend seeing India at the art museum wasn't a big deal. Tried to tell himself he would get used to seeing her in town on dates. He was here on his own date, after all. She wasn't his, wasn't ever going to be his, and even if he decided to try to make her his, Elaina would plot to kill him and Grant would help dispose of his body.

The museum had a small section set aside for local artists. One of his paintings was displayed in that corner. One among a half dozen other local artists. A feel-good display for the people in town to see what their neighbors could do. He'd asked Camille to come tonight so she could see, but he hadn't told her about his work on display. He hadn't told anyone.

Outside of the Robidoux family, not too many people knew he painted. That part of himself had never been up for public knowledge. But after the divorce, when he'd started indulging in his hobby again, he'd taken a portrait-painting class at the museum. The teacher was also one of the new employees at the museum who hadn't known him as a Robidoux family attachment. They'd sparked a friendship and begun discussing art. Now, not only had that friendship led to Travis becoming a member of the museum's board, but he'd also been convinced to add one of his portraits to the local artists tribute.

He'd held his breath in anticipation when he took Camille to the section to view the paintings. Waited anxiously for her to scan the various works, read the names of the local artists, see his and turn to him with surprise in her eyes. Instead, she'd scanned the paintings, ignored the names of the artists, then looked around, noticed they were alone in the secluded corner and immediately tried to put her hands down his pants.

He didn't typically have a problem with women being forward, but not when he was trying to share a piece of himself. He wanted to find out if Camille could be *the one*. The one he really started over with after the divorce. He'd led Camille away, disappointed but also trying to convince himself that her not noticing his name on the wall didn't mean they weren't well matched.

Then he'd seen India. India with Russell. His entire body had frozen as a wave of happiness at seeing her bowled him over. He'd turned away quickly before instinct overrode good sense.

He'd told himself he would stay away from her. Ignore her. Except, when India wandered over to the local artists exhibit by herself just as Camille said she wanted to check on the people selling her family's beer at the event, he followed India instead of Camille.

He watched her, breath held and heart racing. Her eyes scanned the paintings. She stilled. Her head tilted the side. Her full lips parted, and she slid closer to the painting. Her hand held out as if she wanted to touch. At the last second she drew back.

He came up next to her. She didn't turn his way, but he could tell from the way her body tensed she knew he was beside her. With her back to him, he was free to soak in her presence. The slender column of her neck. The way the simple sheath dress fell over her curves. The citrus scent of her perfume just as bright as her personality.

"Do you like it?" he asked, studying her.

"It's a portrait. You never do portraits," she answered, still examining the painting. "Who is she?"

"It's not really a portrait. Just a profile." He kept his eyes on her, his chest tight with anticipation. The portrait was of a woman with her back to the canvas, her face slightly turned so only the slope of her jaw, soft curve of her neck and the shadow of long lashes on soft cheeks was shown. Her curly hair was pulled back in a thick puff at the base of her skull. Shoulders bared except for the strap of a white tank top.

"A very good profile. You painted her so perfectly. As if you wanted to reach out and touch her."

"Maybe I did." He focused on India's profile. Her distinct beauty he'd tried to capture from memory. His fingers flexed, his hand lifted. He stopped himself just in time.

She wasn't his. He was here with someone else. So was she. They'd create a scandal, and even though he'd accepted the choices he'd made, he didn't want to hurt Elaina or her family. They deserved better than having their family torn apart because he couldn't shake this fascination he had with India.

"Does Elaina know you painted her like this?"

Travis frowned. His eyes shot to the painting. "Elaina?"

"It's her, isn't it?"

He shook his head. Disappointment settled like an elephant on his chest. "No. It's not your sister."

She looked at the painting again. Her eyes widened. She sucked in a breath. When her bright eyes met his, he saw the question, the confusion in their depths.

He looked away first. "It's just an image I had in my mind. No one in particular."

"Oh." She sounded disappointed. "For a second I thought…"

You were right. What would she say if he'd answered the question in her eyes and admitted she was the woman in the picture? If he admitted that he had thought of her too much after she'd left and even more after his divorce. He was too embarrassed to admit any of that and couldn't face her pity, or worse, her discomfort from talking about a situation that couldn't be undone.

You'll never be happy with her, Grant had said in a cold, calculating voice. *You're both too sentimental. Too lost in your artistic sides to amount to anything.*

Don't disgrace Elaina because your sentimental side noticed India.

Grant had been right. He and India wouldn't have been able to make things work after Elaina admitted she was pregnant. He'd taken Grant's offer to cover law school and married the sister he'd already "ruined" according to Grant.

"Oh well," India said when he didn't respond to her unanswered question. "How did you get the museum to display your work?"

Relief relaxed his shoulders. He could let his guard down if they talked about art. "I took a class a few years ago."

"You're taking painting classes?" she asked with surprise. "You didn't mention that the other day in your office."

He shrugged and ran a hand across the back of his head. The impressed look in her eye made him feel as if he'd rescued a box of puppies in the middle of the highway instead of just taking a class. "I was distracted by other things."

Her eyes met his. She chewed the corner of her lip. A dangerous look came to her eye. Dangerous because she wasn't hiding the flare of desire in her gaze. Dangerous because the need to get closer made him clip a few inches off the distance separating them.

"It never hurts to continue to learn," he said to get both their minds off her seeing him shirtless. "I never had formal training. Law school didn't leave me a lot of time to study art. After the divorce, the idea of taking a class that didn't revolve around cases intrigued me."

India broke eye contact. She took a deep breath, then pointed at the wall of paintings. "You can't tell me these are just a teacher showing off a student's work. They are all really good."

He wanted to roll around and wrap himself up in the warmth and praise in her voice. "The board decided to showcase local artists."

"And they chose you?" she said as if he'd won a huge honor instead of being one of many local artists displayed in the building.

Travis chuckled and scratched his jaw. "I'm on the board, remember. Kind of hard not to choose me."

India laughed and playfully slapped his arm. Her touch lingered a few seconds too long. Travis's hand quickly lifted and covered hers. He pressed her palm against his biceps. Her hand was small and soft, but the heat of her touch seeped into his bones. Her fingers flexed as if she were cupping the muscle. She stood close enough for her perfume and a distinctly feminine scent that belonged only to her to invade his system and make him ease another inch closer.

She stared at their joined hands. Her breaths short and choppy.

"I guess they had to include you," she said, her voice low and breathless.

"Would you have chosen me?" he asked quietly. Even with the noise in the museum from the people talking and the band playing, he knew she could hear him because they stood that close.

Her eyes lifted to his. "I would have." Her voice shook. "I'd always choose you."

His hand tightened on hers. Her words were a jolt to his system. Pushed aside all of the reasons he'd just given himself for not admitting his feelings to her. Her beautiful eyes were sad, regretful but also completely honest. She felt something, too. Not just desire. Not just unsettled about the way things abruptly ended between them. The only thing guiding him now was a need to have no more secrets between them. "India, the woman in the portrait—"

She tugged on her hand.

He let her go, but clenched his hand in a useless attempt to hold on to the feeling of her hand in his. India rubbed the back of her neck and put back the inches between them he'd taken away. Shutting him off.

"I mean, you're a talented artist," she said. "I've always thought that."

Her words shut down everything they didn't dare speak. *Don't push this.* They knew something was there. They also knew they couldn't be together.

Travis let the moment slip away. He did what he was supposed to do. "Thank you."

They stood in awkward silence before India snapped her fingers. "You know, we should consider a fundraiser at the museum. I know Byron isn't the biggest fan of the arts, but between the two of us we could at least give him enough information to pull in the artistic people in town."

He put on his lawyer's mask, even though he felt like he'd jumped out of a plane and his parachute opened a second before he would have plummeted to his death. He'd been about to cross a line that couldn't be uncrossed.

"That's not a bad idea," he said, matching her forced enthusiasm. "Occasionally, we hold luncheons for our patron sponsors and have people come in and speak. Byron could talk about his plans to support the arts."

"Do you think they'll let him speak?"

"I'll bring it up at the next board meeting. We're planning the next patron luncheon for the following month and haven't nailed down a speaker yet."

"Great." She looked over her shoulder. Scanned the crowd. "I guess I better get back to Russell."

To hell with Russell. Russell could go jump off the side of the building for all Travis cared. She should stay here with him, but when he looked over the crowd, he spotted Camille searching for him. The woman he should be with.

He looked at the woman he wanted one last time. "Enjoy your date. He's a nice guy." Then he turned and walked away before she could notice he hadn't meant a word he'd just spoken.

CHAPTER TWELVE

"Do you remember everything I told you?"

Byron eyed India over the paper in his hand with a mildly exasperated smile. "You do realize I've made several campaign speeches already? I think I can survive one more."

India held up her hands. "I know. I know. Sorry."

"For someone who wasn't interested in helping, you seem to be really invested in my campaign lately," Byron said.

They were downstairs in the art museum. Travis had worked his board member magic and got Byron on the agenda for the next patron's luncheon. By a miracle, Byron's schedule was clear and he'd agreed to the impromptu opportunity.

The luncheon was in the auditorium in the back of the museum. Byron wanted to stop and review his notes before they made their way to the back. He didn't read directly from his notes when he gave a speech, but India had noticed he always checked, double-, then triple-checked any talking points before going before a crowd. Seeing her brother go after his dream inspired her. His drive for success fueled her own. She hoped to blow away the selection committee if given the chance to audition in California.

So you can run again instead of facing reality.

Refusing to let that thought take hold, she brought her mind to the task at hand: getting Byron through the luncheon. "I am invested," she said. "At first I couldn't believe you actually wanted to run for Senate. Seeing your dedication over the past month made me realize you aren't just doing this for someone else."

Byron folded the paper with his notes and tucked them into the inside pocket of his gray suit. He looked the part of the handsome and debonair politician. No hint of the playboy she remembered before going on tour.

"Who else would I be doing this for?"

"Dad." She raised her eyebrows. Who else tried to influence their lives? Byron had always been optimistic and into volunteering, but he'd never talked about public service before.

Byron nodded and chuckled. "Dad only wants what's best for us."

"I know, but he does like to have his say in what we do." He'd told her flat out she couldn't join the Transatlantic Orchestra. Said she needed to get her head out of the clouds and had gone so far as to reject her offer for her. Thank goodness she'd been able to fix his meddling. The difference between her and her siblings was that Byron viewed their Dad's meddling as strong suggestions and while Elaina fought him often, she also viewed his ways as a doctrine for success.

"I understand where he's coming from," Byron said, sounding slightly defensive. "He's in a tough business and Granddad's legacy means a lot to him. Of course he wouldn't want us to do anything that could jeopardize our future or the company's."

"You're right. It's just…everything is about the family with him."

Byron wrapped an arm around India's shoulder and pulled her to his side. "Would you rather him not focus on our family and only care about business? Besides, Dad just gives his suggestions. As you proved, we still get the chance to make our own decision."

She didn't tell Byron that their dad had stopped her stipend after she'd gone against him and accepted the orchestra's offer. Cutting her off from the family fortune. She hadn't realized just how lucky she was to have her family's backing until there was no more joint bank account, credit cards or anything. She'd been embarrassed and furious when her card was declined for the purchases she'd tried to make after a month on the road. She'd never confronted him on that. Now she viewed what he'd done as a favor. She had learned to live off her income with the orchestra.

Two years later, he'd told her that her stipend was reinstated. She'd thanked him and hadn't touched the money. Defying Grant always came with consequences. Some good, some not so good.

Byron led her toward the back of the museum and the auditorium. India looked at her brother. He modeled himself after their father. He wouldn't fight back against decisions or suggestions Grant had for their future.

"Will you promise me that he won't be the reason you get married to someone you don't love?" she said.

Byron stopped at the door to the auditorium. He slid his arm from around her and frowned. "What's that supposed to mean?"

"The woman you mentioned marrying. Is Dad—"

Byron held up a hand. "Dad has nothing to do with my decision." His voice hardened.

"I want you to be happy."

"Being the next senator from our state will make me happy." Byron leaned in and lowered his voice. "Having a wife I can trust to support my career will make me happy."

"You can have that and have someone you care about."

"Caring about someone doesn't always make things right." His voice was heavy with bitter disappointment. His eyes iced over like the surface of a lake in forty-below temperatures.

His raw emotion twisted her train of thought. Byron had cared for someone briefly in college. He never talked about his conquests with India, but she remembered her mom talking about cleaning up a mess he'd made over a woman that had him hooked like a fish on a line back in college. Whatever the mess, it had been cleaned up quickly, quietly and without pulling India into the loop. Was that why he was willing to settle for convenience instead of love? Was her brother, spoiled, rich playboy extraordinaire, still mending a broken heart?

"What ever happened to—"

The door to the auditorium opened, cutting off India's question. The chair of the board of directors came out. She saw the two of them and a relieved smile crossed her features.

"Oh good, you're here."

Byron immediately held out his hand to shake hers, his eyes melting like that same lake come spring, and his perfect politician's smile took over. "Sorry to keep you waiting. We were just heading inside."

Jocelyn shook her head. The petite brunette just seemed relieved her main attraction hadn't become a no-show. "You're fine. We haven't started yet. Please go on inside. We're just about to start serving lunch."

Byron thanked her and opened the door for them both. After they entered the main auditorium, Jocelyn turned to India. "I'd like to talk with you later, if you have time. We have chamber music once a quarter here at the museum. Usually we have musicians from the local symphony, but we'd love to have you for a special guest appearance."

India put a hand to her chest. "Me? A special guest?"

"Yes. You were the assistant principal violinist for the Transatlantic Orchestra. Your accomplishments are well-known."

"I just kind of fell into that." The principal violinist hadn't thought India was right for the position. In fact, he hadn't thought she was up to the challenge. His doubt had of course pushed her to prove him wrong.

"Aren't you talented?" Jocelyn's voice challenged India to deny it. As if India's talent was a fact known by everyone far and wide. Jocelyn's confidence sent sparks of pride through India's chest.

"I am. It's just I'm not…" What, worthy of being a special guest? She'd gotten a degree in music appreciation. Traveled with the Transatlantic Orchestra for six years. Practiced daily and knew every nuance of her violin as well as she knew her own skin.

"Not what?" Jocelyn's voice rose at the end of the question.

India waved a hand, whisking away any lingering

doubts about her abilities, and smiled. "Nothing. I'd be happy to participate, and I'm honored you thought of me."

"Great." Jocelyn beamed. "I'll get in contact with you soon to talk more."

"Thank you. I look forward to your call," India said with a broad smile. She'd been asked to perform, not because of her name but because of her accomplishments. Something she never would have expected in her hometown.

Maybe you don't have to go to LA for recognition.

India let the thought play in her mind for a second before pushing it away. One request to play at the museum wasn't worth giving up her hope for a call from the LA Philharmonic. Staying in Jackson Falls would come with a unique set of complications.

India scanned the crowd. Her eyes landed on one of the biggest complications. Travis spoke to a man and woman India assumed were museum patrons. As if her gaze was a touch he couldn't ignore, Travis stopped talking and looked her way. Their eyes locked, the corner of his mouth tilted up, and he nodded toward her in acknowledgment. India smiled and returned his nod.

They were so civilized and appropriate with each other. In the weeks since Arts and Drafts, they'd been extra careful in each other's company. She hated being extra careful. Ever since that moment after her quick touch—when his hand had gripped hers, and she'd said she would have chosen him, but hadn't meant the words in any relationship to art—she'd felt anxious. Restless. As if the words and questions she wanted to suppress were bound tight inside her and fighting like cats in a bag to get out. That moment had been nothing and everything.

But pretending it didn't matter when your heart knew the truth of things was hard as hell.

India looked away first. Before she went with the urge to go to him. Maybe she would call Russell later. That would be good for her.

But she knew she wouldn't.

INDIA SPENT THE afternoon after the patron's luncheon practicing in the music room. She practiced daily but today she was inspired. Byron's talk at the luncheon had gone remarkably well. Her brother's charming personality was enough to win most people over. He'd gotten them not only with that, but also by expressing a genuine affection for the arts. An affection he said had blossomed as he'd watched India grow as a violinist.

The pride in Byron's voice had blown her away. Until that moment she wouldn't have said her brother was proud of her. Sure, he was happy for her, maybe a little impressed, but proud to have such a talented baby sister? That was a confession she'd never forget.

After his speech, the patrons had bombarded him with questions and comments. There was a lot of interest in his promises to continue to support the arts, and a lot of hope that he'd stand by his word. India knew he would. The group had also wanted to know more about India's time playing for the Transatlantic Orchestra. Most surprising was being complimented by Arthur Manke, the music director with the Tri-City Philharmonic out of nearby Raleigh.

"Your work is impressive, India. We could use someone impressive working with us," he'd said with only a slight hint of the arrogance that some musicians wore like silk cloaks.

"Nikolas Kastikov is our conductor," he'd added when she'd hesitated.

Nikolas was well-known in the classical music scene. He'd served as conductor for many large philharmonics, was a guest lecturer around the country and held celebrity status in his home country of Norway. To learn that he was the conductor of her hometown's symphony was surprising.

She'd never considered staying and playing close to Jackson Falls as a kid. Her dreams had always been of far-off places. New York, London, Rome. Today's luncheon had opened her eyes to the serious underestimating she'd done of her hometown. Thanks to the town's proximity to the capital, Jackson Falls had a thriving arts scene including music, theater and even film.

Arthur's hints about the need for an assistant music director hadn't gone unnoticed. Honestly, if she were staying in town, she'd probably jump at the chance. Except, she'd caught Travis's eye again over Arthur's shoulder and once again she went tumbling down the slope of forbidden promises and shattered dreams. She'd changed the subject.

The murmur of voices followed by the sound of laughter drifted from the hallway. She recognized that laugh. Patricia's laughter always made her muscles go rigid and acid burn in her stomach, because every time she heard Patricia laugh, she thought about how she was here and happy while India's mother had died. Her mother's death wasn't Patricia's fault, but Patricia laying up with Grant while her mother was sick was her fault.

She pulled out her case to quickly pack away her

violin. The voices got closer, pushing her to hurry. She wouldn't be able to avoid them. If they walked by, they'd see her. If she hurried from the room, she'd run into them, and she was too grown to hide like a scared kid.

Her dad and Patricia breezed into the music room arm in arm. They looked good together, like a happy, long-married couple in some television advertisement. How obviously they complemented each other only made the acid in India's stomach bubble violently.

They both froze for a second when they saw her. That same awkward moment of silence descended whenever India and Patricia unexpectedly ended up in the same room.

Patricia slipped her arm from Grant's and took a step away. India barely stopped herself from rolling her eyes. They were past the point of hiding their everlasting affections. As if India would suddenly forget Patricia had been her father's mistress while her mother was still alive.

"I was just finishing up," India said.

"No need to run off," Grant said. He took Patricia's hand in his, a deliberate movement, and came farther into the room.

She wasn't running off. She just didn't like being in the same room as her dad and the woman he'd betrayed his wife with. "I've got to get ready. I'm going out with Russell tonight."

She'd called him after leaving the art museum. They'd agreed to meet for dinner. Just as friends. He still had the connection to his ex, and India had enough baggage to deal with, wanting her brother-in-law and all. But she enjoyed his company and she preferred going out for dinner instead of staying in.

Patricia's brows rose. "Oh good. He told me you two were hitting it off."

India cocked her head to the side. Why would Russell tell Patricia that? "Really? I didn't realize you two know each other."

"He's my nephew," Patricia said.

India's gaze snapped to her dad. Grant straightened his shoulders.

"Her nephew?" India's voice was a sharp whip of accusation.

He'd set her up with his mistress's nephew? In what world was that a good idea? India had barely been able to forgive him and accept that he wouldn't give Patricia up. How could her dad possibly believe she'd want to be more deeply involved with Patricia's family? Just because Byron and Elaina had gotten used to Patricia in the time India had been away didn't mean India wanted to be closer to her and pretend as if they could one day be on good terms.

"Another way for our families to grow closer," Grant said easily. "Especially now that our families will be truly connected." Grant's voice was calm. Too calm. The way it got when he was about to lay down a law he expected to be followed with no arguments.

Truly connected? India's eyes dropped to their joined hands. A new, sparkly engagement ring reflected the light from the third finger on Patricia's left hand. Her mouth went dry.

"You're engaged." Her voice was flat, emotionless.

Her father smiled. Patricia lifted her hand so India could see the ring.

"We aren't going to announce it until later. We don't want to take anything away from your brother," Patri-

cia said the words as if they were being so considerate. Making sure they didn't cause any undo harm with Byron's campaign.

"How could you do this?" India asked her dad.

Grant's calm expression morphed into one of cold resolve. "Patricia, do you mind giving my daughter and me a second to talk?"

Patricia looked between the two of them. She nodded and slipped back out the door. India and Grant stared at each other. India tried to get a handle on the hurt and betrayal reeling within her. She wanted to scream, kick something and demand that her father change his mind. The anger didn't surprise her as much as the tightening of her throat. The burn of tears she would not allow to fall. Her mom would never come back, and he'd chosen to blatantly put Patricia in her mother's place.

"I thought you'd be happy for me," Grant said as if he were the one hurt.

Happy for him? She'd been able to tolerate Patricia in his life, but to actually make the woman her *stepmother*? "Why?"

"Do you want me to be alone for the rest of my life?" His face hardened even when his voice remained calm and condescending.

Anger rushed through her like a gale force wind. He was not about to make her the villain in this situation. "I'd be happy if you chose anyone else. Not her." She pointed at the door.

"I've always loved Patricia."

"Love? You're going to use that?" India said with a caustic laugh. "Was it love that made you go to her arms when mom was dying of cancer and you were supposed to be taking care of her? Did love take you to Patricia's

house the night of mom's funeral instead of staying home with me, Elaina and Byron?"

He had the nerve to nod. "It did."

"That's bullshit, Dad." Her voice cracked. The pain of that memory like a fresh burn to her heart.

He walked forward. "Don't you ever talk to me like that. I know you've longed to hold this grudge against Patricia out of a sense of loyalty to your mom, but your mother knew about Patricia." Frustration entered his voice as he spoke words she assumed he thought made the situation acceptable.

"Is that supposed to make this better? Easier?" she said between clenched teeth. Her muscles vibrated with the heightened emotions pulsing through her veins.

"It's supposed to make you understand things aren't as simple as you want to make them," he shot back. "I loved your mom. I took care of her. I made sure she had everything she needed. I mourned when she died. I've always done what I needed to do to keep our family legacy strong. But sometimes love isn't enough."

He turned and paced toward one of the windows, his body tense. "Love changes and turns into something different. Enough time has passed. I've respected your mother's memory and your wishes long enough." When he spun back to her, there was no apology in his eyes, only resolve. "Now I'm doing what I've wanted to for too long. You kids are old enough to accept that, even if you're not happy about it."

"Do we get the same consideration?" Would the man who preached God, family and company accept it if his children did what they wanted? Would he give his blessing without forcing them to give in to the needs of the family?

"As long as your decisions don't go against the goals of the family or our company," he replied. "No matter what you think about Patricia, our relationship won't cause a rift in the family we can't recover from."

"Really? I won't step foot in this house again if you marry her." India walked past her dad toward the door.

"You will step foot in this house and you'll pretend as if you're deliriously happy about me and Patricia."

She spun back to face him. "You can't tell me how to feel."

"But I can remind you where your ultimate loyalties should lie." The sharp preciseness in his words sent a shiver of warning down her spine.

"Excuse me?"

He walked slowly toward her. The anger and hurt in his eyes were the only outward clue she'd pissed him off. Otherwise his shoulders were relaxed, his stroll leisurely and his voice calm. His fuck-with-me-if-you-want-to swagger in place, the one that said if you crossed the line, he would cut you hard and deep.

"You don't get to be emotional when it comes to being a part of this family," Grant said with a cold smile. "I've given you leeway and let you have your rebellions, but at the end of the day, the most important thing is keeping our family together. Like it or not, your loyalty to the family isn't something you can just toss aside. That's not why your grandfather fought so hard to keep our family together and the business strong. It's not why I fought just as hard to give you, Byron and Elaina everything you need to succeed in this life. Are you really willing to turn your back on everything he fought for?" He didn't yell, but his voice had risen, vibrated and rang with disappointment.

Memories rose of her grandfather and the pride in his voice when he'd talked about the tobacco farm his own father started. The fierce determination in his face as he made India, Elaina and Byron promise to always put their family's legacy first.

Survival of our family and what we built is more important than anything else we may want.

Her grandfather's words rang through her head. Their grandfather had given up the woman he'd loved and married someone else to bring in the money needed to build Robidoux Tobacco. He'd encouraged their dad to date their mom because of her family's connections in retail. He'd even sued his uncle and won when he'd tried to take half of the company. Doing what was best for the family always took precedence over anything else.

She loved her family. Even her dad, despite his faults, but she wasn't sure she could stick around and accept this.

"I'm here for Byron and I'll be the perfect daughter and sister when it counts *for him.*" She lifted her chin and hardened her voice after it wavered. The tears she'd held back burned like acid. "But I can't get over you and Patricia."

Pain flickered across Grant's expression before he shrugged and nodded stiffly. "You don't have to get over it. You just have to accept it."

CHAPTER THIRTEEN

Travis SKIPPED UP the stairs to the front door of the Robidoux estate and rang the bell. He and Byron had made plans earlier to grab a beer. They needed a night out after a long week, at least Travis sure as hell did. Jury deliberations had twisted him inside out. He'd agreed to meet Byron at his family's estate because Byron said he would be there this evening. Travis agreed, even though he'd been avoiding the place ever since that moment with India at the museum.

Grant's warning to stay away from India was very clear in his head. Grant had done a lot for Travis. More than his own dad in some cases.

Despite that, he no longer had a say in what Travis did. A part of him wanted to tell Grant to go to hell and tell India exactly how he felt about her. As much as his former father-in-law's meddling ways jabbed into Travis like a rusty nail, he hadn't told any lies. Dating India might make Travis happy, but his happiness wasn't the only thing at stake.

The door swung open and the main reason Travis shouldn't touch India stood on the other side. The surprise on Elaina's face probably mirrored his own. He'd expected their lead housekeeper, Sandra, to answer the door. Just like fate to step in to remind him of the consequences of going through with his actions.

"What are you doing here?" Elaina asked in an unwelcoming voice.

Like putting on a heavy winter coat, he braced himself for her cold treatment. They hadn't always been this cold. He and Elaina had been the poster children for a young-adult, hormone-influenced, good-girl-bad-boy love affair. She was beautiful, and when he'd first met her at seventeen, his body had reacted but he'd never thought he'd have a shot. Until one day she caught him in the laundry room, slid her hand across his dick and dared him to show her if the rumors about sex with him were true.

Until then he hadn't known there were rumors about him, or that Elaina was interested, but his hormone-influenced brain hadn't thought to ask questions. That was the start of their not-quite-clandestine affair. Marriage, a miscarriage and maturity quickly showed them that hot and heavy teenage affection didn't always sustain a marriage.

Now he met Elaina's eyes and wondered what he could have done differently. If he'd really tried hard enough to make her happy or if they'd always been doomed. "I'm meeting Byron."

She crossed her arms over her chest. "He's not here."

Travis checked his watch. He was ten minutes earlier than when he and Byron planned to meet. Usually with Byron, ten minutes early meant on time. He pulled out his cell phone to check for any missed calls or messages but there were none.

"I'm meeting him at six." Travis slid his phone back into his pocket and met Elaina's gaze. She always managed to look at him as if he were wasting her time. Like he'd purposefully rang the doorbell as she walked by just to force her to answer for him. "He said he'd be here already."

"Obviously, he was mistaken." Elaina eyed him impatiently.

Sometimes he still couldn't believe this was their new normal. They'd been pushed into their young marriage, but even then, their relationship hadn't been terrible.

Maybe he'd been foolish to think they could have turned physical attraction into a lasting relationship. They'd tried to put up a front of happy and in-love newlyweds. Then the miscarriage happened two weeks after the wedding. In one painful night, the entire reason they'd agreed to the marriage was gone. He'd been devastated by the loss. Elaina had been angry. An anger that had morphed into the cool indifference she wrapped herself in that eventually carved a canyon between them.

A breeze brushed the back of his neck. Travis shifted on the porch. "Can I come in and wait for him?"

She sighed as if he'd asked her to help him change a tire on a monster truck, but she backed up so he could enter.

Travis crossed the threshold and closed the door. "Elaina, we can be friends. At least during the election."

Her arms remained crossed as she watched him with a bland expression. "How do you suggest we do that?"

"I don't know, maybe the way other people are friendly? Talk and ask each other about our days. We didn't divorce on bad terms."

Their divorce talk had probably been the easiest in the history of divorces. Both of them lying in bed staring at the ceiling after another tedious Friday night dinner with Grant and one of his business partners neither wanted to attend. She'd said, "Maybe we should get a divorce."

His reply: "Maybe we should."

The next day, he'd gotten a call from her lawyer to start the proceedings.

She cocked a brow and took a step forward until only a few inches separated them. "Talking isn't what we were good at." Her voice lowered to the low, suggestive tone that used to make his young-adult heart jump and his dick stiffen.

Travis stepped backward. "Let's not go there." He didn't want to relive the night when Elaina's indifference had turned into resentment.

"I forgot. You're having fun with Camille now," she said sarcastically.

"Even if I weren't, we can't go back."

"Oh, that's right. You're *noble* now." She made air quotes with her fingers. Derision crept into her voice. That, and hurt. Though he'd never been able to truly tell if Elaina was hurt.

Travis regretted to this day almost sleeping with Elaina after their divorce. His grandmother had died. Surprisingly, when Elaina heard, she'd come to his house. Grief, bourbon and months without sex almost made him accept what she offered. *That's what happens when the wrong head takes charge.* He'd sent her away. Not willing to start something he knew would be a bad decision in the glaring light of day.

"That was almost two years ago. We were both—"

"Not thinking straight," she cut in. "Yeah, I've heard."

Sending her away had been so hard. Sex had never been a problem for them, and even though he didn't regret saying no, he'd considered the pros and cons of his decision long into that night. Sleeping with Elaina would have made everything worse. Would have blurred lines they'd both agreed to. That night was why he'd kept his dating life secret for so long. She never came back to him again, but he didn't know if that night was her expressing regret for the divorce or just her showing affection in the only way she ever had with him... through sex.

"Save your friendship, Travis," Elaina said in a bored voice. "I don't want it." She turned away and left him standing in the hall.

"Elaina," he called.

She flicked her wrist dismissively and disappeared around a corner. Travis pinched the bridge of his nose. He tapped his foot several times instead of screaming in frustration. Would there ever come a time when he and Elaina could be in the same room?

Travis checked his watch. If Byron didn't show up in the next fifteen minutes, he was leaving. He was not risking the chance of running into Elaina again and going another round with her. He pulled out his cell and texted Byron to see where he was. A second later he got the return text. Five minutes away.

Travis headed in the opposite direction from Elaina to reduce his chances of running into her again. He wandered toward the back of the house instead of going to the upstairs family room. He wasn't feeling running into Grant either. He could hide out in the back sunroom or on the lanai until Byron got there and was ready to go.

The faint sounds of violin music stopped him.

His feet changed direction and instinctively followed the music. How many times when he was younger had he gone to the music room after a stressful or frustrating encounter with his family, Grant or Elaina? Lured by the sound of something smooth and soothing like a balm to his hollowed emotions. He stopped at the door and watched India.

He didn't recognize the song she played. The music was a strong, fluid sound laced with an edge of anger and passion. Her eyes were closed, a line between her brows as she focused on the intricate pattern of notes. She'd been a great player before leaving with the orchestra, and now she was outstanding. The complicated and intense execution of the music fascinated him.

Something was bothering her. She lost herself in music and practiced daily, but he could feel the deeper need in her to express what she couldn't say. The idea of something, someone, putting her in a mood caused a restless energy to bubble inside him. The need to fix whatever obstacle stood in her way turned him over like a plow in the tobacco fields.

India finished with a flair. Her body stilled as the last notes echoed in the room. Slowly her arm lowered, her shoulders slumped, and she let out a deep sigh. She was both utterly beautiful and deeply sad.

Travis's chest ached. He'd stopped breathing. He slowly drew in a breath as the memory of the sad notes lingered in his mind.

"You play that perfectly," he said in a quiet voice.

She didn't jump, which told him she'd known he was there. How did she always sense when he was in a room? Was she just as aware of him as he was of her?

"I've had a lot of practice." She leaned over to set the violin in the open case next to her chair.

He approached her slowly instead of walking away as he should. "What's got you riled up?"

She snapped closed the violin case with a frustrated huff. "Two guesses."

Travis grabbed the black folding chair next to the music stand, flipped it backward and straddled it. "What did he do?" Only her dad had the ability to really anger her.

"He's marrying Patricia." She finally looked at him. Her eyes narrowed. "You knew?"

The news hadn't been unexpected. Grant had made Patricia more a part of the family in the years India had been away. Elaina and Byron had been given time to get used to the idea of their father marrying his longtime lover. For India the hurt of Grant's indiscretions would still feel new and tender.

"Byron mentioned it the other day. Your dad talked to him about it. He doesn't want it to affect the campaign or take—"

"Attention away from Byron. I know, he told me." She rolled her eyes. "It's just…I can't believe he chose her."

Her arms crossed over her midsection. The anger in her eyes gave way to a deep sorrow that made Travis wish he could stand up, wrap his arms around her and hold her until the pain subsided, even though pain like that never truly went away. It could be painted over like a stain on a wall, but beneath the new layers of shine, the stain would always be there.

"Your father has wanted her for a long time," Travis said slowly. He kept his voice neutral, not taking sides in this family fight. How could he? Grant was marrying the woman he'd wanted for years. Something Travis would never experience. A small knot of envy twisted his stomach. "I don't condone what went on with him and Patricia when your mom was still alive, but I do know she makes him happy."

India snorted. "I didn't realize we valued happiness in this family anymore. I thought happiness came second place to the family, our legacy and the business."

"Maybe it did once, but I think your dad's coming around. If you really wanted something that made you happy, he'd understand."

Soft amber eyes met his. "Not if I told him what I really want." A wistful smile lifted the corner of her mouth.

His heart shot into second gear. The need to do something, touch her, hold her, tell her how he felt tempted him. He shifted in the seat and broke eye contact. India sucked in a breath. Had she seen his thoughts? Was his longing written all over his face?

He cleared his throat and gripped the back of the chair he straddled instead of giving in to the urge to reach for her. Not in Grant's house. Not with the cloud of his conversation with Elaina still in the air. "Things all set for the fish fry next week?" he asked.

India's brows drew together before she turned away and fingered the sheets of music on the stand. "Yes, Frank is going to have most of his people there frying the fish. You got the DJ, right?"

She'd chosen Frank's Fish and Chicken to handle cooking the food. A perfect choice. Frank's was a Jackson Falls staple almost as much as the Robidoux family. The small place that started as a fish market serving quick lunches of two pieces of fish, a slice of bread and hushpuppies during lunch hour had quickly become a community hangout on the side of town where Travis had grown up. Choosing Frank's was a textbook way to use a local business that was loved and trusted by the community for the event.

"I've got two lined up," Travis answered her question. "I don't want us to be stuck with no music because my DJ didn't show up."

"Good. I think everything will go well." She glanced around before standing and walking over to one of the wooden tables where she knocked three times. "I hope so."

He smiled at the superstitious gesture. "Still knocking on wood for good luck?"

"Always. I'm not tempting fate." This time her sweet smile reached her eyes. "We threw this together via email and phone calls. I'm worried sick everything will go crazy."

"Well, I won't tempt fate either." He knocked on his head. India laughed, like he'd hoped she would, and his chest expanded. "I need to get through this so I can finally relax and take a quick vacation."

"How can you vacation in the middle of a case?"

Not easily, but he needed the time away to clear his head. He stood and crossed over to her. "I'm going out of town for a very quick weekend. I'm hoping it will help me recharge and get ready for the trial."

"You and Camille?" she asked casually. Too casually.

"No. I don't think things will work out with Camille." She was part of the reason he needed to clear his head. He couldn't force things with her anymore. He'd tried to force a happy marriage for years. He'd be damned if he'd do that while dating.

Interest brightened India's eyes. She eased closer. "Why not?"

Travis didn't back up. His heartbeat hadn't recovered from earlier and despite himself he didn't want to put distance between them. "She's not the woman I want." One small confession, that's all he'd allow himself.

India chewed the corner of her lip. Her chin lifted and yearning flickered in her gaze. "Who do you want?"

The hesitant question cracked his resolve. Her fingertips still rested on the wooden table. Travis slid his hand across the smooth surface until his fingers lightly brushed hers. Awareness scattered across his senses.

India's eyes widened slightly. Then her gaze became bolder. Desire expanded like a hot air balloon inside him. Bigger. Wider. Adding pressure to the cracks in his resolve. Years of denial whispered, *Do it* in the deep recesses of his mind.

"Travis, I knew I'd find you in here," Byron's eager voice interrupted just in time. He walked in all smiles and easy swagger.

India slid her hand away from his and turned toward her brother. Disappointment and relief plowed over Travis after Byron's interruption. He'd seen his own feelings mirrored in India's eyes. *If Grant can have who he wants, why can't I?* Things were about to get out of hand, and right now Travis wasn't sure if he trusted himself to regret what almost happened.

Travis stepped back from India and greeted his friend. "Just listening to India practice. You ready? I've waited on you longer than I should have." He needed to go and think. There were too many things that could go wrong if he went with the emotions churning in his gut. He couldn't be ruled by those emotions without considering all of the consequences.

"I know, my bad," Byron said. "Let's get out of here." He gave India a quick hug and kiss. "See you later, India."

India smiled at him. "Don't have too much fun."

Byron winked. "Just hanging with my boy. I'll tell you the same thing. Aren't you going out with Russell later?"

Travis felt like he'd been punched in the chest. Jealousy crept deep in his bones. He didn't look at India as she answered.

"Not tonight. I'm staying in."

He glanced at her, a wave of relief sweeping away the jealousy that sprouted so quickly. Her bright eyes darted to him quickly, as if checking to see if he cared? He cared. Cared a lot more than he wanted to admit.

"Well, I'm coming over for dinner tomorrow," Byron said. "We can talk about the final details for the community fish fry next weekend." He glanced at Travis. "You should come to dinner, too."

And sit across the table from India and Elaina for a few hours? Hell no. "I've got plans. Come on, let's get out of here."

They said goodbye to India. On the way out, Byron started talking about his long day and how he was looking forward to getting a drink.

Travis looked over his shoulder as they left the room. Caught India's eye.

She lifted a hand in a slow wave. A spark of disappointment crossed her face before he turned the corner and couldn't see her anymore. He'd been so close to saying everything. Ruining everything. Yes, he was on a roller coaster and he needed to get off. If he couldn't suppress how he felt for India, and couldn't express his feelings, then he needed to decide if he was ready to handle the fallout of going for what he wanted.

CHAPTER FOURTEEN

ASHIYA GRABBED INDIA as she dashed from one end of the park to the other. India had been running around since arriving at six in morning. The actual fish fry started an hour ago, at eleven, and to their pleasant surprise, most of the community had shown up. Whether they were there to learn more about Byron's plans if he became the next senator or for the free fish, it didn't matter. At least not now. Byron worked the crowd and planned to talk to as many of the people who came as he could. If the fish didn't win them over, her brother's personality would.

"What's up?" India asked after Ashiya stopped her. She'd been on her way to make sure the audio system on the stage was connected and ready for Byron's speech.

"I just want to make sure you're breathing," Ashiya said with a grin. "You haven't stopped since I got here."

"Byron's speech is in a few minutes. I need to make sure everything is ready."

"You do realize the world won't come to an end if you take a few seconds to enjoy yourself? Besides, you have tons of family here. We can help. Look at Elaina, she's itching to do something." Ashiya pointed across the park to where Elaina hovered near the owners of the seafood restaurant India had hired to cater the event.

Elaina had raised one slim, critical brow when India

informed her Frank's Fish and Chicken was the place she'd chosen for the fish fry. Elaina had suggested Blue Fin, a higher end seafood restaurant instead, but India knew the smaller, more casual place was a staple in the community. If the goal of today's event was to make the residents feel comfortable around Byron without the steep price tag of an expensive fund-raiser, then Frank's was the perfect caterer.

"She's not itching for something to do," India said. "She's looking for something to go wrong."

"That's only because she didn't choose the caterer. Still, you could have her check the audio system and you can get a moment to breathe. Russell got here a few minutes ago. He was looking for you."

India glanced around the crowded park. She didn't want to see Russell. She'd avoided his calls and made excuses via text message ever since learning he was Patricia's nephew. Russell couldn't help who he was related to. He had nothing to do with his aunt's relationship with Grant, yet India couldn't get the idea out of her mind that continuing to hang out with Russell was like giving her stamp of approval to her dad and Patricia. Any kernels of guilt that tried to annoy her whenever she gave him another excuse were quickly flicked aside when she remembered her dad insisting she had to get used to Patricia.

"Did you know he's Patricia's nephew?"

Ashiya tugged on her right ear and glanced away. "I may have heard that somewhere."

Meaning she'd known all along who he was related to. "Seriously? You didn't think to tell me?"

"I didn't think it would matter," Ashiya defended.

"Of course it matters." India turned and stomped

toward the stage where a guy was hopefully correctly setting up the audio system.

"Why does it matter?" Ashiya asked, running to catch up with India. "He's got nothing to do with your dad and Patricia. It shouldn't matter."

"Well, it does." Anyone else. Her dad could marry anyone else and she'd be happy for him. Instead he'd chosen the one woman India could never forgive.

Neither Byron nor Elaina had decided to tell her their dad's relationship with Patricia had gotten serious enough for marriage. Russell had known and hadn't said anything to her either. Which meant he'd known she would be uncomfortable, especially since she'd already voiced concerns about why her dad wanted her to get to know him. Grant probably assumed Russell would be able to change India's mind about his wonderful aunt. No one cared to tell her the truth, so right now, India didn't particularly care about hiding her feelings when it came to her future *stepmother*.

"You know," Ashiya said, "from the beginning you've been making excuses for why you can't be with Russell. I'm starting to think there's more going on."

India caught sight of Travis walking toward the stage with long and purposeful strides. The lightweight white shirt and camel-colored slacks he wore effortlessly enhanced the width of his shoulders, flat stomach, strong arms and long legs. He had a matching fedora on his head, the front tilted low to the right casting a shadow over his eyes. Every time he looked at her from beneath the brim of that hat, her pulse decided to skip.

There is more going on. More reasons why she couldn't focus on the good guy in front of her. Temptation was always sweeter.

India broke her gaze away from Travis. She stopped and faced Ashiya. "There's no big plot. You know how much I don't like feeling as if I'm being controlled by my dad. Russell feels like a type of control."

Ashiya sighed. "Your dad could be leading you to something much worse than dating one of the most eligible bachelors in Jackson Falls."

"Or maybe he's driving me away from something better." She fought the urge to look over her shoulder at Travis. "Look, let me check on the sound system real quick and then I'll find you. After Byron's speech, it's pretty much just hanging around while he talks to people. I'll have plenty of time to chill."

Ashiya didn't look convinced. "If you don't find me, I'll come look for you."

"Please do. Russell aside, I could use some fun later. Find me."

Ashiya nodded and India continued toward the stage. Travis was there, talking to the guy setting up the microphone. He nodded and his teeth flashed as he smiled and patted the guy on the shoulder. India bit her lip. Her steps quickened. She wasn't in a hurry because Travis looked as if he were about to walk away from the stage. She just really needed to make sure he'd verified that everything was okay.

Travis caught sight of her coming. He stopped and waited for her. He didn't smile, but what looked like anticipation brightened his eyes.

Projecting much? One brush of the fingers and an admission that he wanted someone other than Camille, and India's what-if dreams had started again.

He hurt you once. Don't be foolish and let him hurt you again.

"Hey," she said a bit too brightly when she reached him. "I was just coming over to check on the system, but you beat me to it."

He glanced back at the stage. "Yeah, everything is set. I'm going to try to pry Byron away from the folks he's talking to and get him over here to make his speech."

He stared into her eyes from beneath the brim of his hat. Humor danced in the dark centers. Her pulse played hopscotch against her veins. Heat rose in her cheeks.

"Good luck with that," she said. "Prying Byron away while he's campaigning is next to impossible."

"Tell me about it. I can't go anywhere with him anymore. We ran into a gas station yesterday just to pick up soda and chips. He started talking to the man behind the counter and guess how long he kept me there waiting?"

India tapped the corner of her mouth with a finger. "Thirty minutes?"

Travis shook his head. "Try an hour."

India laughed out loud. Travis's answering smile pulled her closer. She lightly hit his arm. "Oh no. You're joking?"

"I wish I were. I ate the chips and drank the soda while he talked to the owner and customers that came in. I can tell you every single item in the Lil Cricket on Jackson Street."

"And I thought I had it bad when he kept me in the produce section for twenty-five minutes last week." India covered her mouth and chuckled.

"Well, you're at an advantage." His laughter slowly died, leaving behind a sexy smile that made her focus a beat too long on his kissable lower lip. "One pleading look from your beautiful brown eyes and we both know Byron will do what you ask." His husky voice slid over her senses.

Her laughter slowly faded. Morphed into a pleasant warmth that spread from the crown of her head to the very soles of her feet. She felt the smile on her face soften along with the rest of her body. They stared at each other, both grinning. The charge of electricity between them buzzed like a hive of bees, pulsing with life and energy.

She needed to look away. No, she needed to turn and walk away. Yes, Travis was funny, interesting and good-looking. Sure, there was a connection between them, one that had been there for years. One that had made them friends long before they'd realized they would have worked as lovers. Yes, they liked the same things, and he made her giddy with just a glance. But she couldn't forget that he was Elaina's ex-husband. More than that, he'd hurt her. The night they'd been together, he'd promised her something more than lust. When he'd pushed her away, she'd asked what was wrong. Why he'd taken things so far just to reject her.

This isn't a rejection. India, I care about you more than you'll ever know. You're special to me. I need time to think.

Do you promise me this isn't a game?

He'd taken her hands in his, pulled her back into his arms and kissed her softly. *I promise you I'd never play you like that.*

Two weeks later, he'd been back with Elaina. A few months later, he'd married Elaina. India didn't want to feel that pain a second time if he moved on once again.

India broke eye contact first. "Well, since I have an advantage, I'll go get Byron."

Travis cleared his throat and took a step back. She hadn't realized they'd gotten closer to each other while they talked. "I won't argue with that."

There was something in his face as he stared at her. His brows drew together. He studied her as if searching for the answer to an important question. Whether the question was for her or himself, she didn't know. If he asked what she desired, what was in her heart when he looked at her as if he wanted to be the man she dreamed of, she wasn't sure what answer she'd give.

Everyone in her family did what was expected of them. Elaina worked for Robidoux Tobacco. Byron was running for Senate to further extend their legacy. India had postponed moving to California to be the dutiful sister. Dad, on the other hand, was marrying his mistress and had told her to deal with it.

Maybe the reason she couldn't shake what she felt was that she and Travis hadn't finished what they'd started. What would happen if she did this one thing she wanted? Why couldn't she have Travis, then let him go?

The thought scared and excited her. His frown deepened as if he'd read her thoughts. She looked around, trying to spot her brother in the crowd. Time to go before that idea led her on.

"I'll be right back," she said in a rush. She spun faster than a figure skater in the Olympics and headed in the direction she'd last seen Byron.

She couldn't have Travis. Even if she wasn't a dutiful daughter, she was a loyal sister. Then there was the question of whether or not Elaina still cared about Travis in some way. India couldn't break her sister's heart by entertaining these thoughts. She looked over her shoulder. Travis still watched her. She couldn't…could she?

"BEFORE I GET off this stage, I'd like to thank the one person I wouldn't have made it this far without. Yolanda, sweetheart, will you come forward?"

India's gaze flew from her brother to his "girlfriend" standing next to Aunt Liz with the rest of the family on the stage. Byron's speech had been perfect. He'd talked about his plans to boost the economy, represent the underserved and fight to lower taxes. The crowd had cheered, clapped and yelled "amen" as if he were the greatest pastor they'd ever heard preach. She had to admit Byron sometimes sounded like a pastor when giving speeches. Once again, she'd been swept into his sincerity and enthusiasm as she stood behind him with the rest of the family. All of them beaming with pride—well, except Elaina. She never beamed but she had looked pleased as Byron promised to be the best senator their area had ever seen.

India watched anxiously as Yolanda crossed over to Byron. A sick feeling swelled in her gut. She'd spoken to Yolanda twice since Byron's campaign manager mentioned his plans to marry her. She and Byron looked like the perfect power couple, but there was no warmth, no swelling of emotion when the two of them were together. Yolanda was a nice person, but she wasn't who India would have expected Byron to marry. Enough time had passed since he'd mentioned getting engaged that she'd hoped Byron would change his mind. Now, as he turned to Yolanda with a grin on his face and reached into his pocket, India knew what was up.

"Yolanda," Byron said. He slipped a small black box out of his pocket. "You have been there for me from the moment I decided to begin this journey."

India shook her head. The sick feeling in her stomach increased. No. No. No. He couldn't be doing this. Not just to win an election. India looked at their dad. He needed to do something. Stop this charade.

But Grant just watched Byron and Yolanda with pride and satisfaction. Elaina's beautiful face was impassive except for a slight quirk to her brow. Her aunt, cousin and the rest of their family and friends invited onstage all smiled warmly at the couple. She had to stop this. She couldn't sit there and watch her brother make a huge mistake.

She took a step forward. A warm hand wrapped around her elbow. Travis stood behind her. He gently squeezed her elbow.

"Not now," he said in an almost imperceptible voice.

India clenched her teeth. If not now, when? If she didn't speak up, it would be too late. Byron couldn't rescind a public engagement. Had he lost his mind? She looked at her brother and opened her mouth to speak but the words died. Byron's politician's grin was wide and warm. Satisfaction apparent in his face, relaxed shoulders, and the way he confidently took Yolanda's left hand in his.

India leaned back toward Travis. He slid to her side and gave her a quick comforting squeeze to her shoulder. Movement to her left caught her attention. Elaina watched her. A frown on her face. She should move away from Travis. Instead, she gave Elaina a weak smile. Elaina darted her eyes at Byron, then lifted her shoulders in a what-ya-gonna-do way before rolling her eyes and turning back to the *happy couple*.

India knew exactly what she should do. Stop Byron in the middle of his stupid proposal. Tell him he deserved more than an arranged political wedding. Like a dutiful Robidoux, she remained quiet and absorbed the heat of Travis's body as he stood beside her. Their shoulders touched innocently, but India leaned into it as if it were an embrace. She forced herself to grin with the rest of her family as Byron asked a woman he didn't love to marry him.

The crowd ate up the engagement almost as fast as they were eating the free fish. Cheers and claps were everywhere after Byron slipped a sparkling diamond ring on Yolanda's finger. Even though she was pretty sure Yolanda was aware this was a calculated campaign maneuver, she played the part of surprised girlfriend so well she should have received an Oscar.

Everyone rushed over to congratulate the happy couple. Travis shifted away. She wanted to reach for him but stopped herself. He leaned down and spoke to her over the noise of the crowd. "Let's go check on the food." The warm caress of his breath was against her ear.

India didn't hesitate to turn away from the show. She'd deal with Byron later. Everyone was so excited about the engagement no one noticed as she and Travis slipped off the stage and walked silently to where Frank and his team battered and fried fish.

They went through the motions of making sure everything was still operating smoothly. The music started again. Hits from the late '90s and early '00s. Dancing started near the stage, with Byron, Yolanda and their father in the middle of the group. The sun glinted off the huge rock on Yolanda's finger. Everyone was happy for the future senator and his perfect soon-to-be wife.

"I can't believe he did it," India said. Watching as her brother smiled at Yolanda as if she had made him the happiest man alive. Maybe she had. All he wanted was the Senate seat and Yolanda would help him achieve that.

Travis placed a hand on the small of her back, the warmth comforting and frustrating. Casual touches, that was all she'd ever get from him. They couldn't laugh and dance and look at each other as if they were in love. She couldn't get what she wanted.

He leaned in close. "Let's take a walk."

She nodded and followed him. He took her to the walking trail that circled the perimeter of the park. They didn't speak as they strolled along the narrow concrete path. They passed the playground, baseball field and man-made pond, eventually reaching the other side of the park. It was a more naturalized area with trees and expanses of grass, but not so natural as to make the area unsafe for joggers and others using the trail. The sounds of the voices and excitement from the campaign event on the other side of the park near the stage became a distant hum in the background.

Travis walked off the trail, stopping near one of the large maple trees. India followed. "Are you going to be okay?" he finally asked.

She crossed her arms and paced. Her agitation hadn't subsided. She felt restless, angry, frustrated. She didn't know what to do, but the need to do something clawed at her. "I can't believe he did it. He doesn't love her."

"He cares about her," Travis said as if caring about Yolanda was all her brother needed to be happy.

"But is that enough?" She slapped the back of one hand into her palm and continued to pace. "He's only doing this for the campaign. Not because he's really ready to settle down."

Travis tilted his head to the side. "I think your brother is ready to settle down."

She stopped pacing and glared at him with her hands on her hips. "How could you let him do this? You're his friend. You know he doesn't want to marry her."

Maybe Travis could talk some sense into Byron. He might not listen to her, but he'd listen to Travis. Or even Elaina. Byron trusted Elaina's judgment more than his.

Travis ran a hand over his face. "I tried talking to Byron, but he's his own man. He knows what he wants, and he wants this. Yolanda isn't a bad person, and she isn't going into this with rose-colored glasses. She knows the deal."

He remained calm in the face of her anger, which only frustrated her more. She wanted to shake him. Was everyone okay now with pretending? "So, you agree with what he's doing?"

Travis shook his head. "Not entirely. I know what it's like to be in a bad marriage."

India crossed her arms. "But you at least loved Elaina when you asked her. Your marriage didn't start off badly."

Irritation flickered over his face. "My marriage never should have happened," he replied briskly. He pushed away from the tree and rubbed the back of his neck.

India stilled. For a heartbeat she couldn't think or breathe as she processed his words. Then her pulse jumped. "Why do you say that?"

Travis took two long steps toward her, then froze. His jaw clenched as he looked left and right. His dark eyes seemed conflicted. His shoulders tight as if he were holding something back.

"Travis," she urged. Her voice sharp and insistent.

He closed his eyes and the tension eased from his body. "Because she wasn't the person I really wanted." The words spilled from him like a long-held confession.

She closed the distance between them. Or maybe he had. All she knew was that in the moments after he spoke, only a couple insignificant inches were between them. Not enough of a buffer when he said things like that and opened his eyes to look at her as if she were one of the greatest wonders of the world.

"I tried to tell your brother that marrying someone out of duty or obligation wasn't the key to happiness. I know because I tried to do that. I did what I thought was right instead of what I wanted. I don't want your brother to go through that, but I also won't turn my back on him, because it's his decision to make."

India licked her dry lips. Blood rushed in her ears. She watched him. His eyes begged her to ask. Her soul screamed for her to get answers. She had to know. Today, while everyone else was okay with not speaking the truth and living with delusions.

"Who did you really want?" she whispered hesitantly.

Travis closed the scant distance between them, his heat and scent surrounding her like a favorite familiar coat. "You know who I wanted. Who I still want."

Clarity made one last-ditch effort to keep her from taking a step she knew she couldn't come back from. She shook her head. "Don't say—"

His hand cupped her face tenderly. His thumb traced across her lower lip. "Don't say what we both know? Your brother is making the wrong decision. I made the wrong decision."

"What was the right decision?" She had to hear him say it. No guessing. No doubt.

"I shouldn't have married her. I should have followed my instincts and found my way back to you."

The words slid inside of her, wrapped around her heart and melted away the chains she'd been using to suppress her feelings for him. A bittersweet joy swept over her. He'd wanted her. She hadn't been the only one who'd felt the landslide change in their relationship that night. He hadn't lied.

He lowered his head toward her. She lifted on her toes and met the kiss. Any reasons why they shouldn't kiss were meaningless when his lips touched hers. He was tall and solid against her. Heat, masculinity and temptation personified. She drank him in. Immersing herself in the fire of his kiss.

The soft touch of his lips quickly hardened into something deeper. His hand traced a hot line down the side of her body. Cupping the side of her breast for the barest of sweet seconds before gliding down to possessively cup her ass. He pulled her against him in a strong embrace. India wrapped her arms tightly around his neck. Indulged in the reckless pleasure of her softness pressed against his hard strength.

He groaned low and deep. The hand on her butt caressed and squeezed. Desire flooded her, washing away her inhibitions until she wanted to rip open his shirt, drag her nails across his chest and kiss every inch of his body.

A bird screeched in the tree above them. Someone yelled in the distance.

Reality snapped her back. She couldn't rip open his shirt. They were in a public park. She couldn't kiss every inch of his body. This was Travis. They weren't supposed to be kissing at all. Regret and guilt stamped out the flames of her desire.

She jerked back. Travis released her. His ragged breaths matched her own.

"India…"

She shook her head. "I can't. Not again." But the denial came out like a question. All of the reasons why she was denying this and her fears of being hurt again no longer seemed important as the feel of his body against hers hijacked her brain.

"I've got to go." She turned and hurried back down the trail. She brought a shaky hand to her lips. They still tingled with the imprint of Travis's kiss. She'd fucked up, and the worst thing was a big part of her didn't regret what had happened.

CHAPTER FIFTEEN

TRAVIS TOSSED HIS overnight bag into the trunk of his car and slammed it down. He couldn't wait to get out of town. He'd thrown clothes in a bag the night before and spent the morning straightening his house so he wouldn't return to a mess. When he'd made the last-minute decision to attend the Asheville Arts Festival, he'd done so because he needed to get out of town and think. After yesterday, he needed to do a lot more than think. He needed deep soul-searching.

He shouldn't have kissed her. Thing was, he didn't regret kissing her. Nor did he regret telling her the truth about his marriage. The time to clean up the entire blurry mess between them had come. He couldn't say they were destined to become something serious, but he could say keeping his feelings to himself was like pulling an 18-wheeler up a hill with a jump rope. Maybe he was being selfish, but he wanted her to know everything. Wanted to see what she'd do with the information.

Travis turned to go back inside for one last sweep of the house before leaving. He heard a car coming down the road but didn't turn to look. His hand touched the doorknob just as the car slowed and pulled into his driveway. In the reflection of his glass door, he recognized Camille's red sedan.

He grimaced and cursed. Camille had been trying to

interject herself into his trip with all the finesse of an unwanted houseguest. He forced the frown off his face, put on his best I'm-not-annoyed-with-you lawyer smile and turned. He walked back down the drive to meet Camille at her car. If she came inside, he'd never leave.

She jumped out of the car dressed in trendy torn jeans and an off-the-shoulder gray sweater. He glanced in the vehicle. A red leather overnight bag sat in the passenger seat.

"Travis, good, I'd hoped to catch you." She grinned from ear to ear. Looking as if she was so clever to have caught him in time.

"I was just about to lock the house and go," Travis replied. "I want to get there early."

"Well, I couldn't let you leave without giving you something to think of while you were away." She slid close and wrapped her arms around his neck. "Maybe you should rethink this idea of going out of town alone."

She lifted on her toes to kiss him. Travis pulled his head back. Camille's brows pulled together. She frowned as if he'd just insulted her family's beer.

Her arms loosened, and Travis pulled them from around his neck. "I won't be rethinking anything. Camille, we need to talk."

Camille's mouth fell open. She sucked in a breath and took two steps back. Holding up a red-tipped finger, she glared daggers. "Oh no, you are not about to dump me in the middle of your driveway."

Was there a better location to end a relationship? "I don't know of an easier way to do this."

"What happened?"

He and Camille had only been dating for a few months. Not long enough to have warranted any deep conversations about their future, but long enough for them to be more than a casual affair. He owed her an explanation for what had to be coming out of left field for her.

"Before you, long before you, there was someone else. I had the chance to fight for her, but I didn't. She's back in town, and I'm ready to fight."

The truth of the words surprised him. Until that moment he hadn't been sure if he wanted to push for something between him and India. He wanted her to know, but had prepared himself to be ready to step back. Not ask for anything more, and accept they'd never be anything more than friends. That wasn't the case. He wanted India. He wanted to know what could be between them. He was ready to accept the consequences if it meant finally being happy.

The anger in Camille's eyes cooled. A look of regret crossed her features. "So if she wouldn't have come back, you wouldn't be breaking up with me."

He considered her statement. Camille was just as compatible with him as Yolanda was to Byron. Grant had introduced them at a dinner party with a hint that it was time for him to get back in the saddle. So, he'd done that. If India hadn't returned and reminded him in person of everything he'd given up following Grant's orders before, he may have let his perfectly companionable relationship with Camille develop into something serious.

Or, he may have gotten tired of her tendency to do things like pop up unannounced or ignore the interests of others, and broken up with her eventually. "I don't know," he answered truthfully.

She nodded. "Well, I guess I'll let you go."

"I'm s—"

She swiped a hand and shushed him. "Don't, just... don't." She jerked open her car door, dropped into the seat and slammed the door shut.

He watched her drive away. Was he a fool for letting her go? No. Camille wasn't the one for him. He knew that now. Grant had assumed if Travis moved on, Elaina would, too. Grant was too sure of himself to realize Elaina hadn't moved on because Elaina didn't want to move on. Travis hoped one day she'd find someone to make her happy. They'd both lost out on happiness in the years they'd tried to make their marriage work.

Grant was right about one thing though. The time had come for Travis to move on, except he wanted to move on with the woman he'd thought about almost daily in the years since he pushed her away. The woman he'd always been able to talk to. The woman who understood his artistic side and his drive to make a name for himself outside of the art world. The woman he'd admired before that night under the stars and craved afterward.

Travis pushed aside thoughts of Camille and India and went into the house. He did his last sweep. Nothing was out of order. All doors and windows locked, security system ready to be armed as he left. He'd checked before putting the bag in the car, but he couldn't help himself. He remembered all too well how easy breaking into someone's house had been when he was a teenager trying to prove himself. His house wouldn't be easy pickings if he could help it.

His doorbell rang right as he finished checking everything. "Who the hell is that?"

He pressed his hands together and looked up, sending a quick prayer Camille hadn't returned to talk about the breakup.

He took a heavy breath and glanced out his peephole. His uncle Mitch stood on the other side. Travis's hand tightened on the door. His uncle had never come to his home. Hell, his *parents* had never visited him there. To say a family member was the very last person he expected was an understatement. He'd be less shocked to find the British prime minister at his doorstep than his uncle.

Travis opened the door. The hard look on Mitch's face said this wasn't a social call. "What do you want, Mitch?" He didn't bother to sound welcoming. Not after his last visit when Mitch hadn't cared about his son pulling a gun on Travis.

"The trial starts the week after next," Mitch said in a deceptively casual voice. His eyes were obsidian hard. His body tense as if he were waiting for an excuse to go for the gun-like bulge on his side.

"I know."

"I'm giving you one last chance to do right by your family."

Travis clenched his teeth. He took a slow breath in through his nose. Tried to tamp down the rampant frustration bubbling beneath his skin. "I've never done wrong by the family."

Mitch raised one bushy brow. "Oh really? You don't think working for that bastard Grant Robidoux wasn't the start of you doing wrong by the family?"

"No. I don't. Grant kept me out of jail when he didn't have to, gave me a job and a means to improve my life."

"Yeah, guilt can make a man do things like that."

Travis tilted his head. What the hell was his uncle

talking about? "Guilt? He had no reason to feel guilty for helping me."

Mitch sucked his teeth like a smart-ass teen and sneered. "But he had every reason to feel guilty for the way he double-crossed your dad."

"My dad? They barely know each other."

"They knew each other. Grew up together. Were friends. Where do you think Grant got the land he needed when he wanted to expand his damn tobacco fields?"

"A tax sale," Travis replied immediately. He'd heard the story from Grant a dozen times. He'd needed more acres. When the land went up for back taxes, he out-bid everyone in the county, including other tobacco farmers, just to get the land. That expansion helped him start Robidoux Tobacco's special selection of tobacco that they used in the high-end cigars. That expansion had given the company the boost needed to survive the decline in cigarette sales.

Mitch's eyes narrowed. "So, you know."

Travis hadn't thought it was possible for Mitch to sound even more disgusted with him, but he'd been wrong. "Did I know that someone didn't pay taxes and Grant legally bought the land? Yes, I knew that."

"And who do you think didn't pay their taxes?"

Travis glared. "How the hell am I supposed to know?"

Mitch rolled his eyes and sneered. "That was your dad's land. Grant Robidoux stole the little bit of property left in our family."

Travis's head jerked back. "Grant bought our family's land?" Disbelief filled his voice. He shook his head. "He would have told me."

Mitch's laugh was mocking. "He went behind your dad's back after promising to help him save it. He didn't give a damn that me and your dad had plans to eventually try to work the land again. All he cared about was making more money. Now do you understand why you working for him, marrying one of his daughters and being a puppet in that family is a slap in the face?"

The words hit Travis and knocked him speechless. He'd never understood why his dad was so against Travis taking the assistance Grant offered him. His dad's animosity toward Grant made a lot more sense now. He'd always called Grant a liar and a thief. A no-good bastard that was only out to get his. He wasn't surprised his dad had left out the details, or wouldn't acknowledge that failing to pay the taxes gave Grant, and anyone else, the right to purchase the land.

His head spun with the new information. Had he been a pawn in Grant's feud with his father? He'd looked up to Grant. Admired him, tried to be like him and married Elaina after Grant accused him of knocking her up and ruining her chances at a better life. To think Grant had only helped and guided him as a way to further antagonize his father felt like a betrayal.

He met Mitch's eye. Recognized the pleased satisfaction in his uncle's expression. He wanted to make Travis mad. Mitch probably assumed spilling this information would make Travis feel the need to do something good for the family. Something like fail to defend Zachariah King.

Just like when he was in the courtroom and hit with unexpected information, Travis schooled his features and filed away the shock of his emotions to process later. Right now he needed to get Mitch off his doorstep.

"I have nothing to do with what happened between Dad and Grant." He gave no hint of the doubt and confusion churning in his belly.

"Is that your excuse for working with Grant?" Mitch asked. "Because it came before your time, you don't care?"

"Because the problems between my dad and Grant are separate from me defending Zach King." He brought the conversation back to the real reason his uncle was here.

"Tell yourself that, but when it all boils down, it's the same. You going against the family."

"I won't go through this with you anymore." Travis didn't want to have to toss his uncle off his porch, but he was sick of this conversation and ready to get the hell out of town.

"Then I don't have to tell you again that if you don't make sure the man who killed my son goes to prison, then I'll make sure he pays. And you along with him." Mitch looked Travis up and down before he turned and casually walked back to his car as if he hadn't just threatened Travis and his client.

Travis stood there and watched as his uncle got in his car and drove away. His heart pounded like an electrocuted rhino. The adrenaline that flooded his system in anticipation of having to defend himself from his uncle pulsed. He wanted to shout, hit something—shit, smoke a blunt like he would have done at fourteen.

Why hadn't Grant told him? Why hadn't his dad elaborated instead of just calling Travis a sellout for working with the family? Would Travis have done anything differently if he'd known? Would he have turned down Grant's assistance if it meant saving the miniscule amount of affection his father had thrown his way before he'd worked for Robidioux Tobacco? His life had gone from complicated to fucked in the space of two days.

For years he'd been split between the loyalty he'd felt for his father and the man who'd treated him like a son. Eventually he'd chosen the path Grant laid out for him. While his father's ideas of what Travis should have done with his life wouldn't have landed Travis where he was today, he damn sure wouldn't be dealing with a threat from Mitch that was deadly serious.

He gripped his keys, locked the door and hurried to his car, now even more anxious to get out of town and process everything. He had a feeling once everything was said and done he may not come out of any of these situations unscathed.

CHAPTER SIXTEEN

THE CHIME OF the bell on the door of Ashiya's consignment shop greeted India. Several women browsed the various selection of high-end fashions. India was amazed at her cousin's success. Not because she didn't think Ashiya could be successful, but because she'd always known her cousin wanted her own business, and seeing Ashiya not only achieve her dream but thrive at it filled India's heart with pride.

"Welcome to Piece Together," the young girl behind the counter called out.

India smiled at her and another woman ringing up a patron's purchase. She did a quick scan of the shop for Ashiya but didn't see her cousin. She looked back to the counter.

"Hi, Lindsey, is Ashiya in?"

Lindsey pointed toward the back of the shop. "Yeah, she went in the office to take a call. You can go on back."

"Thanks," India said.

She maneuvered her way through the various racks of dresses, blouses, pants and everything in between. On her way to the office, a garnet dress hanging on the wall caught her attention. She'd have to check that out before leaving.

She and Ashiya had made plans to go out later that

day, but India needed to get not only out of the house but also out of town. Everything irritated her. Elaina's cool confidence, Byron's jubilation over being up in the polls, the pep in her dad's step now that he was marrying his former mistress. They all were so sure of themselves and their space in the world. Whereas she was twisted in a dozen knots.

Travis wanted her. He'd kissed her! She wanted him, too.

In any other situation, those three things would be perfect, the start of a new relationship filled with all types of possibilities. Yet, there was nothing about her situation that said she should jump in headfirst. Not only was there the potential to cause a rift in her family over this, but despite her excitement, a part of her was afraid to believe Travis wouldn't hurt her again.

Does anyone have to know?

The one thought that had crept into her mind dozens of times since Travis kissed her taunted her. What if what was between her and Travis was just a whim? An itch they needed to scratch and nothing more? Why couldn't they indulge and then put everything behind them without anyone knowing? Without risking her heart with promises of something more?

She tried to push the thought aside, but it lingered. Always there. Always tempting in its weird sort of logic.

That's why she had to get away. She needed time to think. Time away from her family, the campaign and expectations. Time away from Travis. The last thing she needed was to run into him again while these thoughts held her good sense hostage.

"I'm not going there with you again. You started seeing someone else. I don't play runner-up."

The sound of Ashiya's voice carried from the open door of her office. India hesitated. Her cousin sounded angry and hurt. Was she talking to Stephen? The other week when she and Ashiya had talked about men, her cousin hadn't said anything about Stephen seeing anyone else. Anger seeped into India's blood. This was why Ashiya needed to leave Stephen's trifling ass behind. She walked up to knock so Ashiya would know she was there. She didn't want to eavesdrop.

"Don't give me that," Ashiya snapped. "Stephen doesn't matter. I've told you that."

India's hand paused as she started to knock on the door. That was interesting. Not Stephen. Then who was Ashiya seeing?

"You didn't just date someone else, you were with—"

Ashiya looked up, caught India's eye and clammed up. Guilt made India's face burn. She lowered her hand. No need to knock now. She'd hesitated long enough and had been caught listening.

Ashiya dropped her gaze but waved India in. "I've got to go," she said in the phone. She ended the call and tossed her cell on the desk. "India…what are you doing here?" There was a tremble in her cousin's voice.

India entered the office and pushed the door shut. "I decided to stop by on my way out of town. To see if you're okay with rescheduling our outing tonight."

Ashiya rubbed around the neckline of her shirt. A nervous gesture India hadn't seen in years. "Sure, I'm cool with that."

"Are you okay? Who was that on the phone?"

She met India's eyes and the embarrassment in her gaze slowly gave way to relief. Her hand dropped from her neck. "No one important."

She'd already heard enough. No need to pretend as if she hadn't. "It wasn't Stephen. Are you two still together?"

"I don't want to talk about it," Ashiya said firmly. She took a deep breath, squared her shoulders, then smiled the placid Robidoux-family, let's-not-go-there smile. "Out of town? Why are you leaving?"

More questions bubbled in India's throat. She decided not to pry. She had her own messy situation to clean up. No need getting mixed up in Ashiya's. "I just need to get some space. The fish fry was a lot, and I feel like I've done nothing but focus on the campaign. I'm taking a few days to clear my head."

"And think about why you kissed Travis?"

India's heart fell to her feet. Then hopped back up and ran a race in her chest. "What?"

Ashiya shrugged. "Don't worry. I'm not outing you or anything. I just didn't realize there was something going on with you two."

India hurried across the room and gripped the back of the red leather chair in front of Ashiya's desk. "It's not like that."

Ashiya raised a brow. "I saw him kiss you Saturday." Ashiya's voice was smug in a *gotcha* sense without being judgmental.

India opened and closed her mouth. A dozen excuses ran through her head, but none of them came to the surface. "You saw that."

"I saw it. No one else did," Ashiya answered. She looked at her discarded cell phone and sighed. "Your secret is safe with me. I'm not one to judge."

Based on that conversation with not-Stephen, India

had to agree. "There hasn't been anything between me and Travis in years."

Ashiya leaned forward. "Are you saying there was something before?" Her mouth fell open. "While he was married to—"

"No!" India shook her head emphatically. "I wouldn't do that to Elaina. Though, what I did do wasn't much better. It was the night of my birthday the year after mom died. You know I didn't go to the party with you."

"Yeah, you bailed on me and I had to hang out with Marlena Gore all night," Ashiya said with a grimace. "She left me behind once the fight broke out." Her eyes narrowed, and India bet if Marlena was in that room, Ashiya would have cursed her out again for leaving her stranded.

"I bailed because Travis overheard me saying I would go," India explained. "We hung out that night instead. He figured something bad would pop off and offered to help me celebrate my birthday instead. We talked, drank way too much whiskey, and one thing led to another."

Ashiya slapped a hand over her heart. Her eyes wide as silver dollars. "You slept together! Why didn't you tell me?"

"Because we didn't have sex," India shot back. "He stopped before it got there. I didn't tell anyone, and two weeks later he proposed to Elaina."

"Oh." Ashiya's face twisted into a look of distaste. "That doesn't explain the kiss on Saturday."

"I can't explain the kiss the other day. I've felt something for Travis for years. It's why I agreed to hang with him on my birthday. I knew he and Elaina had fought and were supposedly broken up. I'm not saying it's right, but I wanted him to be with me. When he married her, I tried to get over it, forget it, ignore it, and everything in between. I didn't think he felt anything either. Ever since I got back, he's acted as if we're just good friends and that night didn't happen. Then…he tells me he shouldn't have married Elaina." She said the last in a rush. She still couldn't believe the words she'd suspected and longed to hear for years.

"I think we all know that," Ashiya said in a dry tone.

"Ashiya!"

"Come on, everyone knows they shouldn't have gotten married. Your dad pushed the engagement because Travis was going to law school and rumors were starting to fly about Elaina hooking up with the hoodlum Grant took under his wing. Uncle Grant needed to clean everything up and marriage was the best way."

"How do you know that?"

"How do you think? Mom told me," Ashiya said with a shrug. "She tells me everything that goes on in this family. You didn't know?"

"I never asked." Was it true? More questions filled her head than before. Elaina had never indicated their dad played any role in her marriage to Travis. Even though Travis said he shouldn't have married Elaina, he also hadn't mentioned her father. Why would her dad push the marriage? He'd been irritated by Elaina hooking up with Travis, but would he have pressured matrimony to "clean things up"?

In a hot minute.

The answer was clear. No one told her anything, and in typical Robidoux style, if there was a secret to keep, then no one outside of the people who knew was told. If their dad wanted people to believe Elaina and Travis got married because they cared about each other and not because he believed the rumors were getting too hot, then that's what people would believe.

That didn't change her decision today. Grant pushing the marriage back then still didn't make it okay for India and Travis to explore the desire simmering between them today. Did it?

"Look, I don't know what is or isn't going on between you and Travis anymore. And I swear I'm the worst person to give relationship advice but be careful there." Ashiya's eyes were serious. "Elaina isn't very forgiving in most situations. I doubt she'll forgive you if she finds out about you and Travis. Make sure you know what you're doing before you tear the family apart."

CHAPTER SEVENTEEN

GETTING AWAY WAS just what she needed. India had arrived in Asheville the night before and headed out early the following morning to tour some of the many art galleries downtown. The area was alive with music, laughter and conversation. Outside the galleries, craft and food vendors lined the streets. The multitude of people, sights and indulgences for the senses occupied her mind. Almost enough to keep her from obsessing about Ashiya's revelations and words of warning.

India rested in the park downtown. A trio of men performed an upbeat bluegrass melody nearby. Their voices harmonized over the words as they played a banjo, harmonica and guitar with fluid expertise. She settled on one of the small stone walls nearby and watched them while she munched on popcorn she'd purchased from one of the vendors.

"They're really good, aren't they?" said a male voice to her left.

India looked up and met the smiling face of a nice-looking man with interested brown eyes. He was tall and lanky with a stylish haircut and bohemian vibe about him.

"They are," India replied.

The guy eased closer. "The one playing the harmonica is my roommate. He's always practicing."

"His practice is paying off. I've only heard a few people who can play riffs that well."

"You're a bluegrass fan?" His tone indicated he was pleasantly surprised.

"I'm a music fan." She took another bite of her popcorn. The buttery goodness was so addicting she wanted to lick the salt from her fingers, but opted to use the napkin on her lap instead.

"So am I." He held out his hand. "I'm Rick."

She held up her sticky fingers. "I won't shake because I'm covered in popcorn butter," she said with a laugh. "But my name is India."

"So, India, are you here by yourself?" Rick glanced at the empty space on the wall next to her. His eyebrows rose in expectation. He looked like a puppy begging to be petted.

Meeting a new guy wasn't part of her plan. Russell had stopped calling, so she knew he'd taken the hint that they weren't going anywhere. Rick seemed nice enough, but spending the next few minutes engaged in idle chitchat while he tried to hit on her was not how she wanted to end the afternoon. Her mind raced with multiple excuses that wouldn't sound completely lame.

"No, she's not here alone."

Goose pimples sprouted across her skin faster than weeds in springtime. She slowly turned to her right and met Travis's bold gaze. He stood casually, his hands in the pockets of his dark pants with the thumbs out, a dark blue T-shirt fitted against the lean muscles of his body just enough to make her mouth water. Her heart picked up the pace and her breathing fought to catch up.

She was dimly aware of Rick saying something and walking away. Travis didn't wait for her to invite him the way Rick had. He sat right next to her on the wall. His left side pressed against her right. The touch of his bare arm on hers a lightning bolt across her nervous system.

"Wh-what are you doing here?" Her voice trembled, and she wanted to slap herself.

"I came for the arts festival. What are you doing here?"

"I…I needed some time to think." She scooted away from him. The bolt of awareness had fried her ability to talk without stuttering.

"So did I." He watched her.

India didn't meet his eyes. Meeting his eyes would only remind her of his lips against hers. His hand trailing down her side. The fire that erupted when they touched.

"Did Byron tell you I was here?" Had Travis followed her?

"No. This was the out-of-town trip I'd told you about before. The trial starts the week after next. I need the break before things get real."

Her bubble of anticipation burst. He'd planned this trip in advance. Which meant he hadn't come because he needed to think about what happened between them. Hadn't needed to get away. "Oh."

"The timing was perfect for other reasons, too." Travis shifted next to her. He tugged on his pants, then ran a hand over his shirt.

Was he nervous? She finally looked at him. "Reasons like what?"

The wind blew one of her long curls into her eyes. Travis reached over and brushed the strands out of her face before she could. The tips of his fingers were a gentle caress across her temple and cheek before he tucked the wayward strand behind her ear. India sucked in a breath. Awareness prickled across her skin and concentrated in areas that craved his touch.

"I can't get you out of my mind." The words were spoken like a revelation. Quick and tinged with relief and wariness.

If he'd been coy, arrogant or seductive with the words, she would have pushed him away. Well, she was 75 percent sure she would have pushed him away. But no, he had to sound just as tortured by what was between them as her.

"Travis, what are we doing?"

He brushed her cheek with the back of his hand before pulling away with a frown. "I don't know, but don't you think it's time we found out?"

The word *no* formed in her mind. Clear as the sun shining down on them. The automatic, practiced answer to a question she'd never let herself consider another answer. No, she shouldn't tell Travis how she felt. No, she shouldn't believe there was something serious between them. No, falling in love with her sister's ex wasn't acceptable. But as she looked into his dark eyes, she knew she couldn't go with the expected answer anymore.

"Yes."

"This popular candy bar was introduced in 1930 and named for a horse owned by the Mars family."

Travis slapped his hand on the wooden table and pointed at India. "I know this."

She waved her hands in a come-on fashion. "Okay, what's the answer?"

Travis squeezed his eyes while he tried to pull up

the answer to the trivia question from the dregs of his three-shots-addled brain.

After she'd said yes, the only thing he'd wanted to do was pull her into his arms and kiss her until they both were running to the nearest hotel room. Instead, he'd taken a relieved deep breath, taken her hand in his and turned back to the bluegrass band.

They'd spent the afternoon exploring downtown Asheville. It had been like old times. They'd talked about art. Debated current events. Shared an organically grown and locally sourced meal at an Indian restaurant. Now they were ending the day in one of the bars where they struggled to maintain third place in the trivia contest.

The night was still young, not even eight thirty, but if he hadn't run into India, he would have probably already gone back to his hotel. He wasn't ready to say good-night yet. When he'd suggested they get a drink together, he'd expected her to say no. When she'd agreed, he'd chosen to believe it was because she wasn't ready for the night to end either.

Today told him everything he'd already known. There was something real between him and India. He hadn't told her he was coming to Asheville, but he wasn't surprised she'd also chosen the artsy location for her own getaway. There was a vibe between them. A vibe that had always been there, first as friendship, then supplemented with the awareness of each other as a man and a woman. The mistakes of youth led him to jump in bed with Elaina when she'd shown interest instead of practicing restraint. Restraint would have given him time to realize what was developing between him and India before it had been much too late.

India slapped his arm. "Come on, we get this, we move up to second place."

"Time is running out," the bar's announcer/DJ said into the microphone. "No cell phones, table four!"

Travis slapped the table. "Snickers!" he yelled.

"You got it!" the DJ said, then pressed a button and the sound of horns blasting filled the bar. Patrons clapped and cheered.

He and India slapped high five, then turned their triumphant grins on table four, whom they'd just bumped from second place.

"Last question," the DJ said. "We're quadrupling the points. Winner takes all. And by all, I mean another round of shots and bragging rights."

Laughter came up from the crowd of people in the bar. A right answer was rewarded with a shot of your choice. In third place, Travis and India had already had three shots each. The waitress came through the crowd and dropped two shots on the table. Travis was thankful his hotel was in walking distance from the bar. He hoped India's was downtown, as well.

"Here's your orgasm," the waitress said with a wink and grin.

India laughed and covered her mouth. "I can't believe you ordered these."

"I just asked what was in it," Travis answered honestly. "I didn't know we would be stuck with multiple orgasms all night." India covered her mouth and laughed. He held up a hand. "I did not mean that the way it came out."

"I don't know." India lifted her shot glass. "Multiple orgasms all night isn't a bad thing."

The glint in her eye sent a rush of desire straight to

his crotch. Did she have any idea how one look from her turned his body into a tuning fork? How the magical hum from one of her smiles made him perfectly in tune with everything about her? The pace of her breathing, the lift of her lips, the dilating of her eyes... She was his kryptonite.

He lifted his glass and clinked it against hers. "Then I'm happy to provide you with even more orgasms."

India licked her lips and sucked in a breath. He did mean that exactly how it sounded. He would love to see India's face flushed with pleasure. Pleasure he gave. She nodded and brought the glass to her lips. They downed their shots.

India slammed her empty glass on the table. "Okay... we need to lose now."

Travis chuckled and put down his own glass. "That's probably a good idea. I haven't had this many shots since—"

"That night in the tobacco field," India supplied.

The reminder made his dick swell. Travis shifted in his seat. India licked her full lips. She was fucking irresistible. The reflections of red, blue and yellow light from a rotating ball on the DJ's booth played across her smooth skin the way his lips yearned to. Slowly, across every inch of her.

"That was the last time," he answered. He ran his fingers over the back of her hand resting on the table. "You?"

Her sexy smile made him want to pull her into his lap. India flipped her hand over and trailed her fingertips across his palm. "I partied a little while on tour with the orchestra."

He felt her touch all the way to his toes. "Oh really?" He threaded his fingers with hers until their palms pressed together.

"Really." Her eyes were filled with mischief.

Maybe she'd had shots with another guy. Flirted and held hands with another guy. No matter how much the idea of another man touching her made him want to revert to prehistoric days and claim her as his woman, he didn't begrudge her previous dating history. Whoever had kissed or made love to her before didn't matter. He wanted to be the last man she kissed. The last man who made her body tremble with pleasure. No matter what the cost.

"Okay, folks, for the win," the DJ cut in. "The first minimum wage in the US was implemented in 1938 and was what amount per hour?"

India's eyes widened and her hand tightened on his. "I know this." She turned to the DJ and yelled, "Twenty-five cents!"

"Damn, table six, you're our winners!" the DJ announced.

Travis looked from India to the DJ and laughed. "I thought we were going to lose."

"Sorry, I knew the answer and couldn't help but yell it out. I just watched some documentary on labor reform in the US."

The waitress returned with another shot. "I think we should go," Travis said after their fifth orgasm.

India pushed away the latest empty shot glass and nodded. "I think that's a good idea."

He paid out their tab, which wasn't much since they'd won most of their drinks. The other patrons congratulated them on winning and a few even begged for them to stay for a few more rounds. He and India gave high fives and accepted their accolades, but they left.

Travis wasn't a heavy drinker, but he did enjoy the occasional highball or beer after a long day. Still, he felt the effects of five rounds of shots as they left the bar. India was steady on her feet, a testament to the "partying a little" in the orchestra, but her eyes had the bright, slightly glazed look of someone who was buzzed.

Outside he pulled her arm through his. The warm night air caressed their skin and he breathed in deep. "Where's your hotel?"

India frowned and rested her head against his shoulder. "I drove here." She sounded disappointed. "I'm not staying downtown. I wanted to be more toward the Biltmore Estate."

Travis shook his head. "No way I'm letting you drive back there tonight. Come to my room."

Her head popped up and she stared at him with wide eyes. Confusion, desire and hesitancy in their beautiful depths.

He shook his head. He wanted India, but he wanted to make sure she was safe more than anything. "I have a suite. You can take the bed. I'll sleep on the couch."

"I thought you were planning to finally make love to me." Her smile was teasing, but he noticed the relaxing of her shoulders.

Sex between them was a big step. A step he didn't want to blame later on the multiple orgasms they'd had in a bar. As good as her body felt resting against his, her curves warm and soft, her eyes bright with desire, and her mouth full and tempting, he did not want her to wake up the next morning with fuzzy memories of the first time they made love. Oh no. He wanted her to remember every single detail. Every stroke of his tongue, caress of his hand and thrust of his hips.

Travis pulled her fully into his arms. His hands rested on her hips and he eased her closer until the hard press of his dick was noticeable between them. "I want to make love to you. But not like this. I want to be one hundred percent sober when I finally get you in my bed."

"Why is that?"

"Because, India Robidoux, you are worth savoring and I plan to enjoy every inch of your body."

He was a man, not a saint, so he gave in a little and kissed her. She tasted like the smooth buttery flavor of the shots combined with the sweet feminine spice that was all India. Her arms wrapped around his neck. The softness of her breasts cushioned his chest. Travis gripped her hip with one hand, the other cupped her lush ass. His head spun, from the alcohol and the tumultuous emotions stirred by the kiss. Almost enough to make him say to hell with being a gentleman and take India back to his hotel where he could fuck her all night long.

He broke the kiss before he went with that thought. He was crazy about her. He needed to be sure she knew what they were doing. Needed to be sure in the morning she was still okay with going against everyone in her family for what they both wanted. The ramifications of what they were doing were serious. India brushed her lips over his neck and lightly bit him.

We could have sex tonight and talk tomorrow.

Travis wrapped an arm around India and pressed her head against his chest. "Do that again and I might lose the last bit of self-control I have."

India nodded and slid her arms around his waist. "I don't want to think about doing right."

"Neither do I."

They held each other for several long minutes. With every breath, her sweet perfume dug into him. Branding him as hers forever. Eventually he started walking. His arm around her shoulders, hers around his waist. Her body was nothing but warm curves and soft temptation next to him. Thoughts of ramifications began to dwindle away.

India's steps faltered. He steadied her, and she leaned heavily against him as they continued. When they made it to his hotel room, her eyes were droopy and her breathing heavy. He kissed her forehead and took her into the bedroom.

India sat on the edge of the bed. Travis lowered to his knees and pulled her shoes off. When he stood, she reached for his belt. "Stay," she said in a sexy, silky voice. She looked up at him with sleepy, desire-filled eyes.

He kissed her softly. "Tomorrow."

Slowly, he lowered her back onto the bed. India turned on her side, hugged the pillow and sighed. Her lashes fluttered closed and within seconds she was out. With one last longing look, he walked out and prepared for a long, cold, uncomfortable night on the couch.

THE SOUNDS OF running water and off-key singing woke India the next morning. Her eyes popped open. Muted sunlight through the drawn curtains in the hotel room cast everything in a golden glow. Not her hotel room. Which meant she was in someone else's hotel room. She'd come back to Travis's room.

A slow smile inched her lips up. She pressed her hand to her mouth to suppress the giddiness trying to turn her into a giggling grown woman. She shouldn't be giggling or feeling giddy. In the dim morning light, shouldn't she be overwhelmed with regret? Shouldn't she feel bad for spending the day with her sister's ex-husband? For holding his hand, sharing food and agreeing to find out what could be between them? Shouldn't she feel nervous because she was believing the promise in his eyes or terrible because she wasn't filled with guilt? This was wrong…wasn't it? But how could being with Travis be wrong when everything felt right?

Great, next thing you know you'll be singing Luther Ingram.

The water in the shower cut off. Along with Travis's singing. India jumped out of the bed. She examined herself in the mirror over the dresser and cringed. Her hair was a mess. Her face was lined on one side thanks to creases in the pillowcase. Her shirt and underwear were wrinkled. She vaguely remembered getting hot and kicking off her pants last night. Basically, she looked like a hot mess. This was not the way she'd pictured her first morning waking up with Travis.

Water in the bathroom sink turned on. She picked up the in-room phone, called the front desk and ordered an extra toothbrush and comb. Thank God for complimentary toiletries at hotels. She rushed to the closet and opened it. Spotting the bathrobe hanging there, she breathed a sigh of relief and quickly slipped the white terry cloth over her. Travis's overnight bag was open in the closet. She grabbed a T-shirt and a pair of clean boxers off the top. They would have to do while she washed out her underwear in the sink. Or maybe the hotel had laundry service.

Would she be here that long? Did she need clothes once he came out of the bathroom? Maybe the robe was all that would be required. No, she would need clothes if Travis had his own doubts about this. What if he didn't want her to stay long?

It's not like he hasn't changed his mind before.

The water in the bathroom stopped and the door opened before those thoughts could take root like a vine and wrap her mind in doubt. India clutched the robe's lapels and gaped.

Travis stood in the door wearing nothing but a pair of crisp white boxer briefs. Steam from the bathroom billowed out around him. He looked at the bed, then up at her. The corners of his lips tipped up slightly as if unsure if his smile should come out and play.

"You're up. Sorry, I wasn't trying to wake you."

India snapped her mouth closed and dragged her eyes off the damp skin of his chiseled chest. Though meeting his dark eyes across a bedroom didn't reduce her racing heart.

"You're fine. I don't usually sleep in anyway."

They stood staring for several moments. His eyes, intent and sexy, were locked with hers. Each passing second made breathing harder. A wild rush of excitement infused her bloodstream. The softness of the robe brushed her skin with every short breath she took, and she wished Travis's hands brushed her arms, legs and breasts instead.

"Did you need to get in here?" He pointed over his shoulder toward the bathroom.

Her brain cleared instantly. She looked not quite

hungover, but more I-drank-too-much-and-need-a-shower sloppy. India clutched the boxers and T-shirt in her hand and hurried across the room. "Yes, actually, I do."

Travis stepped to the side. Her shoulder brushed his chest as she rushed into the bathroom with her head tucked low. There was no chance in hell she would give him a close-up look of her unwashed, first-thing-in-the-morning face. His fingers brushed her hip through the thick layer of the robe. The robe might as well have burst into flames from the sparks ignited by his touch.

"You okay?"

"Yep, I'm good," she answered without looking up and rushed into the bathroom. She slammed the door quickly behind her, then leaned heavily against it. She was being a tad ridiculous, but she wasn't prepared. What happened next? Were they taking things slow, talking about their next steps, immediately jumping into bed together? Option three made her wet, and she shook her head. Talk first. Then worry about next steps.

She got in the shower and hoped the mundane routine would calm her. It didn't. The warm water on her skin was like a silky caress. Made her yearn for Travis's hands on her body. As her hands slid across her breasts, stomach and legs, desire grew and stretched inside her until she thought she'd explode. Another round of shouldn't-she-feel-bad-for-salivating-to-ride-Travis-like-a-cowboy-at-a-rodeo hit her as she shut off the water.

Travis knocked on the door after she turned off the shower. India wrapped the towel around her and cracked open the door. He held up the toothbrush and other items she'd called down for.

"Oh, thanks!" India held out her hand.

Travis didn't hand her the items. His gaze followed the drop of water trailing down her neck to the tops of her breasts. He swallowed hard. His eyes flared like a torch.

Sweet tingles spread from her breasts to the junction of her thighs. She tightened the muscles of her sex as that cowboy part of her that wanted to jump him whooped in anticipation.

India snatched the toothbrush out of his hand and stepped back. Travis blinked several times. She bit the corner of her lip to stop her grin. "I'll be out in a second."

He nodded as if only half hearing what she said. His eyes were once again following the path of another drop of water as it meandered down her chest.

India closed the door and quickly dried off. She brushed her teeth and put on the clean pair of boxers and T-shirt she'd taken from his suitcase. She focused on the talking points of what would happen next if they proceeded with this relationship. Anything to not focus on the look on his face that said he was just as ready to have her in his arms as she was.

What if he waited on the other side of the door? What if, when she finally came out, he pulled her into his embrace and kissed her before tossing her on the bed and giving her everything that last hot look promised and more?

She checked her reflection in the mirror one more time and ran her fingers through her hair until there was a messy order to the curling strands. Her heart hammered as she wrapped her hand around the bathroom doorknob. She swung open the door, but Travis wasn't waiting on the other side.

India sighed and closed her eyes. She was completely ridiculous. Of course, he wasn't pacing on the other side ready to pounce on her. They were adults. There was a lot to think through and discuss.

"Hey, India," Travis called from the other room in the suite. "I'm ordering breakfast. What do you want?"

Her anticipation dropped even more. So much for the fantasy of Travis being tight with anticipation after seeing her in only a towel. "Give me a second and I'll look at the menu," she said loudly, bending over to pick up her pants.

"What?" he called back.

She tried to slip one leg into the pants and hopped to the bedroom door. "I said, give—" Her words were cut short as she stumbled forward.

She reached for the doorframe to stop her fall. A strong hand gripped her waist. Her fall was broken by Travis's broad—still naked—chest. One hand slapped against the muscles of his torso, the other gripped the biceps of the arm that slipped around her waist, catching her.

"Sorry," she mumbled. Her cheeks burned with embarrassment.

The light in Travis's eyes turned her knees to putty. "I'm not." His voice was low and thick.

Travis captured her mouth in a searing kiss. India's body caught fire. The feelings storming her made her feel like they hadn't just kissed the day before. The press of his body and the taste of his lips were as hot and potent as she remembered. India's fingers snaked down his firm chest and abdomen. The muscles beneath her fingertips flexed and tensed with her touch. His fingers dug into her hair and he kissed her with an urgency that made her pulse pound.

The waistband of his shorts blocked her exploration. She hesitated a beat before slipping her hands past the barrier and wrapping her fingers around the hard length of his erection.

Travis gasped. His mouth broke apart from hers. Dark eyes burned into hers before he pulled her head back and placed hot kisses across her neck. His other hand engulfed her breast, kneading and squeezing until her nipples were hard, aching peaks.

He pulled back, jerked her hand from its greedy exploration of his thick length, and yanked the T-shirt up and off her body. When she reached for him, he shook his head. He took her hands in his and spread her arms until each hand was braced by the frame of the door. With a wicked smile on his face, he lowered to his knees and eased the boxers down her legs. Long fingers pressed against the insides of her thighs until she parted her legs.

Travis stood and watched her. Her body spread open for his review and approval. Her heart pounded an erratic beat. The scandalous look in his eye was kerosene on the flames rushing through her veins.

He ran his hands down her sides, then slowly back up until he cupped her breasts. Gently lifting them, Travis lowered his mouth and took one tight tip between his lips. India felt the pull all the way in her toes. Her chest arched forward, begging for more. He savored one plump mound before gliding his decadent lips across to the other.

Her body quivered and pulsed. Every time her hand

dropped to touch him, he slowly placed it back against the doorjamb.

"Let me savor you," he said in a low growl against her breast.

India moaned deep and loud. "Please do."

She heard the plea in her voice and didn't give a single fuck. She'd wanted Travis for too long. Dreamed of his hands, lips and body near hers like this. As much as she wanted him on top of her, inside of her, she also didn't want to rush. Savor was the perfect word, because she wanted to drown in the feelings he'd awakened.

Travis slowly lowered to his knees in front of her. Hot hands gripped her waist, the tips of his fingers digging into her skin as if she were a lifeline. Boldly, she tilted her hips forward. Through slitted lids, she watched to see his reaction to her decadent request.

His mouth lifted in a sexy smile that would make fallen angels beg for more. He leaned forward. India sucked in a breath. Her mouth fell open and the tip of her tongue touched the corner of her mouth. Travis kissed her inner thigh. She groaned and shuddered.

"Don't play with me," she said in a breathless voice.

His answering chuckle told her he planned to play with her even more. He kissed her thighs. His hand ran up and down her legs, squeezing her thighs, tickling the back of her knees and rising up to squeeze her ass. Trembles racked her body. She was so wet and swollen, she would be embarrassed if she didn't want to kill him for teasing her like this. She was about to grab the back of his head and show him exactly where she wanted him when he finally slid a long finger between her wet folds and pulled it back with a drawn-out, firm stroke.

Her knees nearly buckled. She gripped the door just to keep from falling over.

"Now you're ready," he murmured. Using this thumb and forefinger, he spread her open, exposing her swollen clit before his perfect lips closed over her in the sexiest of kisses.

India's hand fell and cupped the back of his head. Travis pushed one finger deep into her while his lips and tongue made her his. The deep, pleasurable moans he made as he took her to the edges of the universe were nearly as loud as hers. He didn't seem to notice her nails digging into the back of his head. And when her leg lifted to give him a better angle, he took it and placed it over his shoulder.

The orgasm tore through her like buckshot through wet paper, ripping her inside and out. She was falling, but Travis was up and caught her. As her body trembled and aftershocks racked her from head to toe, he carried her to the bed and laid her there. Travis got a condom out of his bag, and quickly covered himself before joining her on the bed. When his mouth covered hers, she wrapped her arms around his body and pulled him closer. His knee slipped between her legs, and India opened them wide to let him settle heavily between them. His hips shifted back, then forward and he filled her.

"Travis..." His name was a prayer on her lips.

His hand gripped her hip. "India...damn baby... I can't..."

Her nails dug into his firm butt. Urging him to keep moving. If he stopped, she'd kill him. He didn't stop. He branded her with hard, deep strokes. His forehead rested against hers. His eyes barely open, but wide enough for her to see the claim in them. The vow that this wasn't the end. The fierce promise to take her to these heights again and again.

India's heart squeezed, and love flooded her system. Tomorrow didn't matter. This was right. The feelings between them weren't wrong and now that she was here, she couldn't imagine trying to go back.

His mouth claimed hers in a hard, demanding kiss. Then his body tensed, and he jerked as a climax took over. Her body squeezed around him and then she crashed over the edge again. She rode the wave, savored the moment and let everything wash away except for her and Travis in this one perfect moment.

CHAPTER EIGHTEEN

"I NEED TO understand why you married Elaina."

The cocoon of contentment Travis had surrounded himself in since making love to India that morning split wide open with those eight words. He shifted next to India on the blanket they'd laid out in one of the relatively secluded areas off the Deer Park Trail on the Biltmore Estate. After the best morning of his life, they'd decided to tour the famous estate once home to the Vanderbilts and explore the grounds. Everything had been perfect, but he'd known this was coming. Not only was the conversation as overdue as milk four weeks past expiration, but she deserved to hear the truth.

India pulled away from where she'd leaned on his arm. She looked at him with a direct stare. Was she bracing herself for bad news?

"The real reason," she said her voice firm. "After the night we shared. That night was so much more than just us drinking and kissing. I thought you felt something. Before we move forward, I need to know why you went through with marrying her."

Travis searched for the words. The confession he'd wanted to give for years. How many times had he imagined calling her and telling her what happened? Felt the urge to explain he hadn't casually tossed her aside as if she were a used piece of dental floss? Now all the reasons felt inadequate. He never should have left her.

"I thought I had no other choice."

Her brows drew together. "So it's true. My dad forced you?"

"Not entirely."

She raised a brow. "What does that mean?"

He thought back to that time and the choice he'd believed was the honorable one to make. "I don't know how he found out, but Grant knew what happened the night of your birthday. He confronted me about it. Accused me of taking advantage of you when I was still… involved with your sister."

Grant's words were cruder than what Travis told India. He'd called Travis a dog who was unfit for either of his daughters. Charged Travis with not only treating his daughters like whores he could use at his whim but thinking Grant's mentorship would protect him.

"He knows what happened?" India's eyes widened. She pressed both hands over her face. "I mean… I suspected but I didn't know for sure." She dragged her hands down her face.

"Sorry to be the one to confirm this for you."

"Did he say you had to marry Elaina because you and she were…" She rolled her hand in a *you know* movement.

He shook his head. "No. That wasn't the reason. Elaina found out she was pregnant. She told me a few days after your birthday."

India gasped and her back straightened. "She was pregnant?"

Travis nodded slowly. He'd assumed she'd known this already, but from the surprise on her face, he guessed

Grant meant what he said about keeping the pregnancy hush-hush. He wasn't surprised Elaina hadn't told India. She wasn't one to confide in others.

"My dad made it sound like it happened after you got married."

His mind went back to that time in his life. "When he found out about the baby, he said if I didn't do the right thing, I'd ruin Elaina's reputation. When he said I'd ruin her...he said it as if I were some type of disease. I'd never felt like trailer trash until that day."

India placed a hand on his knee and squeezed. "You are not trash."

Her touch washed away the leftover bitterness of that day. Bitterness that never quite went away. Despite all Grant had done for him, Travis could never forget his mentor's harsh words. He'd deserved them for kissing India so soon after he and Elaina stopped fooling around, but being called a dog was hard to forget.

Again he wondered if Grant had ever cared about him. He may have insisted Travis marry Elaina, but that didn't mean he'd done so because he wanted Travis in the family. Before his uncle's confession, Travis would have believed Grant wasn't happy about the circumstances, but he'd been okay having Travis as a son-in-law. Now he feared he'd just been a huge kink in Grant's feud with his family.

"I know I'm not trash," he said. "I knew even as he tore into my ass, but I still felt dirty. Disrespectful. I'd never thought of fooling around with one of Grant's daughters, but when Elaina showed interest, I didn't think long-term. She was so far out of my league and so much like your dad and not at all approachable. Hormones took over. I didn't think it would last as long or become anything serious."

"Neither did she," India said.

"How do you know?"

"I overheard her talking to one of her friends. She bragged about sleeping with you. I think she slept with you to make our dad angry. It's why I didn't feel guilty about kissing you after I overheard her say she was moving on to better things."

Travis studied his hands. He'd known what they had wasn't going to last forever, but India's words hit an insecurity he'd tried to hide. "I think we both knew our time was coming to an end."

"You seemed upset the day she said she was through with you."

"Mostly because I found out she was seeing someone else."

India frowned. "Was the baby…?"

He shook his head. "She wasn't sleeping with the other guy. She liked him and had something with him that she didn't have with me, but I trust her. She wouldn't have lied about that. The baby was mine. We were just having fun for a while. The pregnancy surprised both of us."

Whenever he and Elaina had hooked up, there had never been promises of tomorrow or whispers of love, but they'd agreed to not sleep around. When she wanted him, she summoned him. When she didn't want to be bothered with him, she didn't hide that either. He enjoyed the no-strings setup and never considered the consequences.

"I'm sorry about the baby," she said quietly.

His throat tightened. The pain of what had happened

searing him. "I didn't realize how much I wanted a kid until then. Elaina… She was so angry, but I could see she was hurt, too. She asked me if I wanted out afterward. I couldn't leave her alone. Not when she was hurting like that."

They were quiet for several seconds. India staring off at the trees in the distance. He processed the words spoken. Maybe he should have told her the truth years ago, but it wouldn't have changed much. He still would have been tied to Elaina. Grant still would have insisted on a marriage. Things happened that didn't always make sense. He couldn't get lost in what could have been. Instead, he would focus on today. What could happen with India now.

"Was it the same with me?" India glanced at him from beneath lowered lashes. She pulled the corner of her lip between her teeth. "Was I the unattainable daughter of your mentor who hit on you one day?"

The uncertainty in her voice scared him. He took her hand in his and squeezed her hand. "What happened with you was even more unexpected. We were friends. You were the person in the family I could chill and be myself with."

Her shoulders straightened. She tried to pull away. "You didn't see me as a potential lover?"

He didn't let go of her hand. He had to make her understand what he felt for her was different. "I noticed you, but you are the baby girl. That night when we almost had sex, I was just as caught off guard by how quickly what was supposed to be a simple kiss turned into something a lot more. Feelings I never faced before were suddenly slapping me in the face. I panicked and sent you away because I didn't know what else to do."

It would be more accurate to say he'd felt as if his life had been thrown into a dryer and sent him tumbling in circles. India had always been cool. She was just the friend he was trying to keep from going out and getting drunk with a bunch of assholes. That night, his urge to protect her and be the one she celebrated her birthday with suddenly flipped into a toss-up of desire and caring he'd never experienced in his young life.

"But you didn't tell me anything. You kissed me that night and promised me you weren't playing games and then you proposed to my sister." The hurt in her voice was like a razor blade to his heart. "You could have told me. I may not have liked it, but I would have understood. Why didn't you tell me?"

A ball of guilt weighed heavily in his midsection. "Grant insisted we keep the pregnancy quiet. When he asked if I really cared about Elaina or if I was going to keep treating her like a piece of ass, I couldn't bring myself to say I didn't want to marry her. Not when she was carrying my child. Nor could I bring myself to tell him how I felt about you, when I still hadn't processed what had happened between us that night. He said if I didn't do right by Elaina, then all of his plans to help pay for law school and continue to mentor me would go away. I promised him I'd do right by her. When he asked if that meant I planned to marry her, I said yes. I was just a scared young man and I wanted to do right by our baby."

Travis remembered the sense of loss that had nearly choked him. As soon as the words had come out, he'd known he would always be under Grant's thumb. "I don't think he believed me. Then he said he'd hate for the police to reopen the case of the break-ins around town that had happened a few years before. Break-ins your dad knew I was a part of because he'd covered for me."

He met India's wide angry eyes. "I asked Elaina to marry me the same day. She said no. Then two weeks later, she came back and agreed. To this day, I don't know why she changed her mind, and I haven't asked."

Elaina hadn't wanted to marry him any more than he'd wanted to marry her. She hadn't slept with that other guy, but Travis believed she'd cared deeply for him. Deeply enough to fight the idea of marrying someone she didn't love. For her to say yes meant Grant had found one of her hidden weaknesses and forced her to agree.

India eased her hand from his. He didn't hold on. She opened the picnic basket they'd brought and pulled out a bottle of wine. She poured more wine into the red plastic cup she'd used earlier and took a long swallow. "Someone should have told me."

"Pretending that night never happened and that I didn't have feelings for you seemed easier than telling you that night was a mistake. By the time I thought I should say something, things had gone too far. The engagement was announced. People were congratulating us and throwing parties. Reviving what we'd uncovered that night felt messy and disrespectful."

She stared into the cup. "What's different about this time? Why isn't now messy and disrespectful?"

"I can't guarantee others won't see it that way, but what I do know is I've spent the years since that night thinking about you. Wondering what would have happened if I hadn't been afraid to go against your father. If I had done what my instincts told me to do." He placed a finger under her chin and lifted her face until her eyes met his. There was sadness in them and his chest tightened as if a giant squeezed his heart. He never wanted to hurt her. Would never walk away from her again.

"India, being with you doesn't feel messy or disrespectful, it feels right. It feels as if I've been on vacation all my life and I'm finally coming home. I'm finally with the woman I'm supposed to be with."

"Elaina won't see it like that. My dad won't see it that way. They're going to hate us."

"Then let them. Why do you think I left Robidoux Tobacco? I needed the split. I needed to create my own life outside of the shadow of your father. He has no say in this. Unless you've changed your mind."

He held his breath, knowing he never wanted to let her go, but accepting that he couldn't force her into anything she didn't want.

"No." She brushed her fingertips across his lips to stop him from interrupting. "But I don't think we should say anything just yet. There's Byron's campaign, and this would cause a scandal."

"I don't care about scandal." They'd waited long enough already.

"I wouldn't either, but Byron does care about his campaign. He's gone so far as to agree to marry someone he doesn't love," she said bitterly. "I won't cost him any votes with this."

"I don't want to sneak around and hide for the next few months." November was too long to even think about keeping this secret.

She took his face in her hands. "At least through the primaries. It'll give us time to gauge how everyone will accept things. We can break it to the family after Byron gets through that and then go from there. Please."

The arguments against her decision burned his throat. He was tired of lies. He wanted to be selfish. To say to hell with her family and stop hiding their feelings. But loyalty to Byron and the thought of dumping this on Elaina all of a sudden kept him silent. They would need the right time to talk to Elaina that was less likely to result in a multiple homicide. They'd wait and control the fallout. Afterward, they could come up with a way to tell everyone.

He nodded and kissed India. "Fine, but only until the primaries. I'll talk to Byron first, then we'll talk to the family."

CHAPTER NINETEEN

BYRON CALLED RIGHT after Travis got home on Sunday.

"Are you back? I need to talk to you." Byron sounded nervous and stressed.

Travis immediately went on guard. He hadn't hidden his trip to Asheville. He also hadn't asked India whom she'd told where she was going, but he doubted she would have kept her whereabouts from her family. Had Byron put two and two together and come up with questions about him and India?

"What's up?"

"I just need to run something by you. It shouldn't take long. I'll be there in a few minutes."

Travis agreed and hung up. He paced his living room as he waited for Byron to show up. He didn't like the idea of keeping his relationship with India a secret. The only way to move forward was to be honest with everyone involved. Revealing their involvement would make tsunami-size waves with her family, but that didn't mean they'd drown in the aftermath.

His doorbell rang thirty minutes after Byron's call. Travis let out a heavy breath and prepared to pretend he hadn't spent the weekend in bed with his best friend's younger sister. The idea made his neck stiff. Byron was his boy; he shouldn't have to lie about this.

He opened the door. Byron looked just as tense as

he'd sounded on the phone. Lines bracketed his mouth and creased his forehead from the tight scowl on his face. The top button of his shirt was unbuttoned, his tie loose and slightly askew.

"What do you have to drink?" Byron said, coming in and walking straight toward the back of the house.

"Damn, Byron, that bad?" Travis followed his friend.

Byron went into Travis's living area and zeroed in on the bar in the corner. He pulled down a bottle of Crown Royal and twisted off the top. Travis raised a brow. Byron hated Crown Royal. He preferred a more expensive whiskey. He filled one of the shot glasses Travis kept on a small shelf next to the bar and downed the drink.

"The campaign," Byron said in an exhausted voice.

Relief eased the tension in Travis's neck and shoulders. He followed Byron to the bar. "What happened?"

"We're good in the polls. Things were going great. Then we get word the other side has some dirt on me."

Travis frowned and leaned against the bar. Dirt? On Byron? Couldn't be that bad. Byron loved the ladies, but his bachelor lifestyle was tame compared to most men considered playboys.

"What kind of dirt?"

Byron ran a hand over his razor sharp fade. "That's the thing. I don't know."

"Okay, then why are you worrying? I mean, you shouldn't be this upset about possible dirt unless there is something really bad out there." He raised a brow and his tone so that the sentence came out more question than statement. He knew almost everything about Byron, but everyone had secrets.

Byron poured another drink and avoided eye contact.

Travis straightened and watched his friend closely. "Is there something really bad out there?"

"What?" Byron looked up from the dark liquid in his shot glass. He shook his head. "No. Nothing bad. Yeah, there are some things I wish I hadn't done."

"We've all done stupid stuff when we were younger. Unless you've got a murder to hide or you're some kind of psycho, then you shouldn't have to worry."

Byron scowled. "God no! Nothing like that." He sipped the shot. "It's just… I tried to protect someone. To do so I had to lie."

Travis didn't know this story. "What are you talking about? You never told me anything like this."

Byron ran his hand over his head again, then pinched the bridge of his nose. When he dropped his hand, frustration filled his face. "It wasn't my secret to tell. It still isn't, and I'd rather keep it that way. But if the other side knows—"

"Byron, what did you do?"

Byron shook his head. He capped the bottle of Crown Royal and shrugged. "You know what, I'm probably overreacting. There are always rumors of something starting. I'm not even going to stress."

"Obviously you are stressing. Look, if there's something going on, you can tell me. We'll think this through and figure out what to do."

"Nah, it's nothing. I'm just jittery with everything. The wedding on top of a campaign. I'm jumping at shadows."

He gave Travis the perfect candidate smile that typically won people over. Except the smile didn't reach his eyes. Travis didn't buy his jumping-at-shadows excuse at all.

"Why don't you tell me who you're protecting?"

"Telling you or anyone means there's a chance it can get out. Then I've betrayed the trust of someone who doesn't deserve that. I agreed to keep this secret, so that's what I'm doing."

"Do you really think you can run a campaign for Senate and not have this situation with whomever you're protecting come up?"

"There's no way it'll come up. Four people know, and that's four too many. Three of us will never tell. The fourth isn't in a position for anyone to listen."

Byron's voice was sure, overly confident. He sounded like Grant, which made Travis nervous. "You come over here obviously upset and instead of talking to me you're just going to pretend as if nothing is wrong? You aren't going to trust me?"

"I trust you, Travis. I trust you more than anyone else, but not with this. I shouldn't have even said anything. I'm just overthinking. Today it hit me that I'm really getting married." He tugged on his already loose tie. "Brought up all types of old regrets and shit."

Looking down the road to years, decades in a loveless marriage would do that to a person. "You don't have to marry her."

For a second, he thought Byron would agree. Then Byron's shoulders straightened, and he looked at Travis with grim determination. "Yes, I do. I want to win. I'm doing everything I need to do so that I can win. I can't let down the people relying on me because I've got jitters. I'll do whatever it takes to show people I'm ready for this job."

"But showing the voters and being happy don't have to contradict each other."

"It's too late. The engagement is announced. The date is set. We've got an interview on *Good Morning America* in two weeks." He counted off all the reasons on his hands. "I can't call off the wedding now even if by some crazy reason I wanted to."

"It sounds like you're thinking of a lot of crazy reasons."

Byron waved away Travis's reply. "I'm thinking of fairy tales. You remember Zoe Hammond?"

Travis was thrown by the change in conversation. "Yeah, she was a friend of yours in college. You liked her, right?"

"I was crazy about her. She wouldn't give me a chance. She was in love with that asshole who used to…" Byron clenched his jaw. His hand tightened on the shot glass in his hand.

The memory came back. "He used to hit her sometimes." Anger crept into Travis's voice. He'd never met Zoe. Byron only talked about his homegirl whenever he came home from college. He'd been so furious that she went back to her boyfriend. Travis shared Byron's fury. There was never an excuse to beat a woman.

"Yeah. I poured my heart out to her one night. Told her I loved her. I'd do anything to keep her safe. I would have, too. I would have given up everything to show her what she was worth." He let out a low, bitter laugh. "She turned me down. Broke my heart. Right then and there, I knew I couldn't do that shit again."

The lingering pain in Byron's voice was unmistakable. Travis had felt pain when Grant told him he wasn't good enough for India. He'd felt pain and loss when he'd realized marrying Elaina meant the end of what had barely started between him and India. He'd cared about India, but everything had been so new he hadn't realized his feelings for her were a precursor to love. He'd at least been spared having the woman he loved toss his emotions back in his face.

He understood his friend's hurt, but that didn't mean he had to punish himself. Marriage without the hope of love was punishment.

"Byron, that was years ago. She was young and didn't know any better. You can't let what happened with Zoe push you into marrying someone you don't care about."

Byron tapped the counter, his eyes bright with purpose. "But that's the thing. I do care about Yolanda. Do I love her like I loved Zoe? No. That doesn't mean I don't love her enough to want to build something with her. I know you all think I'm being ruthless in my decision, but I'm being smart. I want a woman who wants me and supports me. We may not have the romantic love people cry about in movies, but we've got something. You have to understand that. You can't tell me you would turn away if you found a woman who was really there for you."

He couldn't, but that didn't mean he believed Byron's choice was the right one. *Caring* about his fiancée wasn't the same as being in love with someone. Travis didn't know much about love. He hadn't loved Elaina when he'd asked her to marry him. He'd tried to love her, and after what they'd gone through in their short marriage, he did still care. He wouldn't have hidden his dating life for so long after their divorce if he didn't care.

But what he felt for India was unlike anything he'd felt before. His feelings for her had grown over the years until he'd felt like he'd witnessed heaven this past weekend in her arms. That had to be love, or what would be love once they were finally able to be together.

The urge to tell Byron about his own revelations was strong. He and Byron had no secrets between them. Or at least, he'd thought that. But they both had secrets. He'd never told Byron about the pressure Grant had put on him and Elaina to get married. Byron was protecting someone Travis knew nothing about.

India was right. They didn't need to let anyone know just yet. Byron had enough on his plate today. They'd wait a few weeks.

He reached over and gripped Byron's shoulder. "If you don't want to share your secret right now, fine. But know that I'm your boy and I've got your back."

This time Byron's smile met his eyes. "I appreciate that, man."

"And, if you're sure about this engagement to Yolanda, then I'll support you."

Byron's shoulders relaxed under Travis's hand. "Will you be my best man?" He held out a hand for Travis to shake.

Byron had to make his own mistakes. He'd be there for his friend if he needed him, but he sure as hell hoped everything worked out. He shook his best friend's hand. "I'd be honored."

CHAPTER TWENTY

THE FRONT DOOR slammed so hard the house vibrated. The hard knock of heels in the marble entryway followed immediately after. India stopped her descent from the family room. Elaina flew by the bottom of the stairs toward the back of the house in a whirl of colors. A string of murmured angry words India couldn't make out trailed in her wake.

"What the hell is that about?" India mumbled.

She hurried down the stairs and followed Elaina's determined strides to the kitchen. Her sister was already at the wine fridge. She jerked open the door and pulled out a cold bottle. "I'm going to kill him!"

"Who are you going to kill?" India asked.

Elaina whirled to face her. She held the neck of the bottle in her fist and raised it as if she were ready to butt India in the head with the flat bottom. "Don't sneak up on me!" She relaxed and lowered the bottle.

"You would have heard me if you weren't stomping and cursing through the house," India replied.

Elaina glared. She snatched open a drawer next to the fridge, dug around and pulled out a corkscrew. "I don't stomp," she said haughtily before stabbing the cork with the screw and twisting it roughly.

India barely suppressed a chuckle. "Fine, we'll call what you were doing heavy walking."

"Are you on your way out?" Elaina looked pointedly at the purse on India's shoulder. "If that's the case, please go on about your business." She popped out the cork and poured wine into her glass.

India had been on her way to the art museum to talk about the guest performance with the chamber orchestra. She'd avoided Elaina in the two days since she'd gotten back from Asheville. She hadn't known if she would be able to look her sister in the face and not say anything about what happened between her and Travis. Except for a few calls, they hadn't been able to spend much time together. He couldn't visit her at home and she wasn't about to risk being seen at his place. She had no idea how they were going to keep things going without getting caught.

"I've got enough time to check on you," India said. She crossed the room and laid her purse on the granite countertop. "What's going on? Who do you want to kill?" A thought made her stomach churn. "Is it Travis?"

Elaina's hand paused on the way to her mouth with a full-to-the-brim wineglass. "Travis? God no, this has nothing to do with him. Though, I wish it did. I could at least get what I wanted most of the time out of him."

India wasn't sure if she should be relieved or concerned by that statement. She hid her confusion by sliding onto one of the barstools at the countertop. "Okay, then who?"

"Alex. Alex Tyson," Elaina said the name with a sneer.

India raised a brow and shrugged. "Who?"

Elaina scoffed and looked at India as if she'd admitted to not knowing who was president. "He's the new head of Research and Development at Robidoux

Tobacco, the bane of my existence and the world's biggest asshole."

India leaned back in her chair. "Okay…" She drew out the word. "We don't like Alex."

"We don't." Elaina scowled and took another sip of her wine. She gripped the corkscrew, cork still attached, in her other hand. She looked as if she were imagining poking Alex in an eye with the sharp end.

India reached over and took the corkscrew out of her sister's hand. "Why exactly do we not like Alex? Other than him being the bane of your existence and world's biggest asshole."

Elaina rarely got worked up by people in the office. For this guy to have her stomping…walking hard… through the house and gripping a corkscrew like a weapon, he must have gotten under her skin like a splinter.

"I can't get anything done out of that department since he's taken over. He doesn't respond to my emails or requests for meetings. When we do meet, he looks at me as if I have a…a kindergarten education instead of an MBA." She sniffed and lifted her chin. "As if having a doctorate in chemical engineering somehow makes him superior to me."

"A doctorate in chemical engineering. That's impressive."

Elaina's eyes shot poisoned daggers at India. "So is an MBA." She ground the words out through clenched teeth. The exasperation in Elaina's voice made India wonder if her sister had said as much to the man under fire.

India held up her hands in a conciliatory gesture. "I know. Believe me. You are way smarter."

"Don't patronize me, India. It's not cute." But the irritation melted from her voice and her shoulders relaxed as she took a long sip of her drink.

One well-placed compliment always did the trick with Elaina. Her sister was smart, tenacious and shrewd, but she wasn't vain. Though most people thought she was. India saw that Elaina wanted approval, acceptance, which was why she didn't mind throwing out compliments to remind her sister of her abilities.

"Tell me what happened," India said. "You haven't said why you're so upset today."

"Because he completely overrode me," Elaina said as if no one had ever not complied with her wishes. Come to think of it, few people had. "I issued a directive to his department and later discovered he told his team to ignore me. When I confronted him on it, he admitted telling them to ignore me."

India's eyes widened. She didn't know Alex Tyson, but he had balls of steel or a death wish to go against her sister. "What did you do?"

"I fired him," she said with a snap of her fingers. "Immediately."

"Are you sure that was right? I mean, can't he file a complaint?"

"I fired him for insubordination." She lifted her glass and took another sip.

"And I rehired him because you were wrong." Grant's voice came from the door.

Elaina slammed her wineglass on the counter with such force India was surprised the glass didn't shatter. "You. What?"

Grant strolled into the kitchen not looking the least bit affected by the hellfire in Elaina's eyes. "I rehired him. He was right, Elaina. You gave Research and Development that order because you were being petty. Not because the work needed to be done."

"People can't ignore directives I send out," Elaina fired back.

"I hire smart people so I can be confident in their decisions. We're fighting on all ends to keep this company on top, not micromanage our employees. The sales of cigarettes have gone down, and unless we look into expanding the market on cigars and other tobacco uses, we'll be left behind. You worry about making sure the books are good and production is high. Let Alex and the other managers figure out how to keep our product out there."

"I'm going to be the CEO of this company one day," Elaina said. "He along with everyone else has to understand that."

Grant pointed one long, accusing finger in her direction. "You have to understand being CEO doesn't make you a dictator."

Elaina scoffed. "That's hilarious coming from you. The man who lives by ultimatums and manipulation to get what he wants from everyone."

"What I've done has nothing to do with what we're talking about now," Grant continued. "Work things out with Alex or else I'll look for someone else to take over when I retire in a few years."

India jumped off the stool and stared at her dad. He may be right that Elaina needed to back off her subordinates, but to threaten to take the company from her? That was ridiculous. "You can't be serious. Elaina deserves the company."

Everyone in the family knew that. Elaina was the

one who'd worked next to Dad in the office and in the fields. She knew Robidoux Tobacco inside and out. She could recite the company mission and vision statement in her sleep.

"No one deserves anything," Grant said with a shake of his head. "I've given you kids everything I could, and I'll admit sometimes I was harsh in my decisions. But you've always *earned* everything I gave you. If I didn't think you deserved it, then you wouldn't have gotten anything. This isn't any different. Alex is the best engineer out there. I had to do a lot of work to get him at Robidoux Tobacco and you're not going to run him off just because he won't bow at your feet the way every other manager does when you give them the evil eye."

"I'll never forgive you if you take the CEO position from me." Elaina's voice shook with emotion. Her face remained ever cool, calm and poised, but the tremor of fear and hurt was unmistakable.

Grant shook his head as if Elaina's rarely shown distress were nothing more than an expected tantrum. "I'd rather you hate me than ruin our company."

Elaina picked up the wineglass and tossed it across the room. The glass shattered, spraying wine everywhere. The sharp scent of the spilled liquid filled the room.

India jumped at the uncharacteristic show of emotion. Not just emotion. Rage covered Elaina's face. Rage and pain. Their dad didn't flinch. India held her breath. Too shocked to know how to respond.

Grant pointed to the mess Elaina had made. "Clean that shit up."

Elaina grabbed the bottle of wine. She stalked around the counter toward the door. When she got to their father, she stopped and glared at him. "I'm sorry, I have to go read up on being a good supervisor. Find someone else to clean up the wine." Her voice was syrupy sweet and laced with bitterness. Without another word, she went to the door.

"Elaina, wait," India called.

Elaina waved a hand over her shoulder. "Not now, India. Not now." She didn't look back as she walked out. Eventually the echoes of her defeated footsteps disappeared.

India spun to her father. "Daddy, why would you say that to her? Why would you threaten to take the company from her?"

"Because your sister has problems she needs to work out." He looked at the broken glass and spilled wine. The anger and unflinching determination he'd shown Elaina faded away. Weariness she'd never seen on her father replaced the other emotions. "If she doesn't realize that... Well she won't be any good as the head of Robidoux Tobacco. She's interfering in areas she doesn't belong. This fight with Alex only proves it."

Elaina was a workaholic and she had difficulty showing emotions, but that didn't mean she had problems. The smell of spilled wine filled the room. India stared at the mess. Unease pouring into her system the same way the wine had poured down the wall.

"Is he really disrespecting her at work? That could be the real problem." Not anything else.

"He's not letting her run him over. Nothing he's done so far has been disrespectful. Your sister is trying to force his hand. Her stubbornness will cost the company, and she's only being stubborn because Alex won't kiss her ass the way the rest of the directors do." He sighed and shook his head. "Enough about Elaina. She'll pout in her room and be fine tomorrow. How are you? I haven't seen you since you got back. Did you have a good weekend?"

India chewed the corner of her lip. He didn't sound as if he were prying. If he'd known she'd spent the weekend with Travis, as unexpected as the weekend had been, she was sure he would say something. If he'd stepped in before and pushed Travis into marrying Elaina, then there was no way he wouldn't try to interfere now.

She smiled and tried not to sound as if she were hiding something. "I did. You?"

The tension around her dad's eyes and mouth disappeared. "Spent some time with Patricia." His voice warmed when he said Patricia's name.

India sucked in a breath. Irritation scratched her like a cheap, unwashed sweater. "You know what. Never mind."

"Is that how it's going to be? You're going to ignore it when I bring her up? You can't do that when I marry her."

"Let's not talk about your marriage." She stalked to the door.

"How about we talk about you going to Asheville the same weekend as Travis."

India's heart jumped in her throat. Shit! She felt like an idiot for thinking he hadn't put two and two together, but she'd prepared for her father bringing this up. She raised a brow and tried to look moderately curious. "Travis was in Asheville?"

Grant crossed his arms and called her a liar with his eyes. "Are you telling me you didn't see him?"

She slid her sweaty palms into the pocket of her pants. "Why would I see him? I toured Biltmore and used the weekend to get away from the drama in this house. What was he doing there?" Her voice didn't give away her deception.

Grant's eyes narrowed before he huffed and shook his head. "You know what. Never mind." He used the I-don't-want-to-hear-this tone she'd used on him at the mention of Patricia. "Were you going out tonight?"

"Yes." She looked at the mess on the floor. "I can clean that up before I go." Her dad didn't like giving the staff any additional reasons to gossip about the family.

Grant waved her away. "No. Go on out. I made this mess," he sighed heavily. "I'll clean it up."

He turned away and pulled several paper towels off the roll. India didn't ask what he meant. Elaina had thrown the glass of wine, but Grant's actions had pushed her to it. Actions that may have started long before he'd rehired a headstrong employee.

THE HOUSE WAS quiet when India returned later that evening. The meeting with the art museum had gone better than expected. India was excited about the guest performance. The other members playing chamber music at the museum were fun and interesting. The cellist, Penelope Gumbee, had been very friendly and invited India to meet up for coffee the next day. She had musical connections in town again and that was great.

She'd gotten the invitation for first-round auditions for the LA Philharmonic today. The anticipation of being a part of a large symphony again was still there, but the idea of moving across country wasn't as tempting as it had been when she'd first come home.

She should be eager to get out of town. Her dad was marrying the woman he'd betrayed their mom with. Her brother was marrying someone he didn't love as a political stunt. Her relationship with Travis was going to create a missile explosion in her family. All reasons to be excited about moving. But all the problems with her family didn't stop her from loving them. She'd missed them when she traveled, and the comfort of being home—despite the hang-ups—was still there. She'd missed being on the estate. Missed hanging out with Ashiya. Even missed her sister's prickly form of affection.

But if you stay and tell her about Travis, she'll hate you.

That was it. The real reason she had to leave. Staying meant hurting her sister. Elaina was strong, but there were cracks in her armor. The scene earlier had proved that. India couldn't be the reason her sister finally shattered.

Then there was Travis. How could she be sure he was really ready for the potential fallout? He'd succumbed to her dad's pressures before and followed his advice. Grant would definitely advise against any relationship between them. Travis was older and had branched away from the family, but that didn't mean he no longer sought her father's approval.

At the top of the stairs, the sound of male laughter in the family room stopped her. She recognized both laughs. Byron and Travis. Her heart did a triplet rhythm against her ribs. Her path changed, and she went to the family room instead of her room.

Byron and Travis sat in the leather recliners. They were both dressed as if they'd left the office and hadn't changed. Wrinkled dress shirts, ties tossed on the floor, and slacks. Papers were strewn across the coffee table along with large Byron for Senate coffee mugs and a few dirty plates.

"What are you two doing?" she asked.

Travis sat up straight. His dark gaze snapped to her, the smile on his face softening along with the look in his eyes. She returned his smile. The pull to cross the room, wrap her arms around his neck and kiss him tugged her like an invisible rope. She forced her gaze to Byron before she went against her own plan to keep their relationship a secret.

Byron waved her over. "We had a meeting with Dad and Roy about the campaign. I dragged Travis over because he needed a break from trial preparations."

India focused on Travis again. "How are things coming with that?"

Tension crept back into his features, the stress of his job immediately apparent in the tightening of his lips and shoulders. "They're coming. I don't see how any outcome is going to be good."

"Why?"

Byron answered, "Family drama. He wins, and his family won't be happy."

Winning would put further pressure on his strained family relationship. Travis acted like the rift with his family wasn't that big of a deal, but India knew how much their lack of support bothered him. He wanted their acceptance, and everything he did seemed to only tear them further apart.

"Are you okay?" she asked Travis.

He nodded and shrugged, but the effort looked stiff.

"I'll be fine. It's no big deal. My main goal is to represent my client."

Byron sighed and ran a hand over his legs. "Before we go back down the road of what could go wrong, how about we call it a night?" He checked his watch and stood. "I've got a long day ahead of me tomorrow and I still need to do a few things."

Travis stood, stretched his arms backward, and rolled his head in a circle like he was working out the kinks. "I'm cool with that. I'll help you straighten up before I go."

Byron looked around at the mess and rubbed the back of his head. "I appreciate that. Sandra might make me pick my own switch and wear my tail out if I leave too much of a mess," he said with a chuckle.

India grunted. "Doubtful. Sandra likes to pretend you're some type of prince."

Byron winked and picked up the mugs. "Which is why I've got to stay on her good side."

"Well, I'm going to get ready for bed," she said. She hesitated and bit her lip. Her gaze darted to Travis.

Travis had looked up quickly when she mentioned going to bed. Longing flared in his eyes so deep it made her bones ache. India's body caught fire. Raw, aching hunger pulsed deep within her.

Byron leaned in and gave her a quick hug and peck on the cheek. Breaking the spell. "Good night, sis."

India blinked and hugged him back. "Night."

Byron went back to stacking up the dirty dishes. Her eyes locked with Travis's.

"Good night, India."

Did he mean to sound so sexy when he said that? His voice was a deep rumble that sent waves through her body. She bit the corner of her lip, then lifted her hand for a brief wave.

"Good night," she said softly.

She felt his gaze on her as she walked to the door. She looked over her shoulder once more. He straightened the papers on the table, but covertly watched her while Byron still talked. Her head nudged slightly to the right in the direction of her room.

Travis's eyes widened, and he raised a brow. The question clear. Was she sure?

Her chin lifted and lowered, then she turned and hurried to her room before she thought about what she'd just done.

In her room, she carefully closed the door before crossing to the window and dropping her purse on the desk. When had she suddenly become a thrill seeker? Of course, Travis wouldn't come to her room. For one, her dad was home. The house would implode with Grant's anger if he found them together in her room. Two, she had no idea where Elaina was. She could picture the awkward scene: her leading Travis out of her room and Elaina bumping into them. Yeah…she shouldn't have given any type of invitation for Travis to come to her room.

Thirty minutes later, Travis hadn't come to her room and she stopped fretting about the stupidity of her move. By now Travis and Byron would have finished straightening up. Byron would have walked Travis out. It's not like Travis could say, "Hold up, I'm going by India's room before I go."

India slipped out of her blouse and unbuttoned her slacks. There was a knock on the door right as she slipped her pants off. Her pulse skyrocketed. She grabbed the satin bathrobe draped over the end of her bed and slipped it on. She hurried to the door, took a fortifying breath, then cracked it open.

Elaina stood at the door. India tried not to show her disappointment.

"Do you have any ibuprofen?" Elaina pressed a hand to her temple. She was still in the clothes she'd had on earlier. Her eyes were red rimmed, and stress lined her mouth.

India opened the door wider. "You okay?"

Elaina grimaced. "Headache. I don't want to go searching through the medicine cabinet for something."

"Yeah, sure. Give me a second." India went to her purse and pulled out the bottle of ibuprofen. She took the medicine back to Elaina. "Keep it. I'll buy another tomorrow."

Elaina was already nodding and walking away. "Thanks."

"Elaina, are you sure you're okay?"

Elaina threw a haughty look over her shoulder. "Of course, don't be ridiculous, India," she said in a voice that made India feel ridiculous for even asking.

She went back into her room and closed the door. Now irritated and edgy. She loved her sister, but Elaina sure as hell made it hard to care about her sometimes. She went to get pajamas out of the drawer.

Her bedroom door opened and closed. India spun around, then sucked in a breath. Travis stood just inside the door.

"Sorry, I was going to knock, but I heard a door open," he said in a hushed voice. His eyes ran over her, raising the temperature in the room by a thousand degrees. "I had to see you."

India didn't care about getting caught. The stupidity of having him in her room. The fallout of their relationship. What choices they'd make tomorrow. He'd come to her. She was across the room and in his arms in a blink.

His arms wrapped around her, his hard chest pressed into the softness of her breasts, the strength of his legs sliding across her bare legs. Travis kissed her like he'd waited his entire life for this moment.

"I didn't think you would come," she whispered against his lips, not bothering to hide how much she missed him.

His hands eased inside the robe, caressing her skin. One slipped beneath the silk of her underwear to grab her ass. The other tugged on the strap of her bra. "Did you think I would stay away when you looked at me like that?" He sounded as desperate as her.

"Like what?" Her head fell back.

His lips trailed down her neck. He pulled down the cup of her bra. His mouth brushed the top of the full mound. His tongue ran across the sensitive tip. Sucked deep and hard. She felt the pull all the way down in her core. She pushed her chest forward. Needing the reassurance of his touch. That he was just as caught up as she was.

"Like you wanted me to do this," he whispered, his lips brushing her nipple.

India bit her lip to keep from crying out. Her sex clenched. "I want more than that." She pulled his head up and met his eyes. She wanted forever. She wanted to kiss him in front of everyone. For him to take her hand in his without fear of repercussions. She wanted to believe everything would work out and they'd have time to explore and grow the love blossoming between them. She wanted that so badly tears burned her eyes.

A line formed between Travis's brows. He cupped her cheek in his hand and ran a thumb across her lower lip. "You can have all of me, India. My heart, my fears, everything." His eyes didn't waver. His voice was thick with emotion.

Her heart felt as if it would explode, it was so full. She was desperate to believe this time was real.

They both rushed in for a kiss. India kissed him with a fierceness she wasn't aware she was capable of. Travis held her as if he feared she would let go.

They moved across the room. His mouth never left hers. Their bodies bumped and rubbed against each other as they stumbled their way toward her bed, each frantic brush and frenzied caress heightening their need to get closer to each other. The need to feel Travis inside her, on top of her, as a part of her guided her every movement.

India hurriedly worked the button of his slacks and jerked down the zipper. She pulled on the opening of his boxers until his dick spilled out. She wrapped her hands around the length of him, caressing the long thick flesh with worshipful hands.

"Damn, India, I love it when you touch me like that," Travis said in a deep, trembling voice.

His body shook and the fingers in her hair tightened. Their tongues danced decadently as India savored the swollen, heavy heat in her hands. Travis broke away from her long enough to push down his pants and sit on the edge of her bed. India tossed off the robe. Emotion flared in Travis's gaze. She slowed down as she unhooked her bra and slid down her underwear. Her sex grew more slick and swollen with each ragged breath he drew in.

Strong hands grasped her hips and pulled her forward. "I don't deserve you, but I'm never letting go." The fierce claim spilled from his lips seconds before his mouth closed over one taut nipple.

India clutched his broad shoulders, too overwhelmed to do much more than soak in the glorious things he did to her body. His hand nudged her thighs apart before rising to cup the wet curls at their juncture. Her nails dug into his shoulders. She sucked in air between her teeth and didn't care if she melted into a puddle right there at his feet.

"India." He slid two thick fingers across her plump clit. "God, I love the way you feel. So hot and slick." He kissed the soft spot between her breasts. "So sweet."

"Let me touch you some more," she pleaded. The trembles starting low in her midsection were an erotic warning that she wouldn't be able to hold on much longer.

"You have forever to touch me." He teased her breasts with light nips and soft kisses while his fingers played the most beautiful symphony between her legs. Her breathing shortened and every muscle in her body quivered. Pressure built inside of her until she feared she would explode.

"Now, Travis, please," she moaned.

He slid back on the bed. India crawled onto his lap, and straddled his waist. His lips trailed down her neck, lightly played across her shoulders. The heavy press of his erection between them was a temptation she couldn't ignore. Reaching down, she took his dick in her hand. He grabbed her waist and lifted her. She positioned the blunt tip of him at her slick opening, and Travis brought her down hard. Filling her completely. Touching more than just the tender part wrapped around him, but grabbing her heart and soul with the tender vow in his eyes.

India rotated her hips, pulling him deeper. Their bodies shook. Travis's lids lowered. He groaned into her shoulder and she clenched her teeth to stop the cries of pure pleasure. When he raised his head and kissed her again as if she were the manifestation of every wish he'd ever made, India squeezed him tight and let her emotions take over.

Travis was here, in her room, in her bed, and at this moment she didn't give a damn what it took to keep him there with her.

CHAPTER TWENTY-ONE

TRAVIS FINALLY DRAGGED himself out of the warmth of India's bed at three in the morning. He'd stayed longer than he'd planned. One kiss had turned into another, one caress became multiple, and one quick question led to a conversation neither wanted to end. That was the way things had always been with India. Nothing was ever quick and simple. They'd start a conversation and it would carry on throughout the day via text messages.

But it was more than just how easily he could talk to her—he didn't want to leave her. Ever. Tonight brought everything into crystal clear focus. He'd been so dumb back then to have considered what was between them to only be friendship. He was not going to be dumb now. He didn't care what he had to do, what concessions needed to be made, or even if he had to follow her to Los Angeles. He was not ruining this chance with India.

India shifted in the bed. She reached for him in her sleep, and he smiled while longing pierced his chest. They shouldn't have to sneak around like this.

India's head lifted. She looked around, frowning, then spotted him. "What time is it?"

"Three a.m.," he answered, keeping his voice low. "I should have left hours ago." He found his shirt at the foot of her bed and slipped his arms in the sleeves.

India slid out of bed. Naked and glorious in the

moonlight filtering through the curtains. His hands froze on the buttons of his shirt. The need to wrap his arms around her waist and draw her body back into bed pounded in his blood.

"I shouldn't have told you to come to my room." She took over buttoning his shirt. "It's too risky."

"Which is why we should tell everyone what's going on instead of sneaking around." He placed his hands on her hips. Her smooth skin enticed him to make love to her one more time. Better yet, bring her back to his place where they could be together without the prying eyes of her meddling family.

"I don't know," she said, not meeting his eyes. "Elaina was really upset today. Work is stressing her out. The primaries are in a few more weeks, but I don't think that'll make anything easier."

Travis didn't give a damn about any of that. Not after they'd spent the past few hours in each other's arms. "Nothing is going to make her work less stressful, or make it easier for her to accept what's going on. We've wasted too much time as it is."

She nodded but her full lips tilted down in a frown. "Can we not talk about this right now? I don't want to end the night on a sour note. I don't want to think about the consequences right now. I just want to enjoy this moment."

Travis reluctantly let the topic slide. He needed to get out of the house. The late hour didn't mean someone in the house wasn't up. Patricia had always arrived early to start breakfast for the family. Now that she and Grant were engaged, she might be living there. Travis ran the very real chance of running into her in the hallways on her way to the kitchen. He doubted she used the kitchen entrance anymore.

He leaned down and kissed India. Her body was soft and warm from the bed. Her curves as tempting as a pile of silk cushions after an arduous day. He pulled back before he lost himself in another kiss as he'd done earlier. The ticking of the clock in her room a reminder he was running out of time.

"I'll call you later today," he said. "I'll be in court all day." The reminder was like putting on a coat made of lead. His family would be there. Watching and waiting for him to make a decision. Throw the case, and prove he was still loyal; win, and forever be considered a traitor.

India pressed a hand to the side of his face. "What's wrong?"

He tried not to scowl. The concern in her soft eyes said he'd failed. "Thinking about the day ahead."

"I know this case has to be hard for you," she said. "I'm sorry you're in this position."

"I wish I knew how to fix this," he admitted. "The evidence is clear. My cousin clearly had a motive for going into Mr. King's business. He'd told people he was willing to kill Zachariah if he didn't give him the money he wanted. Zachariah protected his business. Shot him in self-defense. My cousin shot twice. Why did he have to go in there?" He'd been asking himself the question ever since he'd learned about his cousin's death. The question no one would ever get the answer to.

"You know why. That was the life he lived. The life he chose. The same life your family wanted you to choose instead of becoming a lawyer and working for our family. He made the decision, and that decision killed him. You don't have to agree with the outcome, but if your client was really defending himself, then you can't feel bad for taking the case."

"Except my family is viewing this case as the final proof I've turned my back on them. Did you know your father purchased the land my dad inherited at a tax sale? That the very field he hired me to work in once belonged to my family?"

Her eyes widened. "Are you sure?"

"That's according to my uncle. I haven't had the chance to talk to Grant about it. If it's true, does it even matter? He purchased it legally at a tax sale. Not that something being legal will matter to my family. I worked for the enemy, now I'm defending the enemy."

The situations weren't connected, but Travis still couldn't shake the frustration of feeling that every choice he made came with fucked-up consequences. Whatever reason Grant had to help him didn't take away from the fact that Grant had made sure Travis wasn't the one breaking into Zachariah's business along with his cousin, or that in his dad's world Travis making a better life for himself regardless of the means to get there would have increased the chasm of animosity between them.

"You're doing your job," India said firmly. "Don't let your family's beliefs or my dad's relationship with your father make you doubt yourself. The only person who has to live with the consequences of your actions is you."

The memory of the hatred in Devon's and Mitch's eyes flashed in Travis's mind. "I don't think I'm coming out of this either way."

India gripped his arm. "What does that mean?"

He shook his head. She didn't need to know about the threats his uncle had made. He should have gone to the police, but a part of him still believed Mitch was trying to scare him. Despite what his family thought of him, they wouldn't hurt him if this didn't go well.

I hope.

"Nothing. Either way this case goes, I'm going to get flak for it. And you're right, I'll talk to Grant one day about why he helped me after purchasing my family's land, but for now there are more important things to work out." He brushed his lips across hers. Like figuring out how to convince India he meant what he said and tell her family about their relationship with the lowest number of casualties. He glanced at the clock. Twenty minutes had passed since he'd slipped out of her bed. "I've got to go."

She followed his gaze and nodded. "Okay, please call me after court. Tell me how it went."

"I will." He kissed her again. Quickly, then went to the door.

India followed. "I should walk you out."

"No, it'll be bad enough if I'm caught. If I'm caught with you, that'll be even worse. I'll think of something."

She nodded but he saw the reluctance in her eyes. He cracked open her door and listened. The house was quiet. He gave her one last lingering kiss before he slipped out of the door. Hurried down the hall to the stairs that led to the back of the house. Thanked heaven when no one came across him.

Once down the stairs, he crept toward the kitchen. If Patricia wasn't there yet, he'd go that way. He'd pretended to drive off when Byron left earlier and parked his car in one of the tobacco fields behind the estate.

Going out of the kitchen would make slipping through the grounds to the fields much easier. He didn't worry about setting off any alarms or getting caught by surveillance cameras. He knew the codes and where every camera was pointed.

There was a light on in the kitchen. Not unusual since Patricia typically left a light on over the sink or near the pantry. Still, he peeked around the door to be sure. Seeing no one, he silently sprinted toward the door. A groan echoed in the room. Travis froze. His heart pounded as he thought of a dozen lies for why he was here.

This is stupid. They needed to tell someone.

He slowly turned toward the sound and frowned. Elaina sat at one of the barstools at the counter, her body slumped over on the granite surface. An empty wine bottle and glass next to her hand.

"Shit," he silently cursed.

She was still up to this. After finding her like this a few times after they were married, he'd suggested she try talking to him about whatever bothered her instead of a wine bottle. She'd gotten angry, sarcastically apologized for inconveniencing him and worked harder to hide her emotions and her drinking from him. He should leave her there. Let her wake up with a backache from her uncomfortable position to go with the hangover. Heaven knew if she caught him there this late, the fallout would be ten times worse.

He turned to the door, twisted the knob, then cursed again. He couldn't leave her there.

He went over and lifted her into his arms. She groaned, but as expected didn't wake up. Travis carried her to the sunroom next to the kitchen and gently laid her on the sofa. There was no way in hell he'd take her back up the stairs. Explaining that would be worse than explaining being in the house.

He pulled the throw off the back of the sofa and spread the blanket over her. When he looked at her face, her eyes were open and staring at him. In the dim light, he thought he saw traces of dried tears along her cheek.

"You always did try to take care of me," she said in a slurred, sleepy voice. Then her eyes closed, and she was out.

Travis let out the breath he'd held. She wouldn't remember this. If she did, she wouldn't ask why he'd been there. She never talked about these low points. One of the reasons he'd accepted they'd never be able to fall in love with each other. He'd hoped to save her, but Elaina didn't want to be saved.

Travis brushed the hair away from her face, sighed and then left her on the couch. He went back to the kitchen. Threw away the empty bottle and put the glass in the sink before walking out the door.

CHAPTER TWENTY-TWO

"INDIA, THERE'S SOMEONE I'd like you to meet."

India turned away from putting her violin back in the case to face Jocelyn. She'd just finished practicing with the chamber ensemble for the performance in the museum's auditorium. The chair of the museum's board stood with a man who looked to be in his midfifties. He watched India with a steady gaze from behind square-framed glasses.

"This is—"

"Nikolas Kastikov," India interrupted. She grinned and held out her hand to him. "Music director for the Tri-City Philharmonic and music professor at North Carolina State. It's a pleasure to meet you."

Nikolas grinned, creating wrinkles at the corners of his blue eyes. "The pleasure is all mine. When Jocelyn told me you were going to be a guest performer at the museum and that you were practicing here today, I had to drop by and meet you."

He held out his hand to shake hers. India clasped his hand in both of hers and pumped their joined hands enthusiastically. "I'm honored. I wouldn't think you'd go out of your way for that."

"I am a big fan of the Transatlantic Orchestra. You're the assistant principal violinist for them, am I correct?"

India let go of his hand. "I was, but I'm not with the

orchestra anymore. I'm only in town until the end of my brother's campaign."

"And after that?"

She shrugged. "I submitted a request to audition for the LA Philharmonic and got the okay to audition. First rounds are next month."

Nikolas's face fell, and he crossed his arms. "That's unfortunate."

India frowned. True, she wasn't as enthused to have gotten the reply as she'd expected to be, but that was no reason for Nikolas to look disappointed. This would be a big career move. "Why?"

"I'm looking for an assistant director. I'd hoped you would be interested in the job."

She was momentarily at a loss for words. He should have no trouble finding anyone interested in working with him, but for him to come down to the art museum and directly mention the position to her was flattering. She'd expected to be invited to audition if she'd applied. Not to be sought out.

"I would be if I were staying in town." The comment was supposed to be a statement, but her voice rose at the end, making it a question. Did she have to leave town?

"Would you be interested in staying in Jackson Falls for a little longer?" Nikolas asked as if he'd picked up on her own doubts.

She was interested in staying longer. Her family was here. She missed being home. But staying meant telling Elaina and the rest of her family about Travis. Staying meant trusting she and Travis would survive the coming storm. That their feelings were real.

You want to tell them. You want everyone to know. You love him.

She met Nikolas's gaze. "I am interested in staying home longer. I'll consider auditioning for your position."

Nikolas smiled and nodded. "Good. I know Jackson Falls has nothing on Los Angeles, but bigger isn't always better."

"That's very true," India agreed. Excitement crept into her voice, and she worked hard to keep it contained so she wouldn't appear too eager as she and Nikolas chatted for a few more minutes.

India thought about Nikolas's offer as she left the museum. It was perfect. She was spending a lot more time at the museum and had made contact with other local musicians. Penelope had practically jumped with excitement when India mentioned Nikolas's offer before she left. Penelope played with the Tri-City Philharmonic and thought India would be a perfect addition. The reasons to stay home were growing stronger.

Still she kept her enthusiasm and visions of working closer to home very close to her heart. She'd gotten her hopes up once before and that had ended in heartbreak. This time with Travis felt different, more tangible and real. In the week since that night in her room, they'd managed to catch a few moments together, but mostly spent their time on the phone or texting. Maybe the time was right. They were right. But that didn't make her want to dive into anything without being absolutely sure.

Not wanting to go back to the estate, India headed for Byron's campaign office. There were always phone calls to make, envelopes to stuff or fund-raising plans to be made. She'd occupy her time helping her brother instead of sitting at home debating all the reasons to stay home versus leaving.

Even if things didn't work out, did she really want to run away from home again? That was what she'd done before. All those years ago, she hadn't confronted Travis to ask why he'd kissed her but proposed to Elaina. Hadn't admitted to Elaina what happened between her and Travis. She'd backed away without standing up for herself.

She'd grown since then. She'd learned to be stronger and independent. If Travis backed out again, it would crush her heart, but she would survive. She couldn't let fear of what would or wouldn't happen stop her from considering what she wanted in all aspects of her life. Especially the career she'd fought to build. LA had been a decision she'd jumped on out of fear. She didn't want to be afraid to live her truth anymore.

Byron's office was full of the distracting noise and chatter she needed. She waved to the volunteers at the phones on her way back to her brother's office. She knocked and waited for Byron's deep voice to tell her to come in before entering.

"India, what are you doing here?" Byron stood behind his desk. "I was just leaving for a meeting with potential donors."

India waved him off. "That's fine. I wasn't ready to go home after the practice today. I decided to come volunteer for the next United States senator from our area."

Byron grinned and slipped the jacket off the back of his leather chair. "Help is always welcome around here." He glanced her way "And I appreciate the confidence you have in me." His voice filled with gratitude.

"You've got a good heart, Byron. The voters will be lucky to have you."

His eyes filled with appreciation. "How was practice?" He put the jacket on, then moved to the mirror next to his desk and adjusted his tie.

She smiled and hurried over to help him. "Really good. I miss playing with a group. I'm looking forward to the performance." She stepped back so he could see himself in the mirror.

Byron looked at her handiwork with the tie and nodded. "Well, just know Yolanda and I both plan to attend."

She forced the smile to remain on her face. She'd decided to stop arguing with Byron about his fiancée. For better or worse, she was the woman he'd chosen. The least India could do was pretend to respect his decision. Especially since she was currently hiding the fact that she was sleeping with his best friend.

The difference is you love Travis.

"Great!" she said, forcing the thought aside. "I'll be sure to save you both a seat up close."

Byron nodded at his reflection, then picked up his messenger bag and kissed her forehead.

India raised a brow. "What was that for?"

"For not rolling your eyes when I mentioned Yolanda," he said sincerely. "Your support there is appreciated, as well."

She patted her brother's chest. No part of her ever wanted to run for public office, so she couldn't say how she'd deal with the pressures he faced. Her brother would fight for the people in this area, and if she wanted him to win, she also had to live with his campaign strategy. "As long as you're happy, I'm happy."

"I am happy, and I'll be happier when I win." He checked his watch. "I'll come by the house later for dinner. Will you be there?"

"That's the plan so far."

"Good. See you later."

With one last smile, Byron was gone. India went to the office manager to find out where she could help. A few minutes later she was on the phone making calls. The busywork did as expected and kept her mind off the decisions she needed to make. Moving, Travis, the jumble of her life.

After two hours on the phone, India took a break. She grabbed a doughnut from the break room and a bottle of water. She was considering finishing out the day on the phone when Elaina showed up. She came through the door and shot toward Byron's office with a determined stride. She didn't bother to look at the rest of the people in the office and didn't notice India coming out of the break room.

"Elaina, Byron isn't in there," India called out just as her sister put her hand on the knob to Byron's door.

Elaina spun and frowned at India. "Where is he?"

"A meeting with donors." India strolled over to her sister. "Do you need something?"

Elaina looked impeccable as ever in a fitted light gray suit. Her dark hair was pulled back from her face in a sleek ponytail, makeup so flawless India could barely tell she wore anything. India glanced at the doughnut in her hand, then noticed the ink stain on her shirt from earlier when she'd slipped the pen into her neckline while she'd been on the phone. Even in a rush, Elaina looked polished and beautiful.

India had let go of the old feelings of inadequacy

when standing next to her sister. Elaina was so like their mother in the way she went through life, as if daring the world to challenge her. Now India saw Elaina used that as an armor to keep others out. She didn't really know her sister, what she wanted, how she felt, who she confided in. Regret hit India as she realized that if she got what she wanted, she and her sister would never have that relationship.

Elaina's frown deepened. She looked around the room as if expecting to see Byron pop up out of nowhere. "It's nothing."

"He said he was coming by the house for dinner later. You can catch him then."

"I was hoping to avoid dinner at home today," Elaina said sourly.

Elaina and Grant were coolly cordial as ever, but the strain since the night of their fight was like a grenade in the room whenever they were together. While everyone in the room hoped neither would pull the pin. "Everything okay? At the office, I mean?"

Elaina elegantly flipped her wrist. "I'm behaving myself, if that's what you're asking."

"No, I'm asking if everything is okay with you." India met her sister's eyes. "If you need anything. Even if it's someone to talk to."

Elaina's sharp gaze darted to the people in the office, then back to Elaina. She pointed to Byron's door. "Is this locked, or can we go in here?"

Okay, what was that look about? "We can go in. He doesn't lock it when he leaves."

Elaina snorted, something she did only when she was really agitated, and opened the door. "Byron is too trusting. I've always told him that."

India followed Elaina into the office and closed the door behind them. Elaina's brows were drawn together and her eyes were focused on India's shirt.

Elaina's eyes narrowed and she leaned in to inspect. "Seriously, India, what's that on your shirt?"

Of course, her sister would zero in on that. Classic deflection from whatever bothered her. "Ink. It's fine, the shirt is old. Now, can you tell me what's going on?"

Elaina straightened and clasped her hands tightly in front of her midsection. "Well…have you heard anything?"

Cryptic as ever. India took a deep breath. When Elaina was agitated, she used any sign of frustration as an excuse to cut short a conversation. "Anything about what?"

"Travis," she said as if India should have known immediately whom she referred to. "Is he seeing someone new?" Elaina said the words quickly, her face pinching up as if she hated to even reveal that she wanted to know.

If Elaina would have cut a backflip and sung "Yankee Doodle Dandy," she wouldn't have thrown India off more. India's stomach did the backflip instead. "What? Why are you asking me?"

"Because he talks to you." She turned away and paced toward Byron's desk and back. "He always did talk to you more. You were his little buddy, remember?" Elaina said sarcastically. She stopped pacing and rushed back over to India. Her eyes focused and piercing. "I thought maybe you two picked back up with the BFF vibe you had before."

India wanted a hole to open in the floor and suck her to the center of the Earth. "That was a long time ago—"

Elaina scoffed. "Please, you two seem to have vibed again," she said in a tight voice. She'd never made India feel bad about her friendship with Travis, but Elaina also never talked to India about Travis in anything but a superficial way. She'd never come to India asking for information on how Travis was thinking or feeling. India fought not to squirm under the discomforting realization that her family's fears that Elaina hadn't moved on because she still cared may be true.

"We have to work together because of Byron's campaign," India explained and felt worse for the lie of omission.

Elaina crossed her arms and studied India closely. "But he talks to you. I ran into Camille and she mentioned she and Travis were done. Did he tell you why?"

She knew Travis and Camille were done. He'd wanted India to know about their split before he'd come to Asheville. That he wouldn't have slept with her if he were still with Camille.

"Why do you care if she and Travis are done?" She tossed the question back to change the line of questioning.

Elaina blinked several times. Her chin lifted. "I wouldn't typically," she said defensively. "But she also mentioned Travis said he had a second chance with someone. I got the feeling she told me this because she thinks I'm the second chance." Elaina shifted her shoulders as if she were uncomfortable with the idea. Uncomfortable or excited?

India's stomach flopped. Before, the idea of Elaina still having feelings for Travis was an abstract thought. Now it felt very real. She watched her sister closely as icy fingers of anxiety slipped up her spine. "Are you interested in a second chance?" She carefully kept her voice neutral.

"No, of course not." Elaina toyed with the edge of her collar, her artfully manicured brows drawn together. "I mean, I never thought…not since he made it very clear he didn't want to go down that road again."

India stilled. "Did you try to go down that road?"

"Once—it was stupid." Elaina sounded annoyed. "After his grandmother died. I went over to see him. I thought there was something, but obviously I was wrong. He sent me away."

India barely hid her shock. Travis's grandmother died months after his divorce with Elaina was final. Which meant that after they were separated, Elaina had tried to get back with him. If he turned her down, that explained her sister's animosity. Elaina wasn't vulnerable for anyone. For her to have tried to reconcile with Travis must have meant she'd trusted him to see a part of herself she never showed anyone, only to have him reject her.

"I wonder what changed with him," Elaina continued in a distracted voice.

"What changed with you? I thought you hated Travis."

"I don't hate him," Elaina said in a don't-be-silly voice. "I don't like how he thinks he knows me. Then there was the dream the other night."

"What dream?" Her sister was still dreaming about Travis. India's chest hurt.

Elaina looked embarrassed. India had never seen Elaina embarrassed. "I thought he…" She waved a hand and quickly schooled her features into the usual mask of indifference. "It doesn't matter. I just want to know if I have to deal with this along with everything else."

She sounded exasperated. Her sister hit her with a direct stare. "So, do you know anything?"

India's hand clenched. Something soft oozed between her fingers. She glanced down at the crushed half of the doughnut she hadn't finished. She needed a minute before looking at Elaina again. She hurried to the trash can and dusted off the crumbs into the garbage. Crumbs that matched the bruising pain of her chest.

Elaina hadn't said no. Her sister had gone back to Travis once. Now she was here digging for information to confirm if he still cared. If Elaina did still care, how could India be with him? Before, she'd only kissed him because Elaina said she didn't want him. Now if Elaina did care for him, India would be intentionally hurting her sister by admitting they were together.

"India," Elaina said impatiently. "You know something, don't you?"

India brushed her hands together, took a deep breath, then faced her sister. "No." She coughed, then cleared her throat. "I don't know anything. He hasn't said anything to me. Do you want me to feel him out?"

"No. I won't have him thinking I'm trying to rekindle something that should be dead."

Should? Does that mean her feelings aren't dead?

"What would you do if this is true?" India asked. Did her sister want Travis back?

Elaina took a deep breath and shook her head. "I don't… It's just… I don't know. He was always there. Even when I didn't appreciate him. It's nice to have someone there." Elaina cleared her throat and looked away quickly. "I have to go. It's probably a good thing I missed Byron." She walked over to India and placed a hand on her shoulder. "Don't bring this up to anyone.

I shouldn't have even come to ask this question. The past belongs in the past."

"I won't say anything," India spoke past the lump in her throat.

"Thank you, India. I know I'm not the best sister in the world, but I do appreciate you. You've always been the one with the most heart. You're the one who keeps us together." Elaina squeezed her shoulder, then walked out of Byron's office.

India stood there for several long, quiet minutes, the lump in her throat growing with each passing second. Her tears burned as the pain of thinking about potentially breaking things off with Travis hit her. If Elaina had even an inkling of affection left for Travis, could she really be with him? After all this time, Travis didn't hold ill will toward Elaina. He'd hidden his dating life from Elaina for years so as not to upset her. He might come to the same realization as her.

Regardless of what happened next, if her sister found out, India faced the real possibility of having to once again let go of the man she loved.

CHAPTER TWENTY-THREE

TRAVIS WAS MESMERIZED watching India's solo during her performance at the museum. He'd always enjoyed watching her play. To see her get completely immersed in the music and lose herself in creating something beautiful reminded him of the way he felt whenever he was able to paint. Happy and content doing something he loved.

Her arm flowed effortlessly as she played. Her eyes were on the sheet of music, and a small smile played across her full lips, proof she was enjoying herself. She was beautiful.

I love her.

The thought rammed him in the chest. Falling in love with India wasn't the smartest thing to do, but—despite his law degree—he didn't claim to be a genius. Maybe he'd always loved her. Even when he'd just viewed her as a friend. Maybe that was why, even though years passed, he never could get her completely out of his mind.

Didn't that happen when you were in love, thoughts of the person you loved always at the forefront of the mind? Now that he knew how he felt, he didn't want to hide his emotions. What was he supposed to do with his love if they were keeping things a secret? Was he supposed to shove it back down into a box and pretend as if he didn't care?

The music ended, and everyone clapped. Travis snapped out of his trance and joined in the applause.

India smiled at the crowd. Their gazes locked, and her smile softened into something sweeter. He itched with the need to hold her in his arms again. To be able to pull her into a hug and kiss her openly after her performance. He was not going to lose her.

He turned away before he did something stupid, like walk over and go with what he wanted. There was a cash bar set up and he decided to go have a drink.

"The music wasn't that bad." Ashiya's voice came from over his shoulder.

"The music was great," he told her. He glanced at the bartender. "Whiskey neat." He pointed to Ashiya. "And whatever she wants."

"You know I won't turn down a drink." Ashiya slid up next to him. "Chardonnay please."

The bartender walked away to make their drinks and Travis focused on Ashiya. "I haven't seen you in a while. How have things been?"

"Great, business is good. I'm not directly involved with the campaign, so that's always a bonus in my book. How is the trial going?"

"Excellent," he said with forced enthusiasm. "Each day I make my case, my family looks even more like they want to murder me."

Ashiya threw him a sympathetic glance and patted his arm. "I'll pray for you."

"Please do." He might need more than prayer. A bulletproof vest and twenty-four-hour security.

"I'll pray on that and other things."

"What else could I need praying for?" he asked.

The bartender set their drinks in front of them. Travis gave him cash, then took a sip. Ashiya toyed with the stem of her wineglass.

"I'm praying you and India come to your senses and stay away from each other."

What the hell? The whiskey bypassed his throat and trickled into his windpipe. Travis coughed into his hand and slowly set the glass down. "Come again?" He looked around but there was no one close enough to overhear their conversation.

Ashiya appeared unfazed by dropping her bombshell. She watched him unsympathetically. "I saw you two kissing. I can't believe you two have been fooling around for years."

Travis cleared his throat again. The burning tickle of the drink faded along with his initial shock. "It hasn't been years. Don't say it like that."

Ashiya gave him a pointed look. "Pining for each other for years is fooling around. Elaina's going to be crushed when she finds out."

Angry, yes, but crushed? Travis didn't buy it. "She won't be crushed."

Ashiya leaned closer. "Where do you think this can go? Nowhere?"

"I want it to go somewhere," he said fiercely. "I'm not going to settle for it not going somewhere."

"Are you crazy? Uncle Grant isn't going to let that happen." She said the words as sure as someone saying grass is green and pigeons will shit on your windshield.

Bitter frustration tightened his shoulders. "Your uncle doesn't rule my life anymore, Ashiya. I love India. I won't let her go this time."

Ashiya's eyes widened. "What?"

"Look, I appreciate that you want to step in and give advice, but that doesn't mean I'm going to take it. I bowed under the pressure of your family before, I won't do that this time. I'm my own man."

"You'll tear them apart."

He tried to pretend as if the words didn't bother him. India and Elaina weren't the closest sisters, but they cared for each other. They supported one another and he knew loyalty to each other was important to both women.

"Elaina won't blame India. I'll make sure of that."

"You can't make sure of that. If you won't do this because it will go against what my uncle wants, then at least think about what you're doing to Elaina and India's relationship."

Valid points he didn't want to dwell on. He loved India. He'd walked away before. Why couldn't he just finally have the woman he wanted? Finally be happy? "Why do you care?"

Her spine straightened, and she looked put off that he'd even question her. "Because I love India, too. She's the closest thing I have to a sister. If you push this, then she'll leave instead of facing a fight with her sister she can't win. I'm sorry, Travis, but I'd rather you two be apart than lose my best friend again. Maybe you should think about that."

Ashiya picked up her glass and stormed away. Travis gripped his whiskey in a fist. He wanted to kick the bar, but didn't. After finally admitting how he felt about India, now he had to be faced with the noble decision to let her go. When the hell had he ever been noble and why should he start now?

He looked across the room and caught Elaina watching him. To his surprise, she crossed the room to him. Travis took a fortifying sip of the whiskey and faced her.

She stopped in front of him and clasped her hands in front of her. "I've been thinking about you," Elaina said in a crisp, no-nonsense voice, her chin high.

"Thinking about shooting me?" he said, only partially joking.

The corner of her lip lifted in a hint of a smile. "Always that. No, I dreamed about you the other week."

She remembered. He forced his hands to unclench the whiskey glass in his hand and appear unfazed. "You did?"

"I dreamed you were carrying me."

"It wasn't a dream," he said. "I moved you from the kitchen to the sunroom. You'd…had too much to drink again."

Her lips pressed together. She looked away. "Minor slipup."

"That's what you always called them." How many minor slipups did a person have to have before they became a major problem?

"Don't start this again," Elaina said, exasperation clear in her tone. "I'm not an alcoholic."

"I never said you were," he said evenly.

"No, you just insinuated that I drink too much."

A headache started in his left temple. He'd been hit with enough tonight. He didn't want to add *fight with the ex-wife* to the list. "Can we not do this tonight, Elaina?"

"Have you looked at the calendar?" she asked in a rush. "Do you know what's coming up?"

Pain ripped through his chest. No matter how much

time passed, the pain hadn't lessened. He wondered if it ever would. "I do."

She tossed her hair over her shoulder. "Then maybe you can cut me some slack."

He took a step closer to her. No matter what happened, they'd both always share the pain of that loss. "Elaina, if you need to talk…"

"Then I have friends I can talk to." She stepped back and turned to walk away.

Travis reached out and placed a hand on her elbow. "Elaina, I never wanted to hurt you."

She pulled out of his grip. "You never wanted to love me either."

The words startled him. She didn't make it easy to love her. Outside of their physical compatibility, she'd never opened up to him. Not even in the early days of their marriage. Eventually he'd stopped trying and went along with the charade of happiness they put on. "Did *you* want to love me?"

She glared at him with cold eyes. "What do you think?" Her voice dripped with scorn. "I don't know why I came over here," she muttered before walking away.

Travis groaned and picked up his drink. No, he didn't think Elaina ever wanted to love him. If she had, they'd had years to try to make things work. He downed the rest of the whiskey. Frustration ate at his insides like rabid termites. Ashiya's accusation and Elaina's confrontation forced him to face the difficult hill he and India had to overcome. A hill he was willing to climb if it meant a lifetime with India.

"I REALLY SHOULD GO," India said for the fifth time.

Unlike the four other times, she slowly peeled herself from Travis's side and sat up on the couch. The movie they'd been watching was close to the end and she'd seen it plenty of times before. She'd only suggested watching it to prolong her time with Travis. She'd taken a risk and asked Ashiya for a favor in order to spend time after the concert with Travis instead of going home.

Maybe one of the last times.

Ashiya hadn't been happy and told India she was playing with something dangerous. India brushed off her cousin's warning, but as much as she craved being with him and couldn't imagine pretending like she didn't care, she also hated the deception. The lies made her feel like a teenager who had to sneak and hide to be with the unwelcome boyfriend.

Travis ran a hand down her back. "I think you should stay and we should tell your family and stop hiding what's between us."

India stilled. An incessant flutter of nerves attacked her stomach. Where had that come from? She got it, the night had been perfect…her performance, the hot glances and secret touches they'd exchanged after the performance, and coming back to his place to make love. Who wouldn't think they were ready to "go public"?

Still, she intended to tell Travis she still didn't want to let her family know about them. She wanted to keep things between them a little longer. She didn't want to be faced with giving him up.

"And after we do all that, we can run off to Vegas and get married," she said, trying to tease.

Travis didn't crack a smile. "If that's what it'll take to get you to marry me. Then sure."

India's heart raced. Her lungs tried to supply oxygen, but her brain remained muddled. He couldn't be serious. "You're joking."

Travis took her hand in his. "I'm not. What are we doing here, India?"

"We were having a good night." Telling people could ruin everything.

"And snatching one night here or there so no one can find out isn't enough for me. India, I told you that you could have all of me. I didn't just say that because I want to sneak around with you. I said that because I want to spend my life with you."

"Travis—"

"I've got closing arguments tomorrow in a murder trial and every day I'm in the courtroom I'm reminded tomorrow isn't promised. I think about everyone wanting to pull me in a different direction. All of the various expectations for me to do what other people want. But the only thing that I want is to be with you. No secrets. No hiding. I want you to marry me."

The word *yes* clawed at her heart and soul. She'd loved Travis for years. Had longed for him even when she'd left the States and toured. To be with him forever would be more than she'd ever asked for. She'd be happy. At what expense though?

Elaina would hate her. Byron's campaign would suffer, and he'd hate her. She didn't care what her dad thought, but she didn't want to hurt her siblings. She wanted to enjoy the finite amount of time she had with Travis without facing the realities of what being with him really meant.

She pushed down the happiness and hope before it could spread and take over her rational mind. "I can't."

"Why not?"

She jumped up from the chair. "You know why not."

Travis got up and turned her to face him. "Your family will be fine. Life will go on."

"Life may go on, but that doesn't mean it'll be the same," she argued. "I won't tear my family apart."

"You said you didn't want to live by your family's rules anymore. That you didn't want them to control you again, but you're letting them do exactly that."

"How? By not betraying my sister?"

"In case you didn't know, you *betrayed* her the moment you slept with me."

India pushed away from him. The truth of his words shined a light on something she didn't want to face, that she'd already crossed a line she continued to say she didn't want to cross. That she'd known what she was doing. Using the repercussions of Elaina finding out as an excuse to not move forward was just that. An excuse.

"She doesn't know, which means there's no chance what we've done will come back to bite us in the ass," she argued. "I've done my part for Byron's campaign. I've been invited to audition for the LA Philharmonic. I can go to California and start over. Let's not ruin our time together fighting."

"Ruin our time together?" he said incredulously. "India, for the first time I'm not worried about the next big step in my life. I want to spend the rest of my life with you. California is your excuse to get away from the family instead of telling them what you really want. You'd rather run than face your family."

"I'm not running. I'm trying to make things work out."

"Is that why you left the country before?"

"I left because you married my sister!" Her mouth snapped closed.

The words stunned Travis to silence.

She almost laughed at the absurdity of it all. "We both know that's why I left, despite my dad sending the letter declining the offer. I put my hope in us once before and you chose Elaina. I understand your reasons now, but you didn't tell me then. Knowing the truth now doesn't take away the hurt from before." How could she alter her family on just the hope that she and Travis could work out?

He rushed around the couch and took her hands in his. "This time is different. There's no one who can keep us apart."

She shook her head. "We don't know that. What if my dad comes to you with another ultimatum? What if Elaina still cares?"

Travis closed his eyes for a few seconds. When he opened them, he spoke in an even voice. "Your dad can't push me into anything. Elaina and I are through."

"But has she accepted that?" She'd seen Elaina talking to him earlier that night. Elaina had left shortly after their brief conversation. Outwardly, she hadn't appeared to be bothered by their talk, but India couldn't help but remember their conversation in Byron's office a few days before.

"India, don't go creating problems that aren't there. I'll always care about your sister, but I don't love her and I don't want to be with her. I love you." He spoke the last three words so simply and earnestly that her heart squeezed.

Any lingering doubt about Travis's feelings flickered away. She saw his love for her in his face, heard it in his voice, felt it in his touch. But was love enough?

"This time is different because of the choices we both made then. Back then, it would have been a minor scandal. Rumors would have circulated, and Elaina would have been upset, but she would have eventually moved on and forgiven me. You would have been an ex-lover she didn't care about. Now you're her ex-husband. You were a power couple in the area for five years. You're the best friend of a high-profile political candidate and one of the most popular defense attorneys in the region. The scandal would be huge, and the family would never forgive me."

He shook his head as if he didn't want to soak in the truth of her words. "We can get through this. India, I love you. Can you honestly stand here and tell me that you don't feel the same?"

She couldn't do that. She'd been away too long, and being back revealed how much she'd missed Elaina, Byron, Ashiya and her dad. Her chance at happiness would come at the expense of creating a distance no amount of time or travel would lessen.

She lowered her eyes and tried to pull away. "Loving you doesn't change anything. Please, Travis, don't make this harder than it has to be. Let's not ruin lives over something that won't last."

His grip on her hands tightened. "India—"

She leaned up and kissed him quickly. "Shh. Please, let's not do this tonight. Everything has been perfect." She leaned forward to put her forehead on his chest, but he stepped back.

His face was hard and determined. "Tell me you love me, too."

"You know how I feel." Saying the words would only make her decision harder to deal with.

"I need to hear it. Because no matter what you say, I don't think your family will be torn apart by this. They've done too many other things and played unfair in so many situations that us being together will not be enough to make the Robidoux family fall. So, tell me that you love me. Let me know how you feel so I know I'm not fighting a losing battle."

She crossed her arms over her midsection. "We can't get married."

Travis stepped forward. "Do you love me?"

The sliver of doubt that crept into his voice broke her resolve. "Yes, Travis, I love you."

The relief on his face made her heart ache. He grasped her waist and pulled her close. "Then there's still a chance I can change your mind. Don't let your family keep us apart. Don't answer me tonight. Don't even answer me in the next few days. Think about what you want. What you really want, and know that I love you. I will fight anyone I have to to make you happy."

His voice was so sincere. His dark eyes fierce with the promise to love her and fight to make them work. After performing tonight, she didn't want to leave. She wanted to stay in Jackson Falls, but would that mean letting Travis go? Marriage, a future, how would that work without Elaina's blessing? India would teach an elephant to play her violin before her family accepted her and Travis together.

"We can make this work," Travis said with the confidence of a successful defense attorney. "Believe me. We can be together."

She swallowed hard but nodded. Travis kissed her,

and she kissed him back with all the hope and desperation in her heart. When he picked her up and carried her to the bedroom, she didn't argue about needing to get home. She had to savor each of these moments, because no matter what Travis said and how much he promised, she feared the fallout of their decision would be bigger than either of them could handle.

CHAPTER TWENTY-FOUR

INDIA STARED AT the text message on her phone. She wished she could delete it. Move on with the rest of her day as if the two words on the screen didn't make her insanely happy, extremely frustrated and sick with longing.

Marry me.

She squeezed the phone. To her surprise, she'd fallen immediately asleep when she'd gotten home the night before. A deep sleep full of dreams about telling her family she and Travis were in love and getting married. In the dream everything had gone smoothly. Her dad wished them well. Byron had been excited to make Travis his true brother. Elaina had even hugged India and said she and Travis should have always been together.

She'd woken up smiling and full of hope. Then the sunlight hit her eyes and she realized dreams were not reality. The perfect outcome in her head was far from the outcome that would happen.

The dream had done something else. In her dream, Travis faced everything with her. His hand in hers. Not an ounce of reservation about the decision they'd made. She'd woken up with no fading of the trust she had in his love for her.

But dreams weren't reality. Her dad would try to

force them to change their minds, Elaina would be upset and Byron would question how the entire move affected his political campaign.

The sun would continue to rise. People would continue to get on with their daily lives and eventually, hopefully, hearts would heal.

She left her room and went down the hall to Elaina's room. Her heart pounded harder and harder with each step she took. She didn't know what she wanted to say to her sister. Only that she needed to say something. Feel her out to see how she might react to India and Travis being together. She knocked on Elaina's door. The sound of a thud from the other side was the only greeting.

India didn't wait for an answer. She pushed open the door and rushed into her sister's room. "Elaina, what was that?"

Elaina stood at the foot of her bed. She looked up at India, surprised. "What?"

"I heard a noise. I thought…"

Elaina smiled but it didn't reach her eyes. "I dropped something." She knelt and picked up a book. "I was reading." Her voice broke on the last word.

All thoughts fled India's brain. She went to her sister, her pulse racing erratically. Elaina never cried. What the hell had happened to make her sister cry?

Elaina pressed the book to her chest and turned away before India could touch her. She went to the desk and put the book on the surface. She sniffed and hastily wiped her eyes. "Did you need anything?" Elaina asked in a steadier voice.

Frustration almost made India say no and walk out. Love for her sister kept her there. "Elaina, what's wrong?"

Her sister waved a hand. "I'll be fine."

"I know you'll be fine. You're the strongest person I know. That doesn't mean I don't want to be here for you if you need me."

Elaina's shoulders shook as she took a deep breath. She faced India. She tried to look impassive but her red-rimmed eyes and tightly pressed lips gave away her pain. "It's getting closer to the day. The one day of the year I'm not as strong as I'd like to be," Elaina said in a soft voice.

"The day?" The answer to the question hit India as soon as she said the words. The day she'd miscarried. India pressed a hand on her sister's arm. "Elaina, I'm sorry."

Elaina brushed the hair out of her face. "I don't usually get upset until the actual day, but…well, I got some bad news and it's making everything worse." Her voice was apologetic, which broke India's heart. How long had Elaina pretended to be okay when she hurt that she felt the need to apologize for showing her feelings?

India swallowed and asked the hard question. "What news?" Had she found out about India and Travis?

Elaina's lips pressed together before she moved so that India's hand fell. "Do you think I don't know how much of a disaster it would have been if Travis and I had had kids? How it would have made the divorce even messier?"

"That doesn't take away the hurt."

Elaina pushed away from the desk. "We were done, you know. I was free to do and see whomever I wanted. Then I found out I was pregnant." She shook her head and pressed a fist against her midsection. "Neither of us wanted kids, but after our wedding, he went with me to that first appointment and he got a little excited. Then I watched that excitement disappear in his eyes. Turn into disappointment when he realized he was stuck with me." Elaina didn't sound bitter, just resigned to the fact that she'd been a disappointment.

"Is that what he said?" She couldn't believe he'd be that heartless. Even with Elaina.

"God no. He was more than supportive. That might be the worse part." Elaina let out a dry laugh. "Travis didn't want to marry me any more than I wanted to marry him, but he's honorable like that. I thought I could bring him a bit of peace in our marriage, but I couldn't even do that." She looked at India with confused eyes. "When you're trapped, it's hard to reassure the other person who's trapped with you."

"It's not your fault."

Elaina's hands clenched into fists. "I wanted to make him happy and I couldn't. Now, he's happy, and I'm not. I guess I want a little bit of that happiness, too." A tear trailed down her cheek and she quickly swiped it away. "I can't catch a damn break." Her hands balled into fists.

India's heart broke. Her sister's truth finally became clear. Elaina may not have wanted to marry Travis, but like Travis, she had wanted their family to work. Her sister wasn't good with emotions, so of course she would go back to what was familiar instead of seeking something new. Travis was the only person who'd been there for her when she'd gone through one of the worst times of her life. Elaina may not like it, but she couldn't escape that.

How can I tell her about me and Travis now?

India crossed to her sister and wrapped her arms around her in a hug instead of dwelling on the answer to that question. "Stop. Don't think about that. Don't think of any of that. It's okay."

Elaina's body was stiff, then she relaxed and hugged

India back. She didn't sob, Elaina never sobbed, but the heat of her tears soaked through India's shirt.

India wanted to hit something. Scream at the unfairness of their lives. She knew why Grant had pushed Travis to marry Elaina, but she didn't know what Grant had done to make Elaina say yes. Her sister had been trapped in that marriage, but she'd wanted to make Travis happy.

Elaina pulled away not long after she'd started crying. She swiped her eyes as if the tears annoyed her. She avoided India's gaze and went to her dresser. "Thank you for letting me blubber like that."

"I'm your sister, Elaina, you never have to apologize for letting me be there for you."

Elaina pulled out a handkerchief and wiped her eyes. "What did I say? The heart of the family. You're so perfect." She didn't say it with malice.

Still the words made guilt twist India's insides. "I'm not perfect. Elaina… I need to tell you—"

"You know what, let's do something today," Elaina said, spinning around. "I don't want to face Daddy. He knows the date is coming up and acts extra careful around me whenever it does. We've never done one of those sister days. You know, manis, pedis and stuff. We can even go by Ashiya's shop and buy something sexy. I need to be sexy. Let's do that." Her sister's abundance of enthusiasm did not hide the pleading look in her eyes. Elaina needed a distraction and out of this house.

India swallowed the guilty confession that crept into her throat. Instead she smiled and nodded. She'd do anything to keep her sister from crying like that again. Even breaking her own heart. "Sure, whatever you want, Elaina."

CHAPTER TWENTY-FIVE

THE JUDGE SLAMMED his gavel. "Court's adjourned."

The rumble of voices started as the judge stood and the jury prepared to exit the courtroom.

Zachariah slapped Travis on the back. "You just pulled a miracle out of your pocket with that closing argument."

Travis raised a brow and shook Zachariah's hand. "We'll see when the jury comes back in."

Travis was proud of the way he'd closed the case. He hadn't tried to pretend as if King was a good guy. In fact, he'd made sure to point out that a person with an imperfect life still had a right to defend themselves. Sugarcoating King's history would have only played into the hands of the prosecution. Each time they tried to bring up King's past, Travis had a counterargument. He'd defended King the best he could.

King laughed. "If they don't come back with a not-guilty verdict, then something's fucking wrong with all of them. Hell, I should get you to argue the case for me to enter heaven. Otherwise my ass is going straight to hell."

Travis forced a smile on his face. Zachariah would need a lot more than Travis arguing his case to get him into heaven. Thankfully saving Zachariah's soul wasn't what Travis was getting paid for.

"How long do you think they'll be back there?" Zachariah asked.

Travis shrugged. "Not sure. Hopefully, they won't drag this out. All we can do now is wait and see." He checked his watch. "I'm going to go back to my office and make a few calls. I won't be far if they call us back in."

He turned away from King and met the angry eyes of his dad. Mac crossed his arms and glared. Travis barely nodded his head. The looks from his family had gone from angry to don't-let-me-catch-you-on-a-dark-street furious over the course of the trial. He wasn't letting them bother him. Not much. No matter what he did, his family wouldn't accept or understand him.

He walked out of the courtroom. In the spacious atrium, his uncle Mitch, cousin Devon and other family members stood near the stairs. Travis did nod at his mother, ignored the glares of the rest of his family and walked down the stairs.

Footsteps hurried down the steps behind him. Then Devon blocked his way down the stairs. Travis suppressed a sigh and squared his shoulders.

"What do you want?" Travis asked.

Devon looked him up and down. The corner of his mouth twisted in a sneer. "You think you're going to be okay if the jury comes back with a not-guilty verdict?"

The urge to shove Devon aside, or better yet punch the shit out of him and get the fight over with flexed and raged inside Travis. Getting a rise out of him was what Devon wanted. Travis breathed in and out slowly, unclenched his fists and met Devon's stare head-on. "Yes. I will be okay." He'd already made the decision to do his job regardless of the threats from his family.

Devon's dark eyes narrowed and he leaned forward. "Don't count on that, cuz. We always get what's due to us."

"That's the same thing Antwan used to say, and look where that landed him." Travis was fed up with having to meet some standard that would have him in the same boat as his cousin.

Devon's head cocked to the side and he pointed at Travis's chest. "Oh, you think you're funny."

"No. I think I'm right." He swiped Devon's hand out of the way and brushed passed his cousin. The rumble of conversation behind him on the stairs increased. The back of Travis's neck prickled. He could hear his mother trying to calm Devon down. The scuffle of his uncle probably holding Devon back with whispers of "calm down" and "not here."

Travis didn't care. Let Devon act the fool. There were enough police in the building to ensure Devon's ass ended up in jail if he so much as tried to swing at Travis. A part of him hoped his cousin did. It would give him one less thing to worry about.

He walked out of the courtroom, got in his SUV and pulled his cell phone from the console between the seats. He didn't bring his phone into the courtroom, but today he'd longed to have it near. Only because he'd dared to ask India to marry him again. He knew what he asked of her was huge. The fallout would suck, and they'd have a mountain to climb with her family, but he wasn't about wasting time anymore. He loved her. He wanted to be in a happy marriage with someone who loved him back. He wasn't willing to wait around and hope her family would one day approve.

He was happy to see two missed calls from India.

Grinning, Travis dialed her back via Bluetooth after he turned on the car. India picked up on the fourth ring.

"Hi, Travis."

The sound of her voice blew away the tension from dealing with Devon. None of the courtroom drama seemed important knowing he had India in his life. That they would finally be together. "Did you get my message this morning?"

A heartbeat passed before she answered, "I did."

"And have you thought any more about what I said?" He put the car in gear and drove out of the parking lot onto the main road.

"Travis, do you know what's coming up?" India's voice was sharp and tight.

He did a mental scan of upcoming events. "I don't know, one of Byron's campaign events?" Where was she going with this?

Her sigh echoed in the interior of his car. "No, I mean do you know *the* date that's coming up. What *happened* on that date?"

His hand gripped the steering wheel. The only date coming up that he wasn't looking forward to was the one Elaina mentioned at the concert. The old hurt he'd compartmentalized to deal with after the trial throbbed. "Why?"

"How can you ask me to marry you knowing what's coming up?" Accusation filled her tone.

The pain of his loss didn't have anything to do with why he'd asked her to marry him. Nothing between him and Elaina had a thing to do with why he asked India to marry him. "Because when I asked you, I wasn't thinking about the pain of loss. I asked you to marry me yesterday and decided to remind you of that today."

"Elaina will be heartbroken."

"I know the day is hard for her." It was hard for him, too. Which was why he usually spent the day drowning in work. After the divorce, when he'd called to check on Elaina around that time, she'd rushed him off the phone after telling him she didn't need him to treat her with kid gloves.

"Then how can you even think about marrying me? There's so much between you and Elaina. So many reasons why we can't do this."

Travis shook his head and gripped the wheel. "India, don't do this. You know we're good together."

"Being good together doesn't erase your history with my family." The sadness in her voice was like a dagger in his stomach. "Or make the pain of us being together easier moving forward. We've got to stop."

"No, India." He'd never pleaded before, but he was ready to beg now. Not after all this time. Not when they were finally happy.

"I'm sorry, Travis," her voice trembled. "But we're done."

"India." He got no answer. "India!" His Bluetooth disconnected. She'd ended the call. He slammed his hand into the steering wheel. His throat closed up. He felt simultaneously boiling hot and freezing cold. Travis jerked at the too-tight collar of his shirt. The urge to hit something made him wish Devon had confronted him after this call.

He'd pushed too hard too soon. Talking about marriage and forever when they'd only agreed to see how things would be between them. If he hadn't put his ultimate goal on the line, she might not have bolted. He needed to figure out how to make this right.

Is there a way to make this right?

He knew his relationship with India would be difficult for Elaina. He'd never known how to make things work with Elaina. Had always felt inadequate. She bottled up her emotions, making it difficult for him to be open with his own. There was no bottling up with India. Everything was always out there in the open with them. Which was why he hadn't been able to suppress his feelings any longer.

His cell phone rang. His heart jumped until he realized someone from the office was calling instead of India. He answered and was immediately hit with fires they needed him to put out. Instead of going to search for India to try to change her mind, he went to the office. Two hours helping out the other lawyers and returning phone calls flew by until he got the call the jury had made a decision. That was faster than he'd expected.

Back at the courtroom, Zachariah's confidence from earlier had diminished. He was quiet, subdued and drummed his fingers on the desk. Queasiness plagued Travis's stomach. A quick jury decision usually meant bad news.

"All rise," the bailiff said, bringing the rustling noise of the courtroom to a halt.

Travis stood and looked at where his family sat behind the prosecutors. None of them looked at him as the judge entered the room. His uncle wore a pleased expression. His aunt clutched a handkerchief to her chest and stared hopefully at the jury. The sick feeling in his gut intensified and he looked away. Either way, his family ties were ruined.

The judge settled in his seat, then faced the jury. "Have you reached a decision?"

The lead juror stood. "We have." The bailiff took the slip of paper with Zachariah's fate written on it and passed the slip to the judge.

The judge read the paper, then nodded. "Proceed."

"On the charge of first-degree murder, we the jury find the defendant, Zachariah King, not guilty." Gasps accompanied the answer. "On the charge of second-degree murder, we find the defendant not guilty."

The strain in Zachariah's face washed away. His leg shook, and he clasped his hands into fists at his sides. One more charge to go.

"On the charge of manslaughter, we find the defendant not guilty."

More gasps and sporadic exclamations. A few people clapped, Zachariah's slim group of supporters behind them. Rumbles of conversation spread throughout the courtroom like waves.

Zachariah pumped his fist and sighed heavily. He turned and slapped Travis on the back. A wave of relief, nausea and dread crept over Travis. He'd done it. Another case won. He'd proved once again he was the best defense attorney in the area. He should be happy. Ecstatic and ready to celebrate. Instead the sick feeling he'd had before the verdict intensified.

The angry and hateful looks his family threw him as they rushed out of the courtroom snatched away any feelings of victory. He'd known this win would solidify him as the villain in the family. He hadn't expected the overwhelming cloud of defeat as the realization that he not only wouldn't be welcome, but there was also no chance of reconciliation.

He walked Zachariah out of the courtroom and tried to look pleased. The local media had quietly followed the case of the disliked local businessman charged with murder. The thought of answering questions made him want to turn and escape out the back of the courtroom.

Just get through this and you can go home. Call India. Maybe salvage one thing out of this shit of a day.

He placed a hand on Zachariah's shoulder as they left the courtroom. "Remember, let me answer the questions. You smile and nod. Don't give them anything to add to this decision."

Zachariah smiled and waved at people as they left like an Olympic hero returning home with gold. "I got it. I got it. But damn, this feels good."

A decent-size crowd waited outside the courtroom. Zachariah's wife and mother rushed forward, along with reporters. Microphones and cell phones were shoved in their faces.

"Mr. Strickland, did you expect the jury to give you the verdict you received?" the channel ten reporter asked.

"I never expect to get a verdict in my favor," Travis answered honestly. "I know I have to earn every acquittal. All I can do is defend my client to the best of my abilities and believe that the jury will understand."

"How does it feel to get a man hated by much of the community off on a murder charge?" another reporter shouted.

"Mr. King's business practices and personal life have nothing to do with this case. This is about a man defending himself when his business was threatened. My job is to defend my client, and everyone has a right to a fair trial."

Movement in the corner of his eye distracted him. Travis looked away from the next reporter to see the crowd spreading. People running. Time slowed. Devon strode toward him with purpose. His arm raised a gun in his hand. The barrel pointed directly at Travis.

Travis's entire body went numb. *No. Not like this!*

His sense of survival kicked in. "Get down!" he yelled.

The pop of gunfire exploded at the same time. People screamed. Travis turned to run too late. Pain blasted through his chest. His knees hit the ground. Pain shot up his leg. He wondered if he'd broken a kneecap before everything went black.

CHAPTER TWENTY-SIX

INDIA NEEDED TO get her mind off telling Travis they were through. Going to happy hour with Ashiya was the perfect distraction. They were settled in a corner booth at one of the bars downtown, with large glasses of wine in front of them along with an array of appetizers that included wings, potato skins and fried pickles.

"You know we're going to regret eating all of this later," India said. She picked up a potato skin and took a bite.

Ashiya picked up one of the fried pickles. "I went to the gym earlier today, so I'm good."

India laughed. "I hope you spent several hours in the gym. It's going to take that much to work off all of this food."

"Maybe, but sometimes you just have to forget the consequences and enjoy."

India chewed on the potato skin. Forget the consequences and enjoy. She'd tried do to that, and after today she knew she couldn't anymore. After hanging out with her sister, who'd quickly backed out of happy hour by saying she'd had enough "sister time," India knew two things: one, Elaina may not love Travis anymore but a part of her still cared, and two, she felt like the failure of their marriage was her fault. A part of her might even dread the day he found someone who could make him happy when she couldn't.

Elaina and Travis were divorced, but five years of memories and mutual pain would always link them. If India married him, she'd be flaunting their happiness in Elaina's face. She couldn't do that. She'd made the right decision to break things off.

Then why do you feel so terrible?

A fried pickle hit India in the forehead. She snapped out of her thoughts and looked at the appetizer that had fallen in her lap, then frowned up at Ashiya. "What was that for?"

"You looked lost in thought and you were frowning. I want to know why."

"You don't want to hear my problems." *And I don't want to hear I-told-you-so.*

"Why not? Hearing your problems is a good way to get my mind off my own."

"What are your problems?" India took another cheesy bite of the potato skin.

Ashiya wagged one finger. "Oh no, I asked you first. It's about you and Travis, isn't it? You've just spent a day with your sister and now everything is real. You should end it."

Guess she wasn't going to avoid the I-told-you-so discussion. "I have ended it," India said before Ashiya could dive into all the reasons why she and Travis needed to stop seeing each other.

Ashiya dropped the fried pickle in her hand. "You did? Why?"

"For all the reasons you brought up and more. Elaina will never forgive me for falling in love with him." India had had fun with Elaina today. It was the first time the two of them had hung out. Ever. Her sister was figuring some things out in her life, and India wanted to be there for her. Elaina wouldn't accept anything from India if she married Travis.

Ashiya picked up her wine and took a sip. "No, she wouldn't."

India sighed and ran a finger across the rim of her wineglass. "Which is why I told him no when he asked me to marry him."

Ashiya's hand slapped her chest. She swallowed hard, then coughed. "He asked you to marry him? When?"

"Last night and again this morning." Her fingers automatically reached for her cell phone on the table. She'd sneaked looks at the text message several times today. Glutton for punishment that she was.

"He meant it," Ashiya said almost to herself. She noticed India's frown and continued, "He said he wanted to marry you. That he loved you, but I thought he was just saying that to get me off his back."

Cell phone forgotten, India's gaze snapped to Ashiya. "When did he tell you that?"

"At the museum."

"I shouldn't have let things go that far." India propped her elbows on the table and covered her face with her hands. She was tired, confused and elated. "I never should have admitted to him how I feel. But we both ended up in Asheville and we talked and I convinced myself everything was okay." She dropped her hands and took a deep breath. "I just made things worse. You were right."

Ashiya tilted her head to the side. "About you and him?"

"About everything."

Ashiya shook her head. "I can't believe he asked you to marry him. Maybe he is serious. Maybe I was wrong."

"None of that matters. I've told him no. I'm breaking things off and I'm going to learn to live with that."

"Do you really think you can do that?" Ashiya asked doubtfully. "You two have had this *thing* between you for years. You going away didn't clear it up. How is it going to work now?" She sucked in a breath. Her eyes narrowed. "You're moving to California."

India shook her head. "I'm going to audition in California, but honestly, I'm thinking about the offer for the Tri-City Philharmonic. I don't want to be away from the family. Maybe running away is what made it harder to get over Travis. I was filled with dreams of what could have been. If I stay, it'll be easier to get over him."

Ashiya grunted and shook her head. "Easier to fall right back in bed with him. I don't want you to leave either, but I don't think you can get over him just because you will it so."

"I can't keep this up and I can't break my sister's heart. That's the end of it." India picked up her glass of wine and took a long sip. "Now, can we please talk about something else? Today has been too heavy and I don't want to dwell on it."

Ashiya looked like she was about to argue.

India narrowed her eyes and glared. "New topic."

Ashiya held up a hand. "Fine, for now." She lifted her glass. "To forbidden promises and the impulse to make them."

India chuckled and raised a glass. "Amen to that."

They clinked glasses and finished off their drinks. She thought about Ashiya's phone call with the guy who wasn't Stephen weeks ago. Was her cousin also following impulses and making promises she couldn't keep?

"How's Stephen?" India asked.

Ashiya rolled her eyes. "The same. If we're not talking about Travis, can we not talk about me and Stephen? I'd rather discuss baseball."

"You hate baseball."

"How about those Braves," Ashiya said with false cheer. She caught the eye of the waitress and pointed to their two empty wineglasses. "Another round."

Point taken. India let her cousin change the subject. They talked, ate and laughed some more. A band set up and played a few songs. When a crowd got up and danced, India let Ashiya drag her out on the floor. Anything to forget her worries and facing Travis later. Telling him no on the phone had been easy. How could she possibly do so to his face?

By the time they left the bar, it was almost nine. India turned her cell phone on when she got in the car. She knew Travis would call as soon as he got out of court. She'd been a coward and avoided his calls. Her cell phone rang, vibrated and chimed constantly in the seconds after it powered on. Before she could check the various notifications, her phone rang again. Byron's number.

"Hey Byron, is everything okay?"

"No. I'm at the hospital. Travis was shot."

INDIA RAN INTO the hospital. Byron had given her Travis's room number over the phone. She punched the buttons next to the elevator and stopped herself from beating on the doors to make them open faster. She bounced on the balls of her feet as she waited for the people to file off and then for others to get on with her.

Please let him be alive. Please let him be alive.

Fear and stress put the words on repeat in her brain during the long ride to the fourth floor. The fingers of her right hand tapped anxiously against her chest. When the doors finally opened on her floor, she rushed out and down the hall toward the nurses' station.

"India, wait," Byron's voice called.

She spun around. Her brother stood outside a waiting area. She ran to him. "What happened?"

Byron's shirt was unbuttoned at the top, his tie loose around his neck. There was strain around his eyes and he hugged India tight. "Travis won the case! His cousin, Devon, wasn't happy with the verdict," he said after releasing her. "The bullet hit him in the upper chest, but thankfully, Travis was turning and it missed his heart. He's been out of surgery and is in recovery. They're moving him to a private room as we speak."

Her head spun. "His cousin shot him?" He'd feared his family wouldn't be happy with the verdict, but to try to kill him?

"Apparently there had been threats from his family during the trial," Byron said as if reading her thoughts. "Threats Travis didn't tell anyone about."

"Why would he keep something like that to himself?" India rubbed her temples. Her head throbbed.

"We both know how Travis is with his family," Byron said, rubbing her shoulders. "He probably didn't think the threats were real."

Her hands shook. "He's okay though, right?"

Byron didn't nod. "For now. The bullet did cause

damage, and he lost a lot of blood. The doctors say they'll know more when he wakes up."

She looked around the waiting room. No one from Travis's family was there. The realization didn't surprise her, but it did anger her. "Where are Daddy and Elaina?"

"Dad was out of town on business. He's on the way back. I haven't been able to reach Elaina since finding out. Was she at home?"

After she left India and Ashiya, Elaina hadn't said she was going back out that night. "I don't know. I wasn't home. I was with Ashiya. When I left Elaina, she was going by the office to check on some things."

A woman in blue scrubs came from behind double doors and walked over to them. "That's the recovery nurse," Byron said.

The woman stopped in front of them. "Mr. Robidoux, Travis is in his own room now. He's asleep but if you want to check in on him, that's fine. Just keep it to a few minutes."

Byron shook her hand. "Thank you."

He and India left the waiting area and got back on the elevator to Travis's new room one floor up. India's heart beat erratically as they got to Travis's door. Her chest constricted when they saw him in the bed. He was still. Too still, with a gray pallor beneath his dark skin. Tears pricked India's eyes. He'd almost died.

Byron went over and placed his hand over Travis's. He shook his head and pinched the bridge of his nose. India hurried over and placed her hand on his back. She shook with the force of not breaking from the fear and hurt slicing inside of her.

"I've got to get out of here," Byron said in a strained voice. "I can't see him like this."

He turned and stalked out of the room. India didn't care about comforting her brother. As soon as he was gone, she sank onto the side of the bed. Her body trembled uncontrollably, the terror of the minutes between answering Byron's call and getting to the hospital catching up to her. She picked up the hand not pierced with the IV. It was cool to the touch. India bit her lower lip and suppressed a sob. Her eyes jumped to his chest. It rose and fell with his easy breaths. She relaxed slightly. He was alive. She'd almost lost him.

If he had died—

She cut the thought short and clutched his hand to her chest. "Travis, I'm so sorry. Why didn't you tell any of us how angry your family was? Maybe we could have done something." Tears rolled down her cheeks. "I could have lost you today." He would have died thinking she didn't love him. India shook her head. "I didn't mean it, when I said I wanted us to be over. I love you. I don't know how or if we can make this work, but I want to try. I love you so much." She brought his hand to her lips and swallowed a sob. "I'll marry you."

A gasp followed by a crash came from the door. India jerked up. Her wet eyes met the wide shocked eyes of her sister.

"Marry him? Love him?" Elaina asked in a tight voice. She shook her head. "You're sleeping with my ex-husband!"

CHAPTER TWENTY-SEVEN

ELAINA TURNED AND ran from the door of the hospital room. India hurried after. Her feet slipped in the pile of water and broken glass from the flowers Elaina had dropped. She steadied herself on the door, then continued. In the hall she watched as Elaina pushed past their dad and Byron on her way to the elevator.

"Elaina, stop," India called.

Her dad reached for her arm. "What are you two doing?"

India avoided his grip and her brother's gaze. She had to explain to Elaina. The elevator hadn't opened yet, which allowed India to catch up to her sister.

"Let me explain," India said.

Elaina whipped to face her, her gaze as sharp as razor blades. "Are you or are you not sleeping with my ex-husband?" she asked in a crisp, haughty tone.

India flinched and ran a hand over her face. "It's not like that."

"Then what is it like? You said you were going to marry him!" Elaina's voice rose.

India shook her head. "No, listen, let me explain."

Elaina pointed down the hall. "There's only one thing to explain. Did he ask you to marry him?"

Oh God, this was not how this was supposed to go! "He did. I said no but, Elaina, I almost lost him."

"You almost lost him?" Elaina's voice was incredulous. "He wasn't yours to lose!"

Guilt slapped India in the face. The picture of Travis in the hospital bed hit back. She didn't want to fight Elaina, but she couldn't keep hiding the way she felt about him anymore. She couldn't keep this secret anymore.

"Stop this foolishness right now." Grant's low angry voice cracked like a whip. He and Byron had come over to the elevators. "You will not make fools of yourselves fighting over this in the middle of a hospital."

Elaina's eyes flashed. "She's sleeping with Travis."

"You think I don't know this already?" Grant said in a hushed voice.

Elaina's eyes widened. Betrayal and pain flashed in them as she looked between India and their father.

India sucked in a breath. *He knew!* How?

The elevator doors opened. Their dad pointed to the empty car. "Get in there now. We'll work this out at home."

He spoke to them like they were kids. Obediently, India and Elaina complied. Elaina went to the back corner of the elevator. India settled in the opposite corner. Their dad and Byron entered next. Byron looked between the two of them, then his eyes focused on India.

"Is this true?" Byron shook his head as if he couldn't believe what he was hearing.

India couldn't believe this was how things were coming out. The betrayal in her sister's eyes made her want to cry, but she also ached to go back to Travis's side. "It's not what it looks like," she said again.

"It looks like I can't trust you," Elaina spat.

She had no comeback for that. "We tried to ignore our feelings for each other."

Elaina crossed her arms. "Obviously you failed."

"That's enough," Grant's voice boomed. "We'll discuss this at home."

There was silence after that. India tried to ignore Byron's disbelieving looks. Elaina wouldn't turn her way. Her sister stood stiffly, with her arms crossed beneath her breasts, her face a cold mask of fury.

They were all in separate vehicles, so the ride home gave India a chance to think about what she would say and explore her feelings. She hated hurting her sister. The day they'd just spent together, shopping, getting mani-pedis and actually laughing about inconsequential things was the most sisterly bonding they'd ever had. She'd had fun and believed Elaina had, too. They would never get that connection back. She and Elaina had never been very close, their personalities were too different, but they had supported one another, and she loved her sister.

What happened between India and Travis probably shouldn't have. If they'd kept their distance, or never spent that one night together on her birthday, maybe they never would have become anything more than friends. But they *had* spent that time together. They had kissed, and they had realized something deeper and stronger simmered underneath the friendship. Ashiya was right. Could what they felt be short-lived if it was still there after all these years?

She'd run away from her feelings for too long. Life was fleeting and could be snatched away like a snap of a finger. Maybe her family believed things would fizzle out after a few months, but India didn't. She'd loved him before she'd left, and her feelings hadn't changed. She didn't want to go another seven years, hell, the rest of her life, pretending.

They arrived at the house around the same time. No one spoke as they entered. Sandra took one look at their angry faces and turned around. They went directly to the upstairs family room. Elaina crossed over to the bar and mini fridge where she pulled out a bottle of wine. Byron followed and grabbed the whiskey. India went over to the bookshelf and stared at the rows of family pictures and accomplishments.

Grant closed the door, then stood in the center of the room. "Now, India, will you explain what's going on between you and Travis?"

India didn't turn to face them. She stared at Travis and Elaina's wedding picture. She'd been so upset that day. Believing Travis had toyed with her. That he hadn't felt anything for her.

The time for secrets was over. "What's happening between us now is exactly what would have happened years ago if you hadn't told him to stay away from me and marry Elaina," India said evenly.

"What?" A thump India suspected was the wine bottle hitting the bar accompanied Elaina's outburst.

"Are you serious?" Byron said at the same time.

India turned around and met her dad's gaze. She needed the whole story. "Why did you do that?"

"You expect me to sit around and watch him move on to my baby girl after he knocked up your sister?" Grant said, matter-of-fact. "I don't regret my decision and if I had to make it again, I'd do the same thing."

Elaina came around the bar and glared at India. "Are

you telling me," she said slowly, "that you and Travis have been sleeping together for years?"

"No!" India yelled. She took a slow breath and told her sister the truth. "But on my twenty-first birthday, we kissed. That's all. Nothing else happened, but I loved him then."

"Your birthday…" Elaina's brows drew together. "That was right when we found out."

"You two had broken up."

"That makes it better," Elaina accused. Her eyes sharp as flint.

"I'm not saying it does, but you originally turned down his proposal," India countered. "If you still wanted him, why did you say no?"

"Because I didn't want to marry him," Elaina said immediately. She drew back and frowned, then faced their dad. "You told me I had to. You said I'd played his whore for too long. That if I wanted any chance at redeeming myself and running your company that I'd clean up my mess. You pushed me into it and knew he was interested in India?"

Grant squared his shoulders and raised his chin. "He didn't deserve India."

"Why? Because your baby girl is too precious for the kid from the wrong side of the tracks?" Elaina tossed back.

"I wasn't going to watch him move on to your sister while you had his baby," Grant argued. "We weren't going to be some damn daytime talk show entertainment for the town."

"Don't talk like that," India said.

Elaina shook her head and faced India. "Oh no, don't deflect to Daddy. Let's be very honest with each other.

Let's talk about right now. Let's talk about how you thought it was okay to sleep with Travis."

"It's not about sex," India shot back. "I love him. Jesus, he almost died today. I can't continue pretending as if I don't care for him. He wanted to tell you, all of you, about us."

Elaina sliced her hand through the air. "I will never be okay with this."

The vehemence in Elaina's voice silenced India for several beats. Embarrassment and guilt burned her cheeks. She felt foolish for hoping Elaina would feel differently once she knew the truth. "Is it because you want him back?"

"I don't want him back, but that doesn't mean I want to see *you* married to him. To watch you flaunt your sick relationship in front of everyone and pretend as if it's okay. No, you do this, and I'll never forgive you."

"Elaina, don't be that way. I never meant to hurt you. That's why I didn't want to stay long, but we just—"

"Started sleeping together and decided fucking each other wasn't enough. Let's get married and really make a fool out of your sister." Elaina's voice shook with fury.

"Elaina," their dad snapped. "Watch your language."

She pointed at Grant. "No, I won't watch my language." The anger in Elaina's gaze burned like wildfire. "This entire family is screwed up. You never should have pushed me into marrying Travis knowing how he felt. I'll never forgive you for that. None of us would be here if you wouldn't have tried to preserve your perfect Robidoux family empire."

Elaina pushed past Grant and stomped out of the room. The door slammed behind her. India looked at the door. Her stomach rolled as if she were on a ship in the middle of a storm, the clash of emotions and confessions crashing into each other like thunder.

Her hand shook. Her heart pumped furiously. Was this what she wanted? Was being with Travis worth the anger in her sister's eyes?

"Do you see what you've done?" Grant asked.

She was more than clear on what she'd done. As much as she wanted to go away and pretend this never happened, she couldn't. "I'm not running away this time. We aren't letting you dictate what we do."

Their dad pointed at Byron quietly sipping his whiskey at the bar. "And what about your brother's campaign? Don't you think this scandal will ruin him?"

Byron downed the last of his drink. He sighed and spun the glass. "This won't kill my campaign," he said quietly. "Not if we play it right."

Grant took several steps toward Byron. "You can't seriously be thinking of supporting them."

Byron looked at India. "I thought Travis was seeing someone. He was happy. I haven't seen him that happy…ever. Why didn't you tell me?"

"He wanted to say something immediately, but I asked him to wait until after the primaries. I knew this wouldn't go over well." Understatement of the century.

Byron nodded and spun the glass again. "I'd rather handle the way we announce this than force you two apart." He walked over and kissed her forehead. "If this is what you want, then I wish you both well." His smile didn't quite reach his eyes, but sincerity was there. India wrapped her arms around him and hugged tight. Tears blurred her vision. At least she had Byron on her side.

"Byron, you can't be serious," Grant said.

Byron let India go and met their dad's gaze with a

determined stare. "I am. We've accepted Patricia. We can accept this." His voice held an edge of steel she'd never heard before.

Their dad's face tightened. He looked at India. "He's not right for you."

"You don't get the chance to make that decision," India countered. "I don't think Patricia is right for you, but if you want me to be okay with that, then I need you to be okay with this. You said yourself we can't help who we fall in love with. It's not always convenient or easy, but neither is life."

Grant's jaw clenched. He rolled his shoulders and tapped his toe. They had him. He couldn't argue about convenience when he insisted they accept Patricia.

Their father pointed at the door. "And what about Elaina? Are you ready to lose your sister for him?"

India lowered her eyes. She had no argument for that. As much as she wanted Travis, deep down she knew she'd never be able to handle Elaina hating her forever. "I'll talk to her tomorrow. Maybe she'll be okay in the morning."

CHAPTER TWENTY-EIGHT

THE FIRST THING Travis felt was the dull ache of pain. Dull, he was pretty sure, thanks to anesthesia. He knew exactly where he was. He didn't have a moment of wondering what had happened and why.

He'd been confused in the middle of the night when he'd woken alone in the dark hospital room. That had been fucked up. When the memory of what happened rushed through him—the gunshot, waking up in an ambulance and flashes of lights in a hospital room— he'd hoped someone would have been there with him.

Someone was with him now though. Brighter light glowed behind his closed lids, the television was on, and a soft hand clasped his. The anxiety, sadness and fear from the night before dissipated. A smile crept up on his lips. India.

There was a gasp, and she shuffled next to him, her hand tightened on his.

She'd come. She hadn't meant what she said. They weren't over. "India." The hoarse croak of his voice would have made a bullfrog flinch.

Her hand stiffened and slowly pulled away. "Sorry to disappoint you. It's the other sister."

Elaina? What the hell was she doing there? Where was India? He slowly cracked open his eyes. It took a few seconds to adjust to the light. He turned and focused until Elaina's cool expression cleared in his view.

"Elaina? Here to finish me off?" he asked with a twist of his lips.

The corner of her mouth tilted up. "Maybe I should."

Good ole Elaina. "What are you doing here? Is the rest of your family here?" Was India nearby?

She sat stiffly, back straight, shoulders tight. "No. I left early to see you before work."

"Before work?" Travis looked at the clock on the wall. Just after 6:00 a.m. Why was she here so early?

"Yes. I want to talk to you without others around. Before things become even more crazy than they were the night before."

Things had gotten crazy the night before? He barely remembered being in recovery. The first memory after surgery was being alone in the hospital room. He'd wanted India.

"What did you want to talk about?" he asked.

"Why did you marry me? You didn't have to go through with it. We both know we could have worked things out without getting married."

The campaign. Why his family shot him. If he was planning to pick up ballet after getting out of the hospital. He would have expected Elaina to ask any of those things. Not the reason he'd proposed.

"You've never asked me that before."

"I never wanted to hear the truth before," she said simply. "Will you tell me the truth?"

Travis met her eyes. She looked like someone waiting for a slap in the face they knew was coming. What the hell happened the night before? "Does it matter?"

Elaina folded her hands in her lap. "I think it does. Especially since you've asked my sister to marry you."

Travis closed his eyes. His head fell back on the pillow. How had she found out? Had India told her? If so, had India changed her mind? The pain of the guilt that hit him was only second to the gunshot wound. He should have told Elaina straight up. She deserved to have heard it from him.

"She told you."

"Not directly. Her clinging to your hand, crying and saying she loves you and will marry you kind of let the cat out of the bag." Elaina's voice was dry and sarcastic, but Travis didn't miss the flash of discomfort in her eyes.

India had been there. A tightness in his chest unrelated to the bullet hole released. He'd feared she really didn't love him when he hadn't seen her. Finally, things were out in the open. "I wanted to tell you from the start."

"Yeah, well, I guess it's never a good time to tell your ex-wife that you really love her younger sister."

She was deflecting with sarcasm. He'd hated when she did that. He could never get a straight answer out of her. Never knew how she really felt.

"I know we could have raised our child without being married. But when your father accused me of using you, I thought about my dad. I always said if I have a kid, I'd be better than he was with me. When I told Grant I'd do right by you and handle my responsibilities, I thought I had to be all in to do that."

"But when you asked, you knew you had feelings for India."

No need to lie. "Yes."

She looked him in the eye. "Did you sleep with her while we were together?"

"No. I never saw her, and I never would have done that to you. When I said I do, I was committed to you."

She closed her eyes and took a deep breath. When she opened them, her posture relaxed. "I believe you. That was the thing about you, you always did try to make it work."

"When India came back, I'd hoped we could be friends. I thought we'd both moved on, and at first we were okay as friends."

"Then you were both overcome with emotion. It's all really romantic, I guess."

He didn't want her to think this was a game, or that they'd wanted to hurt her. He wished he could make this easier for her. The truth was, nothing about what came next would be easy.

Travis tried to sit up. The dull pain increased, and he sat back. His hand sought out the controls on the side of his bed and he pressed the button to lift the head of the bed.

"Elaina, do you really think we would have wanted to do this? Not because Byron's in the middle of a campaign, but because neither of us wanted to hurt you."

"Do you really love her? I mean with your whole heart and soul and all that other nonsense people talk about in books, movies and songs. Tell me honestly this isn't just lust or an itch or finishing what you started before you thought marrying me was a good idea."

"It's not. I don't want to hurt you, Elaina, but I love India. She's always been the person I could talk to and laugh with. She's the person I want to talk to about my day, the person I never want to see cry, the person I want to make smile for the rest of her life. She's everything to me." He thought about how upset she'd been when she'd called him yesterday and said things were over. How much she didn't want to hurt her sister. "If she says she can't be with me because it will tear you two apart, then I'd accept that. India loves you and I won't be the reason you two hate each other."

A sheen of moisture coated Elaina's eyes. She looked away quickly and stood. She avoided his gaze by walking over to the tray with a plastic pitcher on it beneath the television and pouring water into a paper cup. "You certainly sound sincere."

"I am sincere."

She returned and held out the cup of water. Any hint of moisture in her eyes gone. "I know you wouldn't have purposefully tried to seduce India. You're a good guy, deep down."

That was the first compliment she'd given him in years. He appreciated her honesty. Appreciated she knew that much about him.

He took the cup from her. "What are we going to do?"

She lifted her chin. "We're going to announce your engagement to India. We're going to act as if this is all normal and perfectly okay. We're going to avoid causing any ripples that may cost Byron the election or weaken Robidoux Tobacco. We're going to be one big happy family and give no one any hint this development is in any way unwanted, unexpected or unsavory."

"Why?" He had to ask. The brittle tone of her voice revealed she wasn't happy with the decision.

"Because you love her, and India has such a big heart. Even though I'm furious with her, I don't want her to become bitter. I'd rather her be happy and loved than forced into a relationship with someone she doesn't care about. We both know those types of relationships are disasters."

"You'd be okay doing that?"

She picked up her purse. "I am okay doing that, because it's what needs to be done. Don't worry, Travis. I'm angry about not knowing the truth, and it'll take a while to get used to the idea, but my heart is bruised, not broken. I've lived with so many disappointments I think it's gotten used to taking a beating." She smiled sadly and went out the door.

CHAPTER TWENTY-NINE

INDIA HAD TO get through three security and ID checks before she was finally let onto the top floor of Robidoux Tobacco. When she'd gotten to her sister's floor, she'd been directed to sit in a hard, gray chair in the waiting area outside of Elaina's office. Elaina was there. Her administrative assistant had already called and informed her of India's arrival twenty-five minutes ago.

Coming here had been a risk. Elaina could have flat out refused to see her. Maybe that's what she really wanted to do, but the potential for gossip kept her from kicking her sister out.

India had wanted to go straight to the hospital and check on Travis. She was dying to know how he was doing. Had he woken up? Had anyone in his family come to see him? Did he remember what she'd said? Did he still want to marry her?

She hadn't gone to him. She needed to talk to Elaina first. Last night, after the adrenaline and fear of Travis nearly being killed wore off, all she could think about was Elaina. The look of betrayal in Elaina's face was something she'd never forget. India loved Travis, but Elaina was her sister. Their dad wouldn't always be there. One day he would die—kicking, screaming and fighting the grim reaper, but the day would come.

Elaina and Byron would be all she had left. She didn't want to lose her family over this.

The administrative assistant's phone rang. She brought the sleek black receiver to her ear. "Yes, Ms. Robidoux, thank you." She hung up and looked at India. "She will see you now."

"Thank you." India tried to smile, but her stomach was a jumble of nerves. *How do you apologize for breaking your sister's heart?*

She entered, and Elaina sat perfectly behind her desk. Her hands folded on top of the desk while she watched India enter with cool, impenetrable eyes. India crossed over and sat in the chair across from her sister.

"I didn't expect to see you," Elaina said.

"We need to talk. You weren't home when I got up."

"I had an early appointment. Have you been to see Travis? Is that why you're here?"

India frowned and shook her head. "No. I haven't been to see him."

Elaina's brows rose. "Why not? I thought you'd have rushed to be by his side. Don't you want to know how he's doing?"

She did, but this was more important. "I need to apologize to you."

"For falling in love with Travis?" Elaina's tone implied India was being ridiculous.

"For everything. Falling in love with him. Not telling you what happened between us before you got married. Not telling you how I feel."

"How can I blame you for that? It's practically part of our family motto to keep our real feelings to ourselves."

India shifted forward in her seat. "That doesn't matter. You two may have broken up, but regardless of the circumstances, I shouldn't have crossed that line. I'm sorry. I love you."

Elaina's mouth tilted up slightly. "I know you love me. I know this is killing you. The pain you feel for me is practically written all over your face. You really need to work on not showing all of your emotions."

"Elaina, please don't make light of this. I want to make this better. I broke things off with Travis yesterday before he was..." Her throat constricted and tears burned her eyes. She blinked rapidly. He was alive. He'd be okay. "Before the accident. I want you to know that if this is going to tear you and me apart—"

Elaina slapped her hands on her desk and leaned forward. "You're giving him up?"

India blinked several times. "What?" The frustration in Elaina's voice was the biggest surprise.

"Why would you do that?"

Why? That was not the reaction she expected. "Because being with him breaks us. Last night you said you'd never be okay with us together," India said, even though Elaina's reaction almost made her doubt her own memory. "You're my sister. We aren't always on the same page, but I want to find a way through this."

"You'd really let him go for me?" Elaina sounded as if the notion of India giving up Travis for her was ludicrous.

India didn't want to let Travis go. She'd rather find a way to give Elaina time to get used to the idea, but if Elaina needed a break from her, if she needed space, then India would give it. "I'd really do whatever it takes to keep our family together."

"But you said you love him. Do you not love him anymore?"

With everything in me. "I do love him, but I love you, too. You're my sister. I hope one day you'll forgive me."

Elaina rolled her eyes and sat back. "My God, you're so dramatic. People say I'm like Daddy, but here you are preaching family sticking together. I don't want you to give up Travis for me."

"But last night you were angry." Last night India wouldn't have been surprised if Elaina had sneaked into her room and tried to smother her with a pillow.

"Yes. Last night I was angry. Angry that I didn't see what was right in front of my face."

"You knew…"

"Not that he was sleeping with you. You've always been closer to him. Travis and I were never in love. We were doing something fun and forbidden, and because we were reckless, we ended up in a…delicate situation. But you two…you two actually had something."

"That doesn't mean I should be with him."

"Maybe you shouldn't, but I'm not going to be the person to tell you to stay away from him. We'll spin this and make it work. We can't disturb Byron's campaign, so I agree with your idea of waiting until after the primaries, and I won't watch you try to avoid being around Travis without your heart breaking. Jesus, you two would drive me crazy. Pining for each other with unrequited love. Me, the evil sister who stood in the way of true happiness."

"You aren't evil. You not wanting us together is understandable."

"I don't feel things the way you feel them. But I do love you," Elaina said succinctly. "Please, go to him. Be with the man who should have always been yours."

She couldn't believe the Elaina in front of her was the same Elaina who'd breathed fire the night before.

"Are you sure?" Could her sister really be okay with this? Was Elaina actually giving her blessing?

"I'm more than sure. Now please, go to the hospital." Elaina waved a hand toward the door. "I've got a lot of work today, and I can't sit here and watch you try to make a martyr out of yourself over something that I really don't care that much about."

Elaina stood and walked around the desk. India stood as well and followed Elaina to the door. "I'll be working late, but we can talk more later."

India wrapped her arms around Elaina. Her sister was stiff in her arms. Caught off guard by India's show of affection. "Elaina… I can't tell you how much this means to me."

Elaina relaxed slightly. Her hand patted India's back. "Please, let's not make a big deal out of this. I'm still mad you didn't tell me, but I'm going to be okay with you two together."

India pulled back. Tears clouding her vision. The day before with Elaina was the closest they'd ever been. Even though she'd given her blessing, India knew she and Elaina would never have another day doing "sister stuff" again.

"Please don't cry," Elaina reprimanded. "You're always so emotional. No wonder you're in love. You've got too much heart."

India wiped her eyes. "You have heart, too, Elaina. I love you."

Elaina's eyes shimmered. She blinked and turned away to open the door. "I've really got a lot to do."

India left her sister's office. A bittersweet joy filled her heart as she left the building for her car. Her life was changed forever and she was excited about the future.

CHAPTER THIRTY

"Where do you think you're going?" India said to Travis.

She rushed across his living room and gently eased him back onto the pile of pillows behind him on the couch. She'd walked out for just a few minutes to check on the meat loaf she was preparing. She hadn't cooked in years but remembered meat loaf was one of Travis's favorite meals. So far she hadn't burned anything or had any major kitchen mishaps. When she'd left, he'd been about to doze off. Now he was trying to push himself up.

"The doctors said it was okay for me to get up and move around," he said, humor shining in his eyes.

She placed her hand on his shoulder and tried to ease him back down. "For a little bit and only if you really need to."

Travis laughed. "I've got to go to the bathroom."

She looked down the hall toward the door to the powder room, then back to the couch. She should have insisted he stay in bed. The bathroom was much closer to his bed upstairs. What if he fell and opened his stitches? He could bleed out all over the floor and die on her watch before an ambulance ever arrived.

"Hey." Travis cupped her cheek gently in his hands. He forced her to meet his eyes. "I'm okay. You don't have to worry." His voice was calm, soothing and full of understanding.

She knew he was okay. He'd survived with minimal damage. He was already itching to go back to work. His cousin had been arrested. His family hadn't been able or willing to pay his bond. There were no direct threats on his life. Still, the memory of almost losing him…of her plans to give him up after he'd been shot, of never seeing him again…

"I know. I just don't want you to break your stitches."

He leaned forward and brushed his lips across hers. "I'm not. Did I ever tell you how cute I think it is that you've moved in to take care of me?"

"Someone's got to make sure you don't start lifting weights and overexerting yourself."

She wasn't officially moved in. In the aftermath of everything, her family asked for her and Travis to keep their relationship out of the public eye until after the primary election. After watching Travis recover, India didn't want to pretend anymore, but for her family's acceptance of her and Travis together, it was a concession she was willing to take.

Travis shifted forward so he could stand. Even though he didn't need her help to move around anymore, he didn't shoo her away when she placed her hand on his elbow to try to guide his movements. "Do you know how happy I am that you're the one taking care of me?"

She smiled and relaxed. "Well, it was me or Camille, and I really didn't feel like scratching out eyeballs."

Camille had come by the hospital to visit Travis. India arrived right as she made the offer to nurse him. Travis firmly told her he didn't need any assistance.

India believed Camille finally got the hint there would be no rebounding with her and left shortly after.

Travis chuckled and kissed her again. "Everything is fine. We're fine. I survived, and I will live a very long time, God willing. It's okay for us to be happy."

India closed her eyes and let out a slow breath. When she opened them, she felt calmer. She'd never forget the fear that clutched her heart after hearing Travis was shot, but she was going to appreciate every damn day they had together from here on out.

"I know," she said. "But I may need you to tell me that again later on."

"I'll be happy to." He nodded toward the hall. "Now, can I go to the bathroom?"

She scrunched her brow as if thinking about it. Travis gave her a don't-play-with-me look. She laughed and stepped back. "Yes. Go on and be careful."

She watched him walk steadily and surely to the bathroom. He was recovering quickly, but he was still in pain. The doctors had once again told him how lucky he was the shot hadn't been a little more to the left. Though Travis said he understood he'd lost a lot of blood and needed to take it easy, he was also a man used to being active. Sitting around waiting for others to do things for him made him irritable. Except when it came to her. He seemed not only grateful but amazed she'd left the estate to be with him.

Honestly, there was no place she'd rather be.

The doorbell rang shortly after Travis disappeared into the bathroom. He'd gotten a constant stream of visitors since returning home. Friends, clients, neighbors all wanted to wish him well, drop off a casserole or just check in while blatantly trying to get the story about why Travis's cousin shot him. Visitors that were noticeably absent: his family. He hadn't said anything, but India knew his family's lack of concern bothered him.

Which made it even more surprising to open the door and find Travis's mother standing on the other side.

"Mrs. Strickland, what are you doing here?" The words were out before India could consider how they might sound. Yeah, it might be rude to ask a mother why she'd come by her son's home, but only if the mother had bothered to visit any other time. Travis's parents hadn't shown up in the hospital or called after the incident.

"I came to see Travis," she said. Her lips tightened and she looked at India as if she came to visit Travis once a week instead of when hell froze over. "Can I come in?"

India glanced over her shoulder toward the car. "Are you here alone?" She didn't see anyone in the car. She eyed the woman's bag, which was large enough to hold a gun.

Mrs. Strickland sighed. "I'm not here to finish what my sorry excuse for a nephew started," she said irritably, as if she'd read India's thoughts. "I just want to check on my son."

India studied her for several seconds. She didn't want anything to upset Travis, but she knew he'd want to hear whatever it was his mom came to say. India nodded and stepped back. "Come on in."

Juanita stepped over the threshold and looked around. India didn't have to ask if it was her first time in Travis's home. She led his mom farther into the house, toward the living room.

Travis came back down the hall as they walked into

the living room. He froze midstep. Staring at his mom with the same wariness India had at the door.

"Mom. What are you doing here?" His voice was guarded.

Juanita rolled her shoulders. "I can't come check on my son? You're just as bad as her." She pointed to India.

"It's not as if you've visited me before." His voice remained cool, but India noticed the stiffness in his shoulders. She went to his side. She wanted to take his hand, but she didn't know his family and obviously couldn't trust them not to let the entire town know she and Travis were together. She guessed Travis understood because he shifted closer to her.

"Well, you'd never been shot before," Juanita snapped. She nodded toward one of the end chairs. "Can I sit down?"

"Yes," Travis said stiffly.

India glanced at Travis. "Do you want me to give you some space?"

He shook his head. "No, you can stay," he said before focusing on Juanita. "So, why are you really here?"

Juanita sat in the end chair. "To check on you. Your dad didn't want me to come, but here I am." At first she sounded defensive, but when Travis winced as he lowered to the couch seat, her tone and face softened. "I swear I had nothing to do with Mitch's boy shooting you. I've told Mitch not to come around anymore. We may have our differences, but you're still my son. I know things have been rough, but I don't want you dead." She lifted her chin. "I'm sorry. I'd like to come see you more often, if that's okay."

India and Travis both stared at his mom. India remembered the stories Travis told about his family. For years

Juanita never went against his dad when he'd pushed Travis away. India had seen the hurt he tried to hide as he talked about his family. She hoped this wasn't some sort of joke, because if it was, India would go to hell and back to make sure his family never got to him again.

Travis cleared his throat. "Does Dad know you're here?"

Juanita gave a stiff nod. "He does."

"And what does he have to say about this?"

"He doesn't think I should be here. He's stubborn," Juanita answered, straightening her back.

"I know."

Juanita glanced at India as if looking for a way to get through Travis's monotone responses. India just stared back. If Juanita wanted to fix this, she'd do it on her own.

"Believe it or not," Juanita said, "he thinks Mitch and Devon went too damn far."

"Did he say that?" Travis asked skeptically.

"He did. He was afraid you were dead. Give him time. He'll come around," Juanita said softly.

They sat in silence for several heartbeats. Unable to help herself, India placed her hand on Travis's back and rubbed. She didn't care if Juanita gossiped. She couldn't let Travis go through this without knowing he had her support. No matter the decision.

"If you want to come around…I won't turn you away," he said slowly as if he couldn't believe he was making the admission. "Dad's another story. I don't want to see him. Not for a while."

His mom nodded. "I understand." She looked around and her shoulders relaxed. "You've got a really nice place. You have done well for yourself."

Travis shifted and shrugged. "Umm…we were just about to eat. You're welcome to stay."

Juanita said she couldn't stay long, but she did ask Travis about his recovery. India left them alone and went into the kitchen to finish dinner. When she came out of the kitchen, Juanita was gone. Travis sat on the edge of the sofa with his head in his hands. India immediately rushed to his side.

"What happened? What's wrong? Did she say something? I swear, if she said something to hurt you—"

Travis let out a surprised laugh and raised his head. His eyes were wet. "She said she loves me." He sounded astonished. "I don't think she's said that since I was little."

India's heart squeezed. "Travis…" She didn't know what to say. The wary hope in his eyes brought tears to her own.

"Do you think…after all this time… I don't know if I can believe her." He shook his head.

India wrapped an arm around his shoulder. "One day at a time. That's all we can do."

He smiled and faced her. He kissed her so hard they were both breathless when they came up for air. "I love you, India. Thank you for being here for me. And, thank you for being willing to toss my mom out if she hadn't come in peace."

She grinned and wiped the lone tear that leaked from his eye. "There's no need to thank me. Just promise me you won't get shot again."

He pulled her closer. "Not if I can help it. I need a lifetime with you."

CHAPTER THIRTY-ONE

"I THINK WE can call it!" Byron's campaign manager, Roy, yelled out to the crowd of supporters.

Cheers went up. Streamers and confetti fell like multicolored snow over the people in the downtown restaurant where Byron waited for the primary results. Projected on the walls were the numbers from the polls. Byron was up by 54 percent and most of the polls were closed.

India joined in with the cheers. Her brother had done it. He was one step closer to making his way to the Senate and she couldn't be prouder of him.

Elaina was next to her. She raised a champagne glass as Byron went on the stage set up at the front of the restaurant and hugged Roy. She turned to India and placed a hand on her arm. "I'm going to go up there with him."

"Go ahead. I'll wait until things die down to congratulate him," India replied.

Elaina nodded, then wove through the crowd to the stage. In the eight weeks since everything had come to a head, she'd expected things to be strained between her and Elaina. They weren't. Elaina either really didn't care about India and Travis being together, or she was a supreme actress. The thing was, India couldn't really tell when it came to Elaina. She was just glad her sister didn't hate her.

A hand pressed against the small of her back. Travis. She'd know his touch anywhere. "Your brother did it."

Her body sizzled where he touched her. They were no longer hiding their relationship with the family, but they were keeping things under wraps publicly. They'd agreed to not steal the focus from Byron during the primary run, but not being with Travis in public was hard.

"I know. I'm so proud of him." She leaned in closer to Travis.

"I am, too. He seemed worried earlier tonight."

"About the election?" She'd noticed Byron had seemed a little off, as well.

Travis's hand rubbed her back. Tingles went through her body. "No, something else is going on, but he and Roy are keeping it close to their chest."

India frowned. "I hope it's not too bad."

Travis moved and blocked her view of the stage. "I don't care about campaign things anymore. The primaries are over. Your brother won. You know what this means?"

"That we've got an even bigger climb to the election?"

Travis grinned and shook his head. "It means that we don't have to hide anymore." He wrapped an arm around her waist.

India glanced around and put a hand on his chest, but she didn't push him back. "Travis, he just won."

"India, I've waited long enough. Life is short and there are no guarantees we'll see another sunrise. I love you. You are the person I think of every minute of every day. I want to spend the rest of my life with you. We've honored your family's wishes, we've done everything they asked, but please don't ask me to wait any longer. Tell me you love me."

Her hand on his chest wrapped around the lapel of his suit. Whenever she thought about him in that hospital bed, how he'd almost been taken away, her throat wanted to close up. "You know I love you."

"Then marry me."

"I am going to marry you." They'd talked about marriage while he recuperated. After almost losing him to a bullet and getting Elaina's blessing, she hadn't thought about not marrying Travis.

Travis shook his head. "Not in the future. Marry me tonight?"

She drew back. He couldn't be serious. "Tonight? How?"

"Vegas."

"Are you joking?" she said with a laugh. "We can't go to Vegas tonight."

He lifted one shoulder and pulled her closer, the strength of his body so tempting against hers. "Why not?"

"The party. The family. The…" She couldn't think of other reasons.

"The party will go on without us. Your family only asked that we keep things under wrap until tonight."

"But…" The excitement to do exactly what she wanted fought to overrule all reasons to say no.

"India, I want to spend the rest of my life with you and I don't want to wait another day." Fierce love shone in his eyes. "I almost lost my chance to be happy. You don't know how scary that was."

"I was petrified." She dropped her head to his chest. She didn't want to think about him dying.

He lowered his head and kissed her ear. "Then let's go. Let's not wait anymore. Marry me, India. Tonight."

She lifted her head and looked around the room. Byron celebrated onstage. He was giving a speech. Her dad and Patricia were wrapped in each other's arms in a corner. Everyone was happy and celebrating the win. No thoughts of tomorrow. No fears about what could go wrong.

India slid her hand up to where the bullet had hit Travis in the shoulder. Everything could go wrong in the blink of an eye. Her answer was as strong and steady as Travis's heartbeat beneath her palm. She didn't want to wait a minute longer either. Their time had come. Finally, there were no excuses. She was going to hold on to forever.

She looked up and met Travis's eyes. "Let's go."

* * * * *

ACKNOWLEDGMENTS

FIRST AND FOREMOST, I have to thank the Destin Divas. Specifically, K.D. for listening as I talked about this story walking on the beach and Seressia for giving me a mental kick in the pants when I said I didn't think this idea was good enough. You ladies are such a support system to me, and I wouldn't have finished this story without your encouragement.

Thank you to my awesome agent, Tricia Skinner. It's nice to have someone on your side in this business, and I truly appreciate your efforts on my behalf.

Thank you to my fantastic editor, Michele Bidelspach. All of those words of encouragement sprinkled in with your edits made me smile and your suggestions pushed me to work harder to make this story better.

Finally, to my family. I love you with all of my heart. Thank you for always being there.

Turn the page for an excerpt from Synithia Williams's next sexy contemporary romance featuring the Robidoux family, coming to HQN soon!

CHAPTER ONE

BYRON WAS AT the top of his game.

His heart pumped with exhilaration. His cheeks hurt from the smile that refused to leave his face. He stared out at the crowd surrounding the stage, and the eyes looking back at him were bright with enthusiasm, hope and determination. Signs with the green-and-blue logo of his campaign flowed like waves in their hands. A blend of people from all races, economic classes and social backgrounds packed in the brewery he'd chosen to hold his watch party.

And he hadn't let them down. The results were in. He'd won.

The fervor of his supporters was like a tidal wave. Bowling him over with its strength. He'd done this. He'd actually gotten this far. The primary win wasn't a guarantee he'd make it to the Senate, but he had lasted far enough to beat out an opponent with experience as a state legislator and a much longer record of public service. The weight of responsibility to live up to the expectations of the people who'd voted for him, the people who were currently cheering for him, was something he refused to take lightly.

"I promise you," Byron said into the microphone. In his periphery, Roy, his campaign manager, took a step forward. Byron could hear Roy's warning in his head. *Never make promises in a speech. They come back and bite you in the ass.* Byron didn't care about that right now. This was a promise he planned to keep.

Byron held up a finger and shook his hand with each word. "I promise you I will not forget the trust you all have honored me with tonight. We have gotten this far, and we will keep going all the way to Washington. No more waiting for tomorrow. The time is now!"

The crowd cheered. They held up and waved his signs and repeated his words. "The time is now!" The campaign slogan had come about during a debate after his opponent, state senator Gordan, insisted the time wasn't right to try to fight the administration on progressive ideas. Byron's immediate comeback had been that fifteen years was too long to wait, and the time was now.

A slim hand slid into his left one and squeezed. Byron turned from the crowd toward his fiancée, Yolanda. Her brown eyes were filled with pride. Tall, graceful and perfectly polished in a tasteful green blouse and navy pants—to match his campaign colors—she complemented him. As Byron wrapped an arm around her shoulders and pulled her into his side, anyone looking at them would see a young, optimistic couple deeply in love.

Byron didn't miss how the gleam of triumph overshadowed the pride in her eyes. Yolanda was a woman on the way to making partner at the reputable legal firm she worked for. A position beneficial for the wife of North Carolina's newest senator.

Byron leaned down and pressed a kiss to her lips. She placed a hand on his cheek. Her nails lightly scratched the beard he'd grown during the last weeks of the campaign. Her gentle reminder to cut the damn thing, before she pulled back and grinned wider. "We did it," she said.

He slid his arm back and entwined their fingers. "Yes, we did."

They waved and shook hands as they made their way off the stage. The band played upbeat music. Champagne corks popped throughout the building and more beer poured from the tap. The party would start now, along with the real work. He needed to finalize the strategy against his opponent. Brainstorm the best way to reach the digitally disconnected constituents in his district. Figure out the best way to utilize his family to spread his message throughout the district. Develop a plan to be more relatable to his constituents. Something even more necessary now that his best friend and former brother-in-law had plans to remarry into the family. This time with a different sister.

"I know that look," came a booming male voice.

Byron shifted and faced his father. Grant Robidoux had a Robidoux Tobacco cigar in one hand and the other slammed down hard onto Byron's shoulder and squeezed. His dad was what Byron imagined he'd look like one day. Skin the color of dark honey, slightly lined due to age, light brown eyes and curly hair with just enough salt-and-pepper to make people say he looked distinguished. Pride radiated off him like sunbeams as he studied Byron's face.

Byron took the glass of champagne Yolanda handed to him off the tray of a passing server. "What look is that, Dad?"

"The I'm-already-planning-the-next-step look," Grant said, pointing his cigar at Byron. "Not tonight. There is enough time for strategy tomorrow. Tonight, you enjoy the win." He winked at Yolanda. "Enjoy the company of the beautiful woman at your side. The real fight is about to begin. Give yourself this moment to bask in the glory."

Yolanda raised her glass and tapped it against Byron's. "I agree with that."

Byron forced the massive list of things he needed to do to the back of his mind. Taking a second to enjoy this milestone wouldn't hurt. "Fine, I'll sit back and enjoy this win, but I'm starting early tomorrow." He glanced around the crowd and caught the fierce glare of his older sister. "Uh-oh."

Grant's brows drew together. "Uh-oh? What's wrong?"

"Elaina is scowling. Do you know why?" Nothing good ever followed one of Elaina's scowls. She'd just been smiling and clapping with the rest of his supporters.

Grant's gaze shifted away. He brought the cigar to his nose and sniffed. "No idea."

"You're lying." Byron didn't hesitate to call his dad out. He loved and respected his dad more than any other man in the world, but he also knew when Grant tried to keep something from him. "What happened?"

Grant shrugged. "Nothing big. India and Travis ducked out right after your acceptance speech, and she's worried they've run off and done something stupid."

Byron relaxed. "They're probably just getting out of here to spend a few minutes alone together. I don't blame them after we spent the last few weeks pretending as if they weren't together. You tell Elaina to do exactly what you told me. Enjoy the win and strategize tomorrow."

Byron wasn't concerned about his younger sister and best friend leaving his party early. They were crazy about each other—God help them—and they wanted to spend time together. Elaina being upset, well, that made more sense. Even though she'd given her blessing to India and Travis after discovering they were together, the situation was still awkward as hell.

"Why do I have to tell her?" Grant asked, sounding genuinely put out.

Byron lightly hit his father's shoulder. "Because it's my party and I don't want to." He wrapped his arm around Yolanda's shoulders and maneuvered her away from his dad in the opposite direction of Elaina.

"You know you were wrong for doing that," Yolanda said, chuckling.

"He's the one who told me to relax. Dealing with whatever is bothering Elaina is not my idea of relaxing."

Yolanda sighed and leaned farther into him. "I still can't believe you're okay with India and Travis. God knows how we're going to smooth over this situation with them in the media. We don't need anything smearing your campaign."

"Don't worry. This won't smear my campaign. If anything, it'll show how well our family works together." *Or reveal just how cracked we are beneath the polished exterior.*

Byron caught the eye of one of his larger donors. He smiled and waved and moved in that direction. He added worrying about his family's image to the long list of items he'd have to overcome if he hoped to win in November.

Yolanda dug her feet in and stopped him. Her eyes were serious as they met his. "I'm not playing about this. We have to be delicate moving forward. I'm with you to win. Not to let the soft spot you have for your baby sister and best friend derail this train."

Yolanda's words were pragmatic as always. Her practicality and ability to strategize was why he'd agreed to this engagement, but that didn't stop irritation from crawling up his spine. Happiness was hard to obtain. So why get in the way when two people he cared about actually found it? He may not be a proponent of true love, but he also wouldn't begrudge those who were.

"I know why you're here," he said. She reminded him at least once a week. "We need each other, and it'll take both of us to win. Don't worry about India and Travis. That won't be the thing that kills my campaign."

"Byron! Congratulations!" The happy voice of the donor whose eye he'd caught a second ago.

"Hello, Mr. Sparrow. Mrs. Sparrow, so good to see you again." Byron grinned and shook hands.

Yolanda's face became a mask of blissful happiness as they talked and schmoozed their way through the party. This was their future. He'd known what he was getting into when his campaign manager mentioned that proposing and marrying would make him a more viable candidate.

So why was it bothering him tonight?

Things were going the way he wanted them to. Yolanda's business ties, along with her family's history in politics, combined with his family's wealth and influence, was political gold. On top of that, he liked her. She was driven, attractive, passionate and had let him know from their very first date she wanted to help him on his rise to the top. Yolanda was a woman who knew her own mind and didn't apologize for going after what she wanted. He'd never have to guess where he stood with her.

Movement in his periphery caught his eye. He turned and his entire body went rigid. Guess everything wasn't going as planned tonight. Dominic, the consultant he'd hired to help with his campaign, made his way toward Byron, his expression grim and his dark eyes blank.

Nothing good could come of Dominic showing up tonight. He'd hired the guy months ago to handle a situation from his past, one that Byron had paid a lot of money to hopefully fix. Dominic kept in touch to let him know if anything popped up. Mostly via email and the occasional phone call. Never in person.

Byron excused himself from the group. Ignoring Yolanda's concerned gaze, he walked up to Dominic. "What's wrong?"

"Someone is here to see you." Dominic's calm expression didn't waver. Dominic was always calm. An observer who could charm as easily as he could intimidate. Despite his calm, the sharpness of his gaze put Byron on edge.

Byron's heart jumped in his chest. "Zoe?" He'd thought he'd protected her. Had something gone wrong?

Dominic shook his head. "No. She's still back home living her life with no signs of any problems. But I don't know if I can guarantee that much longer."

Byron shifted closer to Dominic. He rubbed his beard, a new habit now that he had one, and tried not to let the fear seeping into him show. "What?"

Dominic nodded his head back toward the door. "Come with me. You don't want him to create a scene."

Him? "Let's go." Byron followed Dominic out of the party, through the kitchen in the back and into an empty office. Once inside, a man he didn't recognize turned and faced him. Slim, with beady black eyes and a shifting stance. Byron immediately didn't like the guy.

"Byron Robidoux, this is Carlton Powell," Dominic said through clenched teeth.

Byron's hands tightened into fists. "Carlton Powell? What the hell do you want with me?" Byron had paid Dominic a lot of money to make Carlton stay out of his business. Carlton had been hired to find the same person Byron had been looking for before announcing his run. Byron thought the payoff would ensure Carlton moved on to other things.

Carlton rubbed his hands together. "Don't be so rude. As you know, I'm here to do you a favor."

"I don't need any favors from you." Byron glared at Dominic. "You brought him here?"

Dominic shook his head. "No. I've kept tabs on him. When I found out he was in town, I followed him here. Stopped him before he went in there to confront you."

"I'm not confronting anyone," Carlton said with the nerve to sound affronted. "I'm just here because I've got an offer I think the future senator can't refuse."

"What offer is that?" Byron asked.

"The offer to keep what I know to myself instead of telling all those happy people out there." Carlton pointed to the closed door. "About you being a deadbeat dad."

Byron's stomach flipped and sweat ran down his back, but he didn't flinch. He hadn't become a defense attorney and served a term in the State House without knowing how to hide his shock. "I'm not a deadbeat dad. I don't have any children."

"That's not what I've heard," Carlton said, sounding like he'd gotten the gospel truth on everything Byron Robidoux. "You see, after you sent me on my way I did a little digging on my own. Turns out the woman you told me to stay away from also told a few people you were the father of her kid."

Byron gritted his teeth. He should have known this would come back. He didn't have any children, but thirteen years ago he'd agreed to help a friend out by keeping her secret and going along with a lie. The image of Zoe in his college apartment, her face bruised and tears in her eyes as she'd clung to him, played like a bad movie in his mind.

Byron, please say the baby is yours. He'll kill me if I stay with him. This is my only way out.

Even now the memory filled him with rage and helplessness. Zoe had been his best friend. His homegirl. He'd loved her with everything he had, but when he'd told her, she'd tossed his love back at him as if playing hot potato. She'd been in love with someone else. A guy Byron had never thought deserved her. A guy Byron discovered way too late that he'd been right about. So he'd kept her secret. Said the child was his and promised never to say anything.

"You're coming to me with rumors," Byron replied coldly. He wasn't playing his hand without knowing exactly what Carlton knew and wanted.

Carlton shrugged. "Rumors can do a lot of damage. You see, I doubt you're really the father. The person who originally sent me to find the old girl was pretty sure someone else was the father. Now, I took your money to lead them off her trail, but then I got to thinking why so many people were interested in this one woman and her kid. Did a little research and here we are." He sounded pleased with himself.

"Get to the point," Dominic said in a deadly voice.

"My point is regardless of who is the baby daddy, I think word getting out about everyone's favorite candidate possibly being on the birth certificate won't be good for this campaign you've got going so well. You know the early polls show you're going to beat the other guy. Be a damn shame to lose because people think you're an absentee father."

Byron didn't have time for this. "What do you want?" he asked instead of going with the urge to shove Carlton into the wall.

"A million dollars," Carlton said without missing a heartbeat. "I know you're good for it. Your family is known for its wealth."

"I don't have a million dollars." He did, but he'd be damned if this guy got any more of his money.

"Oh, I don't want it tonight. I'll give you say…two weeks to come up with the money." Carlton spoke as if he were a debt collector who'd done a client a favor by extending the deadline. "Bask in this win. Let it sink in a little what you stand to lose."

Byron was well aware of what he had to lose. He was also shrewd enough to realize that paying Carlton anything wasn't going to make this problem go away. He needed to know how far this guy was willing to go.

"What if I say no?" Byron asked. He crossed his arms and sized up Carlton. "A DNA test will prove I'm not the father."

Carlton sucked his teeth and shook his head. "But the scandal it'll cause. That, and your playboy ways. Oh, I'm sure there are dozens of other women willing to come forward and claim you're their kid's dad."

The greedy gleam in Carlton's eyes made Byron's stomach churn. He wouldn't doubt Carlton already had women lined up to say they'd slept with him. Even if he had a dozen paternity tests to prove his innocence, the stigma would follow him and cost him the campaign.

"I thought you'd see what I mean," Carlton said. "Just think it over. But not too long." Carlton put two fingers to his brow in a mock salute and walked out.

Byron punched his fist into his opposite hand. "Fuck!"

Dominic frowned. "You can't pay him. Guys like Carlton never go away. I never should have taken his first deal."

Byron paced back and forth. His mind raced with what to do next. He couldn't dwell on previous decisions. They were already done. Byron had agreed with all the choices he'd made, and he'd deal with the results of those decisions.

"Protecting Zoe is what matters," he said. "Carlton just proved what I feared. Her ex is about to get out of jail and he's looking for her. There's no way that man needs to get close to her."

"If you pay him for this, you'll have a paper trail of past dealings with him. He'll make things worse and won't hesitate to out you as a guy leaving babies all over the Southeast."

Byron stopped pacing and met Dominic's concerned stare. "No, he won't. I have no intentions of paying him."

"Then what are you going to do?"

He was going to outplay Carlton. Byron hadn't grown up in this family to not recognize when he needed to make a big play in order to win. "I'm going to see Zoe. It's time we figured out our next move in this game."

"Darius. What are you doing here?" Audra stared at him,
her eyes wide.

She looked adorable in a pair of gray cropped cargo
pants and a long-sleeved white T-shirt. A heart-shaped
gold locket, which matched the color and shape of her
nose ring, dragged his attention to the deep V of her shirt.

"A few of the locals invited me to volunteer. I decided
I could use the mental break." His gaze shifted from hers.

A deep ache in his gut nagged at him for hiding his
connection to the Blackwoods from Audra. But the
runway show was just a few weeks away. He wouldn't
risk the story about the CEO of Thr3d being the "bastard
child" of the late Buckley Blackwood getting out and
overshadowing the show. He didn't believe Audra
would intentionally sabotage him. But what if someone
overheard them or she told the wrong person?

Everything had to be perfect for the show.

It wasn't a chance he could afford to take. "I figured
I'd help out for a few hours. How about you?"

"Sophie, my client—" Audra nodded in Sophie's direction "—asked me to help. Besides, several members of the bridal party are here. This gives me the chance to get to know them as I try to finalize the designs for their custom jewelry gifts."

"Makes perfect sense." He nodded.

They stood together in awkward silence. Close enough that he could feel the heat radiating from her smooth brown skin and smell the sweet citrus scent wafting from her hair. Finally, Darius couldn't take the vivid images of them together—him touching her, kissing her, making love to her—that his brain conjured in the absence of words.

"Have you eaten breakfast yet?" he asked abruptly. "I haven't, and I'm starving. I was about to grab a sandwich, if you'd care to join me."

"Sure." Audra followed him toward the bar where the food was set up. "And thank you for the salad the other night. It was thoughtful of you."

"For you, Audra? Anything."

Will Darius risk everything for one more chance with Audra?

Find out in
Secret Heir Seduction
by Reese Ryan, available March 2020 wherever Harlequin Desire books and ebooks are sold.

Harlequin.com

Get 4 FREE REWARDS!

We'll send you 2 FREE Books plus 2 FREE Mystery Gifts.

FREE
Value Over
$20

Both the **Romance** and **Suspense** collections feature compelling novels written by many of today's bestselling authors.

YES! Please send me 2 FREE novels from the Essential Romance or Essential Suspense Collection and my 2 FREE gifts (gifts are worth about $10 retail). After receiving them, if I don't wish to receive any more books, I can return the shipping statement marked "cancel." If I don't cancel, I will receive 4 brand-new novels every month and be billed just $6.99 each in the U.S. or $7.24 each in Canada. That's a savings of at least 13% off the cover price. It's quite a bargain! Shipping and handling is just 50¢ per book in the U.S. and $1.25 per book in Canada.* I understand that accepting the 2 free books and gifts places me under no obligation to buy anything. I can always return a shipment and cancel at any time. The free books and gifts are mine to keep no matter what I decide.

Choose one: ☐ **Essential Romance**   ☐ **Essential Suspense**
                 (194/394 MDN GNNP)   (191/391 MDN GNNP)

Name (please print)

Address   Apt. #

City   State/Province   Zip/Postal Code

Mail to the Reader Service:
IN U.S.A.: P.O. Box 1341, Buffalo, NY 14240-8531
IN CANADA: P.O. Box 603, Fort Erie, Ontario L2A 5X3

Want to try 2 free books from another series? Call 1-800-873-8635 or visit www.ReaderService.com.